He was a rat. A creep. Lower than the lowest of the low.

He should have found a way to tell Olivia the truth by now.

Maybe, though, as long as he didn't put his hands on her, the lie he was living remained marginally acceptable. However, if he ever crossed that line, he wouldn't be able to live with himself.

But he wouldn't cross that line. The last tattered threads of his mangled integrity still clutched him. He could control himself. Barely.

Besides, Olivia's shyness and inexperience would help. She simply wasn't the type of woman to become aggressive about sex.

Jack sat up and rubbed his eyes.

And all he could do was stare.

There stood Olivia. Wrapped in a sable coat, wearing naughty red high-heeled slippers…and evidently very little else.

Dear Reader,

Welcome to Silhouette Special Edition...welcome to romance.

That telltale sign of falling leaves signals that autumn has arrived and so have heartwarming books to take you into the season.

Two exciting series from veteran authors continue in the month of September. Christine Rimmer's THE JONES GANG returns with *A Home for the Hunter* And the Rogue River is once again the exciting setting for Laurie Paige's WILD RIVER series in *A River To Cross*.

This month, our THAT SPECIAL WOMAN! is Anna Louise Perkins, a courageous woman who rises to the challenge of bringing love and happiness to the man of her dreams. You'll meet her in award-winning author Sherryl Woods's *The Parson's Waiting*.

Also in September, don't miss *Rancher's Heaven* from Robin Elliott, *Miracle Child* by Kayla Daniels and *Family Connections*, a debut book in Silhouette Special Edition by author Judith Yates.

I hope you enjoy this book, and all of the stories to come!

Sincerely,

Tara Gavin
Senior Editor

Please address questions and book requests to:
Silhouette Reader Service
U.S.: 3010 Walden Ave., P.O. Box 1325, Buffalo, NY 14269
Canadian: P.O. Box 609, Fort Erie, Ont. L2A 5X3

CHRISTINE RIMMER
A HOME FOR THE HUNTER

SPECIAL EDITION®

Published by Silhouette Books
America's Publisher of Contemporary Romance

For Gail Chasan,
who thought I ought to write a few books
about the Jones boys.

 SILHOUETTE BOOKS

ISBN 0-373-09908-8

A HOME FOR THE HUNTER

CHRISTINE RIMMER

is a third-generation Californian who came to her profession the long way around. Before settling down to write about the magic of romance, she'd been an actress, a sales clerk, a janitor, a model, a phone sales representative, a teacher, a waitress, a playwright and an office manager. Now that she's finally found work that suits her perfectly, she insists she never had a problem keeping a job—she was merely gaining "life experience" for her future as a novelist. Those who know her best withhold comment when she makes such claims; they are grateful that she's at last found steady work. Christine is grateful, too—not only for the joy she finds in writing, but for what waits when the day's work is through: a man she loves who loves her right back and the privilege of watching their children grow and change day to day.

THE JONES FAMILY TREE

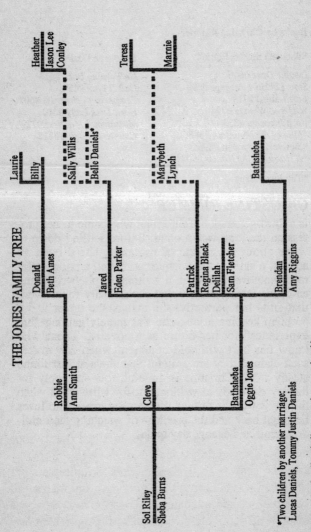

*Two children by another marriage:
Lucas Daniels, Tommy Justin Daniels

Note: Broken lines indicate previous marriage(s).

Chapter One

Olivia Larrabee looked up from the blackjack table—right into the piercing midnight eyes of the most compelling man she'd ever seen.

Something happened in her stomach—that down-too-fast-in-an-elevator feeling. If she hadn't had the high felt-topped table to lean against, she very well might have fallen off her stool.

Olivia's face burned. She knew that to allow herself to be so strongly affected by the mere glance of a strange man at this juncture of her life said terrible things about her character. After what she'd endured just twenty-four hours ago, she certainly ought to know better.

Oh, but he was so...mesmerizing. So completely a *man*. There was humor in the lift of his mouth, strength in the jut of his jaw and danger in his eyes. And there was absolutely no doubt about it. He was looking right at *her*.

"Wake up, dearie." The blue-haired lady with the rhinestone-studded glasses who had the seat next to Olivia's nudged her in the ribs.

Olivia stiffened and blinked. "Oh. Um. Yes." She forced herself to break the hold of the stranger's hypnotic glance and to sneak another peek at the six of hearts and the seven of clubs that she'd been dealt. She beamed a smile at the dealer. "Umm. Hit me."

The dealer peeled off another card. A king. Just what she *didn't* want to see.

"Bust." Olivia said the word she'd heard the other players say when their cards totaled more than twenty-one. She turned her cards over.

The blue-haired lady clucked her tongue. "Bad night, eh, dearie?"

Olivia sighed. Then, trying her best to appear cool and unconcerned, she glanced up and scanned the busy casino, seeking again that incredible pair of consuming dark eyes.

But the stranger was nowhere in sight. She felt ridiculously bereft, more solid proof of the meagerness of her character.

The blue-haired lady was peering at her sympathetically. "You all right, honey?"

"Yes, I'm fine." Olivia forced a polite smile. "Thanks." She gathered up what was left of her chips and slid off her stool. Then she headed straight for the change cage to get coins to play the slot machines.

Half an hour later, her arm was tired from pulling levers. She'd failed to hit even one jackpot, though she'd put more than two hundred dollars in quarters into the machines.

She was feeling glum—and not because she was losing. But because she knew that when her jumbo cup of quarters was empty, all she had to do was get more. All Olivia *ever* had to do was get more. In fact, it was probably silly for her to be playing the quarter slots. The least she could do, rich as she was, was to go and waste her money in the dollar machines. She could be down over a thousand now, instead of a mere two hundred. She could feel more like something was at *stake* here, even though she knew it wasn't.

To the only daughter of Lawrence Larrabee, owner of Larrabee Brewing Company, a thousand hardly rated as pocket change.

It was awful to be rich. Especially when it was your father, not you, who had earned all the money. Olivia didn't know how other undeservedly wealthy people felt. But she herself felt a little guilty all the time. A little wasteful, just on principle. Which was why she'd come to Las Vegas, to learn to lighten up a little.

Or at least lightening up was part of it.

But, of course, there was more.

The brutal truth was, she'd discovered her fiancé naked in the arms of another woman and known she had to get away. The alternative was too dreary: to spend weeks wandering around her beach house in a bathrobe, feeling like it was just too much trouble to wash her hair.

No, she'd decided. She was *not* going to sink into some dismally predictable depression. What she needed was a visit to the gaudiest, most gloriously wasteful place in the United States. In the crowds and excitement, she would forget all about Cameron Cain and the way he'd betrayed her.

And maybe a little of the glitter would rub off on her. She'd pictured herself wearing red velvet and throwing around some of the money she hadn't earned. In her mind had been the idea that such profligate spending would not only help her to forget how empty her existence was, but would also teach her to take life more as it came.

But so far she wasn't doing very well. She was wearing red velvet all right. By Kamali. But every time she caught a glimpse of herself in one of the casino's gold-veined mirrors, she thought of Fantine in *Les Misérables*. She was just one of those women who looked like a refugee from a used-clothing store, no matter what she wore.

Beyond her disappointing appearance, everything she played, she lost. And losing wouldn't have been so bad, really. If she only could have lost *largely*. But Olivia was too naturally frugal to bet large. And even all the tension and excitement around her wasn't helping to change that. If anything, it was only making her failure to do anything on a grand scale seem all the more evident.

The single bright spot in this whole questionable enterprise had been that shared glance with a stranger half an hour ago.

"Pitiful," Olivia mumbled to herself. "Utterly pathetic."

"You using this machine, sweetheart?" *another* blue lady inquired.

Olivia wondered morosely what it could be about her that made older ladies call her things like "dearie" and "sweetheart." Olivia suspected that, though she was a grown woman and had been for years, other people did not consider her fully mature.

"Well, hon?" the lady prompted.

"No. I'm done. You go right ahead." Olivia took the lady's veiny, zircon-encrusted hand and pressed her full cup of quarters into it. "Win a jackpot on me."

The lady's rather faded blue eyes lit up. "Well, thanks, hon. You're a doll."

The woman's obvious pleasure at such an unexpected windfall cheered Olivia. "Think nothing of it, sweetie." She tossed the words over her shoulder as she flicked her crimson skirt out of her way and headed for the craps tables.

There, she stood to the side and watched for a while, thinking that craps was a very fast game. Olivia had heard somewhere that it was the true gambler's game. She didn't know about that, but it certainly was confusing.

Still, she wanted to try it. So once she had the general idea of how it was played, she dared to join in. She put her chips on the numbers and listened to everyone shouting and chattering and watched the man at the money box rake in her chips every time the dice were thrown. She was losing, she could figure that out.

But when the dice came around to her and she tossed them, the other players made appreciative noises. Apparently Olivia had won for *them*.

After she'd thrown the dice twice, everyone else at the table passed up their turns to roll. The dice kept coming back to her. And she threw them, paying no attention to her own bets. The other people at the table cheered her on and threw chips at her. It was actually sort of exciting. And it was nice to have everyone thinking she was wonderful and shouting at her to "do it one more time, baby!"

For a few minutes Olivia almost felt expansive. She tossed her head and laughed and talked to the dice before she threw them. She could have sworn she was actually starting to forget her troubles and have a good time.

But then she was assailed. There was no other word for it. Olivia was assailed by the feeling that someone was watching her. It was eerie. And it broke her concentration on having a good time.

Soon enough she found herself casting frequent furtive glances all around. She saw no one looking at her but the money man, the man with the stick, and the people around the table. And they all had good reason to look at her. They were wondering if she was going to throw the dice or not.

Olivia threw the dice again. But in the very act of tossing them, she couldn't help speculating if it might be *he* who was watching her—he of the mesmerizing midnight eyes.

The very thought that he might be observing her now, during her little moment of glory as the darling of the craps table, sent a sweet shiver all through her. She had a fleeting moment of absurd fancy in which she actually dared to imagine that he'd taken one look at her and known he'd never forget her. Now he was following her around the casino, stalking her, awaiting just the right moment to—

Around the table there rose a collective groan.

It appeared she'd rolled a bad one.

Olivia put her ridiculous fantasies about a man she didn't even know completely from her mind and concentrated on winning more money for her new friends at the table.

But it was too late. Her lucky streak with the dice was over. When she rolled the next time, everyone groaned again. The man beside her grumbled something rude about her under his breath and rolled the dice himself instead of passing them. Suddenly craps wasn't any fun at all.

With a sigh Olivia departed the table. She trudged through the casino, looking for the next diversion. But nothing caught her eye.

So she went out the main doors and stood on the sidewalk for a moment and stared up and down the Strip. She saw bright lights and huge marquees that advertised the ever-popular game of Keno and progressive slots and the most famous entertainers in the world.

And she saw neon, a river of neon. Flashing and flowing. More neon than in Times Square in New York. It pulsed and whirled against the desert night sky. It awed her. And in a strange way it soothed her.

She wondered what time it was. She wasn't wearing a watch, and in the casino there seemed to be no clocks anywhere. As if time were not allowed in Vegas.

She thought of moving on, to the MGM Grand or the Tropicana. She could see what another pleasure palace had to offer. But then again, wasn't one casino like another in all the ways that mattered?

Oh, that was a bad attitude to have. She knew it. How was she going to forget her problems and learn to take life as it comes with an attitude like that?

Determined not to give up yet, she started down the sidewalk. And then she realized she was hungry. The casino where she was staying—the one she'd just left—advertised lobster with drawn butter for $9.95. A bargain.

And, though she knew from long experience that really fine food rarely came cheap, Olivia Larrabee had never been able to resist a bargain. She turned so suddenly that she bumped right into a rather portly urban cowboy who just happened to be walking behind her. He grunted as she stepped on his snakeskin boots.

"Oh, I am so sorry, I—"

"Think nothing of it, little lady." The man was tipping his Stetson at her.

But she hardly noticed what the stout cowboy was doing. Because just past his beefy shoulder, she saw *him*— the compelling stranger who had watched her at the blackjack table.

The stranger had just come out of the casino behind her. And she knew, from the way his eyes narrowed as she spotted him, that he'd left the casino because he was following her.

"Er, miss...you okay?" the beefy cowboy was asking.

She smiled vaguely without looking at him. She was not taking her eyes off the stranger this time. This time, if he turned and disappeared, she would be watching as he did it. She wouldn't be left with the eerie feeling that he had vanished into thin air. "I'm fine. Just fine."

The cowboy grunted and moved on. Olivia stood on the sidewalk and stared at the stranger. He returned her stare for a moment, his look both defiant and knowing. And then he started to turn away.

"Wait!" The plea was out of her mouth before she had time to tell herself that the last thing she needed in her life right now was to go chasing after some man she didn't even know.

The man in question froze where he was, just outside the gilt-framed glass doors to the casino. Around him and between him and Olivia, people jostled and shifted, flowing like so much flesh-and-blood neon in and out of the big doors.

"Don't go." She only mouthed the words.

But he heard them, she was sure he did. He knew what she had said.

Through those deep-set dark eyes he regarded her with extreme wariness. In the garish yellow light of the casino entrance, his pale hair and brows had a gilded look. His skin was rich bronze against the white of his dress shirt. On his tanned cheeks, there was the shadow of a beard. He managed somehow to look both rumpled and lazily elegant.

There was something feral about him. He was like those lions that survive in the African deserts. A little too lean, dangerously hungry. But no less king of the beasts for all that.

Olivia decided all over again that he was the most thoroughly masculine man she had ever seen.

And just as she reached that decision he shrugged and began walking toward her.

Chapter Two

As she watched him stride toward her, Olivia knew very well that she was behaving most unwisely. If she had any sense at all, she would turn quickly and walk away.

But she didn't turn. Somehow, she *couldn't* turn.

He reached her. They stood regarding each other. People going by shot them curious glances, even bumped them once or twice. But they paid no attention.

"Give me a reason why not." His voice, pitched low, was like a long, gentle stroke from a knowing hand.

The desert wind swept up the street, blowing the bloodred velvet in a swirl around her ankles, causing his tie to flip up and over his shoulder. With a boldness she hadn't known she possessed, Olivia caught the tie and smoothed it back into place, then quickly snatched her hand away.

"Well?" He lifted a brow.

"Well, what?"

"Give me a reason why I shouldn't go."

She looked past his shoulder and then back at him once more. "Because..." A few strands of her hair blew across her mouth. She caught them, smoothed them away.

"Yeah?"

She couldn't think of a thing except, *Because I don't want you to go.* And yet that would sound so obvious, so dull. She didn't want him to think her dull. She stared up at him, suddenly tongue-tied, her unaccustomed boldness blown away with the wind. She felt her skin begin to flood with agonized color.

"I, um..."

"Tell you what..." He smiled; a strange smile. Ironic and yet so tender. "*I'll* give *you* a reason. You just say yes or no. And I'll be gone. Or I won't."

She coughed, feeling nervous now. "What reason?"

He actually chuckled. It was a warm, teasing sound, one that enticed and intrigued her as much as his speaking voice had done. Then he asked, without preamble, "Scared?"

The truth was all that came to her, so she gave it. "Yes." Then she asked, "Was that the reason?"

"No. I just wanted to know. And don't be."

"What?"

"Scared. I would never hurt you."

"Oh."

"But take my advice."

"What?"

"Never trust a man who says he'll never hurt you."

She stared at him for a moment. And then she burst into laughter. He laughed with her, standing there on the street, buffeted by the crowds and the night wind. Several people passing by stopped to look at them. Those who stopped smiled knowing smiles. But Olivia didn't notice. She saw only the stranger.

Then he said, "Have dinner with me. Now."

She hesitated. "Is *that* the reason?"

He nodded. "If you have dinner with me, then I've got a reason not to go."

She confessed, "Well, I am a little hungry."

"Is that a yes?"

"I shouldn't."

"Yes? Or no?"

"I . . ."

"Think about it. Take a minute. I can wait." There was a gold pillar behind him, one of the six that adorned the porte cochere of the casino. He backed up and leaned against it. "No rush."

She laughed again, then composed herself and asked, "What's your name?"

He answered after a brief pause, "Jack Roper."

Jack, she turned the name over in her mind and decided she liked it. It was hard and direct and no-frills masculine.

She volunteered her own. "I'm Olivia." But then she hesitated. She dreaded giving him her last name.

Whenever she said her last name, people would ask, "Larrabee, as in Larrabee Lager?" She hated when people asked that. She didn't want Jack Roper to ask that. For once, she just wanted to be a woman, talking to a man who found her attractive. Not the heiress to the third-largest brewing company in the western United States.

So she picked a last name from a marquee across the street, the last name of a certain country and western singer. "Loveless," she told Jack. "I'm Olivia Loveless."

He grinned. "*Loveless?* You're kidding."

"No, I'm perfectly serious."

She gave him what she hoped was a no-nonsense frown. And as she frowned, she was thinking that really, she shouldn't be lying to him about who she was.

But then again it was so nice, for once, not to have to go into all that.

And besides, who was *he* really, anyway? She knew nothing about him or why he seemed to be following her.

Because he thinks I'm beautiful.

Oh, right. Sure, a more reasonable voice seemed to say.

Okay, fine. If not beautiful, at least appealing. He finds me appealing.

And that's supposed to be reason enough that you should have dinner with him, a total stranger?

Given how many fabulous men like him have even bothered to look twice at me so far in my life, you're darn right.

It's dangerous. Downright dangerous, said her wiser self. *Picking up a man on the sidewalk in front of a casino is just asking for trouble.*

I wouldn't be picking him up. I'm not going to his room with him, for heaven's sake. Only out to eat.

Oh, get real.

I need this, I really do. My ego's been decimated by what happened yesterday.

Pitiful. Purely pathetic.

And I've never done anything like this in my life. I never take chances. It's time I took a chance.

Time you acted like a complete idiot, you mean.

So? She threw caution to the desert wind. *I'm doing it.*

Though her wiser self was still calling her a fool, she granted the incredible stranger a nod. "Okay, Jack. I'll have dinner with you. On one condition."

He came away from the pillar. "Name it."

"That it will be my treat."

He gave her that odd smile again. Ironically tender. "Fair enough."

A little flustered by the intense look in his eyes, she cleared her throat and tried to think what to do next. "I, um, don't know Las Vegas very well. In fact, I arrived this morning and I'm staying right here, in this hotel and casino. This is the first time I've been outside of it since I got here. Where are *you* staying?"

"Right here, too."

"Oh, well. Isn't that a coincidence?"

He shrugged.

She forged on. "Anyway, just now I was going to go back inside and try the lobster. But if you—"

He took her arm, causing a pleasant little shiver to course through her. "I'm no native, but I know a couple of good places. Come on. We'll take my car."

She reminded herself that she was not going to get carried away with this. She looked at him levelly and refused to be pulled along. "Jack, I hardly know you. I will not get into your car with you right now."

His expression was rueful as he released her arm. "Sorry. So it'll be the lobster, I suppose."

"Is the lobster that bad?"

"Hell, I don't know. As a matter of fact, I'm not much on seafood."

"I'm sure there are other things on the menu. Choose one of them."

"I will. Let's go."

The lobster, while it didn't compare with what Olivia enjoyed at her favorite restaurant in Malibu, was certainly acceptable. Neither stringy nor rubbery, it had enough flavor that Olivia was sure the crustacean had been alive not *too* long ago. She hadn't been allowed to choose one from a tank, but for the price what could she expect?

And anyway, it was the man across the table, not the quality of the food, that interested her. Not surprisingly he ordered rare steak and seemed quite happy with it when it arrived.

He watched her as she expertly cracked the claws and removed the sweet meat.

"Amazing."

She glanced up from her work. "What?"

"That's a damn messy job. But somehow, you do it—" he sought the right word "—so tidily."

"Yes. I'm a tidy eater, all right."

He must have picked up on her ambivalence because he asked, "You don't like being tidy?"

"I'm not tidy, in general." She sucked the last shred of meat from a claw without making a sound. "I'm tidy when I eat. But in most everything else, I'm a mess."

"What do you mean?"

"I don't pick up after myself."

"You mean you're not a good housekeeper?"

"To put it bluntly—" she picked up her glass of Chardonnay and toasted him with it "—I'm a slob."

He sat back in his chair and regarded her.

She waited for him to tell her in some charming way that it was all right to be a slob. After all, if he wanted to please her, that would be the next thing for him to say. It was certainly what her ex-fiancé-as-of-yesterday would have said. Cameron had been a real pro at telling her how wonderful, how charmingly quixotic, how terrific she was in every way.

But Jack Roper only shrugged, as if whether Olivia "Loveless" was a slob or not was her own problem, not his.

She suddenly felt a little ashamed that she'd never had to pick up after herself, so she added, as if it mattered, "But I'm neat in the kitchen. And I'm quite frugal, as well."

"Why the kitchen?"

"I once took an expensive cooking class."

Very expensive. Olivia had spent six months in Paris studying the art of French cooking. In fact, her dream had once been to become a professional chef. But in the end she hadn't been good enough to get a job in any of the really fine restaurants. And eventually her father had convinced her that it was patently absurd for a woman of her means to be cooking in the kind of restaurants where, as a rule, she would never deign to eat. He'd suggested she buy a restaurant of her own to cook in, which somehow had felt like it would have been cheating. So she'd refused.

She told Jack, "I have a great respect for the art and the science of meal preparation."

They looked at each other for a moment over the candle in the middle of their table. She was aware, once again, of how very dark and deep his eyes were, especially in contrast to his pale gold hair. And of how much he attracted her—and how little she knew about him.

She sipped from her wine again. It was kind of nice, really, she thought. Not knowing him. Like one of those lovely old romantic movies. A movie with the word "stranger" in the title. *Strangers in Las Vegas,* perhaps.

He suggested quietly, "Tell me more. About yourself. About Olivia *Loveless.*"

The stress he put on the phony name made her wonder. Did he know it wasn't hers? She looked down at the white tablecloth and back up into his eyes just as the busser cleared her dishes away.

"I'm..."

"Yeah?"

She squared her shoulders. If he knew, he knew, she decided. And if he wanted to confront her with her lie, he could just go ahead and do it. She told him, "I'm just an ordinary woman."

He lifted a white-gold eyebrow but didn't say anything.

"I'm from Los Angeles." It wasn't much of a lie. She lived in Malibu. Her house was right on the beach. Her father had bought it for her as a Christmas present, a few years ago, from a movie star who'd needed a lot of money fast. "I'm here for a few days while I'm between jobs."

That was the truth. Technically. She'd quit her job as a "regional representative" for Larrabee Brewing Company only the day before. It hadn't been a *real* job anyway, just a meaningless position created by her father to ease her guilt about all the money he'd given her that she'd never earned.

"So while I'm in Las Vegas, I want to forget my troubles," she said, "and have a good time."

"And are you?"

"Forgetting my troubles?"

He nodded. "And having a good time."

She gave him a slow-spreading grin. "Now I am."

"Good."

"Dessert?" the waiter asked.

They agreed they'd have coffee.

Once the coffee was served, Olivia asked the question she'd been trying to form all through dinner. "When I turned around and saw you outside the casino, were you following me?"

His eyes seemed even darker than before, and fathoms deep. "Yes, I was." He sipped from his coffee. "I'd been following you for a while by then."

"You had?"

"Yeah. I was watching you at the blackjack table."

"I know." She stirred her coffee, though there was no reason to. She took it black. "I saw you."

"I felt like an idiot."

She looked up. "Why?"

"No one ever catches me staring." She detected a hint of a smile on his lips. "If I'm looking at all, they don't know it. But there's something different about you."

"Different?"

He shrugged. "Yeah. Different. Unusual."

She frowned. "I'm *unusual?*"

"Yeah. You say that you're ordinary, but you're not."

"How do you mean, *unusual?*"

"Well, it's partly that you're so small boned and pale. And then there's that dress."

"What? You don't like my dress?"

"It's different, that's all."

Olivia looked down and stirred her coffee some more, paying great attention to the unnecessary task. She was thinking that maybe the things Jack was saying about her weren't exactly flattering. But somehow, the way he said them, they made her feel complimented, anyway.

"I watched you at the craps table." His voice was low, caressing.

The surge of feminine pleasure she felt was instant and utterly shameless. She remembered the absurd little fantasy she'd indulged in right before she'd thrown the dice and her lucky streak had ended. She'd imagined him watching her. And now it turned out that he had been.

He added, "But you didn't catch me that time."

"No," she murmured softly, watching the coffee swirl in her cup. "I didn't catch you."

"Stop stirring that coffee."

Her hand went still.

"Look at me."

Slowly she raised her head and met his eyes.

"But you spotted me out on the sidewalk."

"Yes, I did."

"You turned around so fast, I didn't have a chance to disappear."

"Umm-hmm."

"That's twice you caught me."

"That's right."

"Nobody catches me." His gaze was so strange. Unreadable. Far away and yet probing.

Olivia had a sudden, disorienting sensation. A feeling of being utterly, completely, out of her depth. She pushed the feeling away and forced a rather brittle laugh. "Well. Should I be sorry?"

"Probably."

"That's too bad. Because I'm not." She took a sip from her overstirred coffee. "I think it's time to change the subject."

"To what?"

"We could talk about what brings you to Las Vegas."

He considered for a moment. "Business."

"What kind of business?"

"Do you really want to know?"

Now she was the one considering. At last she said, "I thought I did, when I asked."

"But?"

"Well, now that I think twice, I'm not so sure. Is it something that's bothering you, this business of yours?"

He didn't answer right away, but then he said, "Yeah, I guess it is bothering me. Just a little."

"I mean, you don't really want to talk about it, do you?"

"No." His eyes were wary again. "To be honest, I'd rather not get into it."

She knew just what he meant. She had no urge at all to tell him what had brought her to Vegas. Now that she was finally having a nice time, the last thing she wanted to talk about was how she'd caught her fiancé with another woman and run off to Nevada to keep from suffering a major depression.

An idea came to her. "Tell you what."

"What?"

"We hardly know each other."

"So?"

"So let's keep it that way. For now."

He looked flummoxed. "What the hell is that supposed to mean?"

She laughed, pleased that she'd managed to catch Jack Roper off guard for once. In general, Jack struck her as a man who rarely allowed himself to be caught off guard. And he'd already confessed that he'd been unable to stop staring at her earlier in the evening.

Because she was so *unusual*.

Her heart, which up until a little while ago had felt like a lead weight in her chest, was starting to seem as light as spun sugar. Maybe this spontaneous trip to Vegas had been the right idea after all.

It was only a little more than twenty-four hours from the moment she'd discovered her fiancé in the arms of his executive assistant. And yet here she was, having dinner with a mysterious and compelling man and somehow actually managing to hold her own with him. The momentary feeling of being out of her depth was long gone.

"Are you going to answer my question?" he asked.

"What question?"

"You said we hardly know each other and that you wanted to keep it that way. What did you mean?"

"Oh, that." She gave an airy wave.

"Yes. That."

"Well—" she sat forward "—what I meant was, let's not talk about the ordinary things, the mundane things. Not tonight, anyway. We're strangers in Las Vegas. And let's enjoy being just that."

He took a sip of coffee. "It's an interesting idea."

"Does that mean you agree?"

He seemed to study her. "If I did, what would we talk about?"

She put her forearms on the table and leaned on them. She was warming to the idea. "Oh, everything. What we think. What we like. What we don't like. Opinions and observations. But no personal facts. Nothing about what you do or what I do or what our everyday lives are like. Nothing about our family problems or any of that stuff. We could save all that for later." She found she was blushing. She sat back a little and added, "I mean, if there *is* a later, of course."

"Of course."

"So what do you think?" She was so pleased with the idea that she bounced a little in her chair.

He chuckled. "Hell. Why not?"

"We have a deal?" She stuck out her hand.

He took it and gave it a firm shake. "You bet we do, Ms. Loveless."

"Brussels sprouts," he said much later. They were sitting in a pair of wing chairs next to an areca palm in a little alcove they'd discovered right off the lobby.

"Brussels sprouts." She pondered a moment. "In any form?"

"Yeah. It doesn't matter how you serve 'em up. I hate 'em."

She didn't realize that what she was thinking must be showing on her face until he said, "I mean it. There is no way you can serve me a Brussels sprout that I would eat."

"I know this little place on Sunset in L.A.," she told him. "They make a Brussels sprout quiche that is out of this world."

He looked at her sideways. He was clearly disgusted. "Quiche?" he asked. "*Quiche?* Next to Brussels sprouts, I hate quiche worst of all."

"A macho and ridiculous prejudice," she informed him.

"Get that nose of yours out of the air." He reached from his chair to hers and brushed her nose with a forefinger. Then he peered more closely at her. "You have freckles, you know."

"I know. I've always had them."

"They're cute. *You're* cute, to tell you the truth."

He sounded like it pained him to admit this, which Olivia found funny. She laughed.

"What is so funny?" He looked noble and wounded.

"Nothing. Everything."

"Start with everything and go on from there."

"It seemed like it almost killed you to say you thought I was cute. I've noticed that about you, Jack."

"Oh, right. You're some big expert on me already.... You've noticed *what?*"

"That you're not exactly lavish with compliments."

He sat back in his chair and sipped the drink that a cocktail waitress had just served him. In the casinos there were cocktail waitresses everywhere. "I should be more lavish, is that what I'm hearing here?"

She smiled softly. "No. You shouldn't. You should be just like you are. A little too blunt. An honest man."

He looked away. She knew at that moment that he hadn't been completely honest with her. But she wasn't really bothered by whatever he was holding back. She'd had a magical evening, made all the more enchanting by its very unexpectedness. They'd talked of so many things. From football to favorite movies. But they'd held to their agreement to keep their real lives out of it. So Jack Roper had a right to a secret or two.

He was looking at her again. "It's late."

She knew he was right. "Yes. So late, it's practically early."

He set his still-full drink aside and stood. "Come on." He reached down. "I'll take you to your room."

She twined her fingers with his and let him pull her to her feet. His touch was warm, his grip strong. Her heart beat faster. She relished the little tingle she felt all through her body, when all she'd done was take his hand.

In the elevator she pushed the button for her floor. They rode up together in silence, fingers still entwined.

She was careful not to think ahead to the precarious moment that was fast approaching, when they would stand at her door.

And then the moment was upon her. They faced each other.

"The evening was perfect," she said.

"Yeah, it was."

"Thank you, Jack."

"My pleasure."

"I..."

"Yeah?"

He waited, still lightly clasping her hand. She looked at his mouth. She'd been looking at his mouth all night. It was a tempting mouth. Chiseled on top, slightly fuller below.

Oh, what was the use of kidding herself? She wanted his kiss. She wanted to feel that tempting mouth against her own. Just once before they said good-night. Or goodbye.

He let go of her hand. She sighed at the loss of his touch.

But then his palm was gliding up her arm, the caress burning, teasing her through her red velvet sleeve.

"Olivia." He said it so tenderly.

She tipped her face up to his. "Jack, I know we agreed not to get personal." Her voice was more breath than sound. She made herself continue. "But there's something I have to know."

"Name it."

"Are you married, Jack?"

He shook his head very slowly.

"Engaged?"

"No."

"Living with anyone?"

"Well..."

Her heart seemed to sink right down into her red satin shoes. "Oh, Jack."

"There's this damn tomcat, see."

"What are you saying, Jack?"

"There's a tomcat. I've been calling him Buzz, because the hair on his head is so short it looks like a buzz cut, you know? He hangs around my apartment. He seems to *think* he lives with me."

Sweet relief coursed through her. It must have shown on her face because he said, "Don't look so happy. The damn cat won't get lost. I'm hoping by the time I get home he'll have given up and moved on."

She tried to look more solemn. "So your only roommate is a cat?"

"Or so the cat seems to think."

"I'm just so glad to hear that."

And she was, oh, she was! Now, there was absolutely nothing standing between her and Jack and the good-night kiss she'd been dreaming of sharing with him.

And of course Jack must want to kiss her, too. He had followed her around the casino for half the night, waiting for just the right moment to step forward and introduce himself. He'd shared a meal with her, and they'd talked for hours. He desired her. It was obvious. Why else would he be with her now?

But maybe he didn't want to push her. After all, they'd only just met.

Olivia smiled. He was probably only waiting for a little signal from her, that was all. Olivia swayed toward Jack, lifting her mouth and letting her eyelids flutter closed.

Chapter Three

Jack Roper gazed down at Olivia's soft, enticing lips. He wanted to taste them.

But there was no damn way he was going to.

Because he knew that the minute he put his mouth on hers and pulled her slim body close he would completely forget the real reason he'd spent the evening with her.

Suppressing a sigh, he stepped back.

She must have felt his withdrawal, because her cornflower blue eyes popped open. She blinked, and he watched a blush move up her slender neck and steal beneath the freckles that dusted her nose.

"Well." She twisted her hands together. "Um, thank you. For everything. And good night." She began fiddling with the small red velvet evening purse that hung from her shoulder on a silken rope.

Damn, he thought angrily. He liked her. Really liked

her. She was a true innocent. She moved him, in a way he hadn't been moved in more years than he cared to count.

She moved him so much that he felt like a first-class jerk for the way he was deceiving her.

He had a moment's crazy urge to tell her everything, right now, as she frantically pawed through her little purse seeking the computerized card that would let her into her room.

But then she looked up at him, those forget-me-not eyes wide and vulnerable. She held the key card in the air. "Found it." She was striving for jauntiness but missed it by a mile.

And he heard himself saying, "If I knocked on your door at noon, would you be ready for breakfast at the greasy spoon of my choice?"

It broke the heart he didn't even know he had anymore to see the way her face changed. She looked like someone had turned on a klieg light beneath her pale skin. She glowed, brighter than a searchlight on opening night.

He wanted to grab her and shake her and tell her it was a rotten world out there. She had to protect herself, learn to cover her feelings, not let strangers see every little thing that went on inside of her.

But he didn't. He ordered his hands to stay loose at his sides and made his mouth smile an easy smile.

"I'll be ready," she said.

"Great. See you then."

Once inside her suite Olivia tossed her evening bag on the little table by the door and waltzed through the foyer into the sitting room. She danced around the love seat, whirled past the easy chair and spun into the bedroom, where she at last collapsed, giggling joyously across the king-size bed.

She noticed then that the light on her phone was blinking. She sighed. It would be her father, of course. Wanting her to call him back, no matter what time it was.

She wasn't going to do it. She simply wasn't.

But of course, even as she determined to stand her ground on this, she was picturing the way he was probably pacing the floor of his study right now, unable to sleep because of his concern for her.

It was only because she knew how he worried about her that she'd called him when she'd first arrived here in Vegas. She'd felt driven to reassure him that she was all right. But she'd also told him firmly that he was not to call her back.

With a little groan Olivia sat up and rubbed her eyes. Then she buzzed the desk to make sure the message really had been from her father.

"I show six messages here," the switchboard operator said. "All from Lawrence Larrabee—hey, is that *the* Lawrence Larrabee, as in Larrabee Lager?"

"Yes," Olivia said, sighing. "I'm afraid it is."

"Well, what do you know? Anyway, he called six times and each time left the same message. Call him back as soon as you get in."

Olivia suddenly realized she was getting a headache. "Thank you." She hung up and pondered the idea of wandering into the bathroom to see if there was a complimentary packet of pain reliever in there.

But then she decided she only needed to relax. So she kicked off her shoes and sat Indian-style on the bed. She closed her eyes and rolled her neck and chanted one of the affirmations she'd picked up in a stress-management class.

"I am in charge of my life and affairs. I am in charge of my life and affairs. I am in charge of—"

Right then the phone started ringing.

Olivia went on chanting.

The phone went on ringing.

Olivia was determined not to answer.

But somehow, around the seventh ring, her hand reached out on its own accord and snatched the darn thing from its cradle.

"What?"

"Livvy?"

"No, sorry. There's no one by that name here."

Her father let out a tired breath. "It's damn late, Livvy."

She thought of Jack, and her mood lightened marginally. "I know. So late it's practically early."

"I left several messages requesting that you call."

"Well, I told you I wouldn't."

"Are you all right?"

"Stop worrying, Dad. Let it be. I need a little time away, that's all. Can't you please understand that?"

He was quiet for a moment. She heard a murmur on the other end and knew that Mindy Long—a special lady her father had been seeing for the past year—was there with him. She also knew the things Mindy would be saying. More than once Olivia had confided in Mindy. Mindy understood Olivia's position and would be on her side.

Olivia urged, "Please, Dad. Listen to Mindy."

"I *have* been listening to Mindy. I've been listening to Mindy all night. You two women will drive me to an early grave."

"*Please.*" She put everything she had into the word, to try to get through to him. "I love you and I know you'd do anything for me. But this is something you just *can't* do for me. I have to do it on my own."

Her father made a disgusted sound. "But what is it you're doing?"

"I'm . . . finding myself."

Her father swore roundly. "Fine. Find yourself in
Malibu, where you belong."

"No."

"This is insane, Olivia. There is nothing in Las Vegas
that will help you to *find* yourself. There are endless miles
of sagebrush and cactus. And there is gambling. And that
is it."

"Dad—"

"It's absurd. I want you to come home. I'm sorry
about Cameron." Her father felt guilty about what had
happened, because Cameron worked for him. "I never
should have introduced you two, I understand that now.
It was all my fault and I'll—"

"It was not your fault. Please, Dad, don't—"

"Yes, yes it was. I thought he was a nice young man."

"He *is* a nice young man, Dad. Just not a faithful
one."

"He's toast in the brewing industry, I can tell you
that."

"You already told me that. And I told you that he's the
best salesman you've got. And I don't want you to fire
him because of me. Please."

"Livvy, you are too forgiving. You have got to toughen
up a little or—"

Olivia just didn't want to hear anymore, so she prepared to say what she'd been hoping she wouldn't have
to say. "Dad, I want you to stop calling me."

"Livvy, I—"

"Listen. I mean this. If you don't let me work this out
on my own, I'll go somewhere else."

That gave him pause. "What?"

"I said, I'll go somewhere else. And this time I won't
call you to tell you I'm all right."

"Now, Livvy. Don't do anything you'll regret."

"This is the situation, Dad. You leave me alone. Stop
calling me. Let me work this out for myself, or I will get

in my car and drive. I'll disappear. And when I finally stop, it'll be somewhere you've never heard of. Understand?"

"Please don't do that, Livvy."

"Then stop calling me."

The ensuing silence from her father's end was hard for Olivia to bear. But she did bear it, because she had to, even though she knew that he truly did want the very best for her.

"All right," Lawrence Larrabee said at last.

He sounded so weary. Olivia ached for him. But she couldn't give him what he wanted. Not anymore. At some point she had to live her life as she chose to. She had to make her own mistakes and suffer her own consequences. She was almost thirty and she was going to have to grow up.

He asked, "Have you got enough money?"

She wanted to cry. "Of course."

"If you need anything..."

"I know. I love you, Dad."

"I never doubted that. And I love you."

"Bye."

And then he was gone.

Olivia very gently put the phone back in its cradle. And then she stared toward the far wall for a time, questioning everything—all of it, from coming here in the first place to the conversation she'd just had with her father.

She'd said she was "finding herself," and sincerely meant it at the moment. But the more she thought about it, the more she had to agree with her father. Las Vegas was an odd place to go to find oneself.

And then there was Jack, about whom she really knew nothing. Which wasn't his fault, of course. She'd been the one to suggest they remain "strangers in Las Vegas" for an evening. Tomorrow, she was sure, they would get to know each other better.

The wisdom of there even *being* a "Jack" in her life at this point made her wonder. She'd just been betrayed in the worst kind of way by one man. Perhaps that should have told her something about her judgment where men were concerned. She really hadn't had much experience in that area, to be honest. And maybe it would be advisable to stay away from men for a while.

Maybe tomorrow she should tell Jack that she'd enjoyed their evening together more than he could ever know, but she wasn't going to have breakfast with him after all. She could explain gently and regretfully that, while he was the most incredible man she'd ever laid eyes on, the timing was all wrong. She simply had too much work to do on herself before she would be ready to share anything meaningful with a man.

"Yuck," Olivia said to the far wall.

The thought of sending Jack away was just too depressing to consider. And hadn't she come here in the first place to avoid depression? A lot of good she'd do herself if she sent Jack away in order to "find herself" and then became depressed once he was gone. Because, truthfully, the idea of not seeing Jack tomorrow left her feeling more than a little dismal.

And beyond that, there remained the fact that she really didn't know the man at all. Maybe he wouldn't even show up tomorrow. Maybe she was wasting her time sitting here worrying about whether or not she should send him away, because she was never going to see him again, anyway. Maybe he would—

"Oh, stop it," she muttered at the wall. "Stop it right now. No more thinking tonight, and that's that."

With a soft little sigh, she slid off the bed. Once she managed to undo the tiny buttons at the back of her red velvet dress, she slithered it down over her hips and stepped out of it. Then she went straight to the bathroom for a long, soothing soak in the tub.

Behind her, the expensive dress lay on the floor in a crimson puddle, right where it had fallen, next to her red satin shoes. A trail of silky underthings marked the way she had gone.

Olivia woke to the sound of knocking.

After a few grunts and groans she rolled her head and squinted at the digital clock-radio by the bed.

Noon.

Jack was supposed to come for her at noon.

"Omigod!" She leapt from the bed. "Coming!" She looked down at herself. She was wearing black silk shorty pajamas.

"Unacceptable," she decided aloud. She was crazy about Jack, but that didn't mean she could greet him at the door wearing nothing but black silk lingerie. She scanned the room frantically, looking for something to put on over the pajamas, calling out at the same time, "Just a minute! Be right there!"

The short robe that matched the pajamas was nowhere in sight. And anyway, it was too suggestive by far.

She raced to her stack of luggage in the dressing area and plowed through the largest suitcase, which was a total mess even though she'd only been in Las Vegas since early yesterday morning. Already she was missing Constance, her live-in housekeeper at home, who kept everything in order and seemed somehow always to be able to find whatever Olivia was looking for.

"Aha!" she crowed, as she found a huge knit shirt that was supposed to be worn with stirrup pants. The stirrup pants were nowhere in sight. But the shirt was modest enough by itself. Olivia tugged it over her head and smoothed it down.

Then she rushed to the door and swung it wide.

And there was Jack, wearing chinos and a shirt with a designer logo on it. He looked as if he'd been awake for hours.

"Hi."

"Hi."

After that, she wasn't sure what to say next.

The lines around his eyes deepened with his smile. "Forgot to set the alarm, huh?"

She just stared, thinking how absurdly glad she was to see him. He looked her up and down and went on smiling.

She realized that they couldn't stand here all day, gawking at each other and grinning. "I need a few minutes." She almost invited him to wait in her sitting room, but held back. It seemed a little too intimate for right now.

"I'll be in the lobby."

"Okay. I'll be there in twenty minutes. I promise."

Jack took her to a place called Randy Jim's.

Randy Jim's was an actual railroad car parked between a Joshua tree and a saguaro cactus out on Highway 147. The sign in the window said Breakfast Served All Day. They ate biscuits and gravy and drank coffee they poured themselves from the insulated pot the waitress provided.

They were both quiet, but more because neither of them felt like talking, Olivia thought, than anything else. They looked out the window at the highway and then back at each other.

Once or twice Olivia almost broke the companionable silence to tell him that she'd lied about her name. But she was having such a lovely time that she decided she could put it off for a little while longer. She definitely would tell him by the end of the day. But for right now, even though she probably shouldn't, she was going to postpone the unpleasant task for a while and just enjoy being with him.

When they were through eating, they lingered a while, sharing a newspaper that some other customer had left behind.

At one point Olivia glanced over the top of the entertainment section she was reading. She saw the crown of Jack's head, his brown elbows and forearms and his fingers. The rest of him was hidden by the sports section.

And she had the warmest, sweetest welling of emotion within her. She didn't examine it, for fear of losing it. She only smiled to herself and went back to her own reading.

"Ready to go?" he inquired just a little while later.

On their way back to the hotel/casino, Jack asked if she'd tried the pool up on the roof yet. She admitted she hadn't.

"How about now?" he asked.

She agreed that a swim was just what she needed.

The roof pool was open to the sun, with a view of the gray outlines of the mountains that loomed in the distance. And even though it was October, the heat in the middle of the day made the air dance and shimmer.

Olivia was careful of her pale skin, slathering herself in sunscreen and then putting her chaise longue in the shade of a potted palm. Jack put his chaise beside hers, though his bronze skin looked like it could withstand a lot more sun than hers.

After a few minutes in the water they lay down side by side, and for a while neither spoke. Olivia closed her eyes and listened to the splashing and giggling from the kids who were playing in the pool. Once or twice the kids got carried away. The water would splash so high Olivia would feel the cool drops on her legs. It felt good.

She felt good.

"What are you smiling about?" Jack's voice was low and very close.

She turned her head and opened her eyes. He lay on his stomach and had rested his head on his hands at the edge of his chaise, so that his face was less than two feet from her own.

She studied him, her breath catching a little. His lashes were very thick and pale gold, like his brows.

Earlier, she'd had a chance to admire him without being too obvious about it. His body was lean, his shoulders broad, his musculature well developed, though spare. He had more than a few scars—on his arms and shoulders and on his chest. There was one on his leg that ran around the back of his calf, like a white snake against the bronze flesh. A warrior's scars, she thought, and wondered if he'd been in the military.

"Earth to Olivia," he teased softly.

"What?"

"I asked what you were smiling about."

Instead of answering, she asked a question of her own. "You were watching me, weren't you? While I had my eyes closed."

"Is that a crime? If so, I plead guilty."

"No, it's no crime."

"Good. Now, what were you smiling about?"

"I was thinking that I feel good."

The corners of his mouth curled in a lazy grin. "I suppose there are worse reasons to smile."

A word she'd been trying to think of finally occurred to her. "Obsidian," she whispered.

He lifted an eyebrow. "What?"

"Your eyes," she mused. "Like obsidian. That deep black green. Especially for a man with light hair, it's very unusual." She purposely used the word he'd employed to describe her the night before, wondering if he'd remember, if he'd come back with some clever rejoinder.

But instead of a clever reply, he only looked away. "Yeah. So I've been told."

His reaction puzzled her. "What? Did I say something?"

"Nothing. It's nothing."

"Yes, it is. I can tell."

"It's nothing, really. Someone used to say that about my eyes, that's all. But it doesn't matter. It was a long time ago."

"You mean, someone used to say that your eyes are unusual?"

"Yeah."

"Who?"

"It was a long time ago."

"Who?"

"No one. My father."

She turned over onto her stomach. Then she scooted closer, so there were only inches between their noses. She could smell him. Moisture and chlorine. Some kind of lotion or after-shave. And something else, slightly musky and very seductive to her: his body's special scent.

She put aside her pleasurable contemplation of how much he attracted her. She had another thing on her mind right then. She was thinking of how she wanted to learn all about him, but how she had no right to expect him to tell her any of his secrets when he still believed that she was someone named Loveless.

Do it. Tell him who you really are right now, an inner voice urged.

But she couldn't quite say the words.

Instead she decided to lay a little groundwork for the beginnings of trust between them.

"Jack?"

"Um?"

"I think we just broke last night's agreement."

He looked puzzled for a minute, and then he understood. "You mean because I mentioned my father?"

"Yes. You came very close to revealing something about yourself, about who you really are." She laid a hand on his arm. His skin was warm, the muscles beneath hard under her palm. "I'm glad."

"Right." The word was gruff.

"You'll tell me more."

"It looks likely."

"But not right now, is that it?"

He chuckled. And then, with a stunning economy of movement, he was on his feet and reaching for her hand. "Come on."

"What?" But even as she asked the question, she was pushing herself up and swinging her legs to the concrete.

"Time for a swim," he announced, spinning her around and scooping her up against his chest.

She understood what he planned too late. By the time she shouted, "No, Jack!" he had already strode to the edge of the pool and was tossing her in.

They tried some of the other casinos that night.

They crossed an actual moat, complete with drawbridge, to enter the Excalibur. Then they stood on the street gawking with all the other tourists in front of the Mirage, where an imitation volcano spewed real fire into the night sky every fifteen minutes. Inside, they watched Siegfried & Roy perform fantastic illusions.

When the hour grew late, they found their special place again, back at their own hotel, in the wing chairs by the potted palm.

There, as she'd been building her courage all day to do, Olivia ventured, "Jack, I, um..."

He leaned near her chair. "What?"

She swallowed. Sweet heaven, this was difficult.

She didn't even know she was twisting her hands together until he captured them and held them still in his. "Just say it." With his thumbs he idly stroked the hands he held captive. "Come on, I'm listening."

She dragged in a big breath and came out with it. "I'm not who you think I am."

He frowned. "What?"

"I said, I'm not who you think I am."

Suddenly his expression was very strange, very distant. He'd stopped his subtle stroking of her hands.

She forced herself to go on. "I lied, Jack. My name isn't Loveless. My name is Larrabee."

He tipped his head to the side. "You lied?"

She bobbed her head up and down. "Yes, I did. When I told you my name last night, I just wanted to be someone else at that moment."

"Someone else?" He was still looking strange and distant.

She hastened to make him see. "Yes. Someone other than me. Oh, I'm sure it doesn't make any sense to you—"

"I didn't say that."

"You didn't have to."

"Olivia, I—"

"No. Let me finish. Let me explain." Her words came fast, then. They tumbled over each other getting out of her mouth. "You see, I'm rich, Jack. Very rich. My father is Lawrence Larrabee, of Larrabee Brewing Company. And Jack, I hate being rich. I'm just no good at it. And all my life being Lawrence Larrabee's daughter has overshadowed everything. It cuts me off from people, it makes me different. And most of the time I never know if a person likes me for myself or for my money or what. It's very confusing to me. But with you it was different. You didn't have any idea who I was, and still you were . . . interested in me."

Jack had let go of her hand. She looked at him, begging him with her eyes to understand.

But he didn't seem to understand at all. Instead he was withdrawing from her, just as she had feared he might when he learned that she had pretended to be someone she wasn't.

She blundered on, willing him to forgive her deception, to understand how she'd felt. "It meant so much to me, Jack. That you didn't have a clue who I was and yet still you were following me. I couldn't stand to watch your eyes change, Jack. Because that's what always happens with people. They learn who I am and their eyes change. I'm not *me* anymore. I hate that. I…" Her voice trailed off as Jack actually stood and turned away from her. It was obvious he couldn't bear to hear another word.

She pleaded, "Jack? Oh, Jack. Please. I'm sorry. Forgive me."

He turned then. "Stop," he said quietly. He looked completely composed. "There's nothing to forgive."

She stared up at him, bewildered. What in the world could be going through his mind?

"But I *lied* to you."

He put up a hand. "Hey." His voice was so tender. Slowly he sank to his chair again.

And then he did the most wonderful thing. He reached out, hesitantly, as if he were doing something she might not allow, and he touched the side of her face. One feather-light caress, from her temple to her chin. To Olivia it was the most consuming touch she'd ever known. It burned her right down to her soul.

He whispered, "It's okay. It's not a big deal."

"It's not?"

"No."

She blinked at him, bewildered. He was behaving very strangely, first seeming unable to bear what she was telling him and then suddenly turning around and saying there was nothing to forgive.

But then it came to her. Of course, he must have been hurt at first that she hadn't trusted him. And now he wanted to let it go, since he realized that there had been no malice in what she had done.

Like her, Jack only wanted the two of them to go on from here. The important thing was that he wouldn't hold it against her for pretending to be someone else.

He was smiling at her. "It's late."

She bit her lip, since it was trembling a little. "So late it's practically early."

He made a low sound in his throat, and she knew he remembered how they'd shared the same exchange the night before. Then, once more, he was on his feet, holding out his hand.

"Come on. I'll take you to your room."

She pushed away the vague uneasiness that kept trying to sweep over her and went with him.

Like the night before, they rode the elevator hand in hand.

However, unlike the night before, this time she was certain that he would kiss her when they reached her door.

But he didn't.

And for a moment she even thought he was going to leave without a word about seeing her again.

She couldn't let that happen.

She collected all her courage and suggested, "It's my turn to treat for breakfast. There's a café downstairs by the other pool, the indoor one? Meet me there. At noon."

He said nothing. His look was rueful.

She refused to believe that he was trying to think of a way to bow out. "Okay, okay. I know, it's hardly Randy Jim's. But what do you expect? I'm new in town."

"Olivia . . ."

"I promise to set my alarm. I won't stand you up." She held up her hand. "Scout's honor."

Oh, Lord. What if he said no? She didn't even have his room number.

"All right." His voice was grim. "I'll be there."

Before she could drum up the nerve to ask him what in the world was going on with him, he turned and was gone.

She stared after him for a moment, her heart so heavy it seemed to weight her feet to the floor. What had happened? She wasn't really sure.

She was only sure about one thing.

She'd seen the look in his eyes just before he turned away from her. And she knew what that look meant.

He never intended to see her again.

Chapter Four

In Jack's room the message light was blinking.

He knew who it would be. But he buzzed the switchboard anyway, just in case it might be someone else.

It wasn't.

"Lawrence Larrabee called," the switchboard operator said. "He wants you to call him back as soon as you get in."

Jack punched up the home number Larrabee had given him. It was answered on the third ring.

"Hello?"

It was the aged housekeeper, Zelda, whom Jack had met on the interview two days before, when Larrabee had hired him. Zelda was a tank of a woman, a true family retainer. Zelda did not approve of private investigators; that had been clear to Jack from the moment she'd opened the door of Larrabee's huge Bel Air mansion to him. She'd looked at him as if he were something she'd found stuck to the bottom of her shoe.

"Let me speak to Lawrence Larrabee," Jack said.

"Who is calling?"

"Jack Roper."

There was a disapproving pause, then "One moment, please."

Larrabee was on the line in seconds flat. "Roper. What the hell's going on? It's the middle of the night."

"Fine. I'll call in the morning." Jack started to hang up.

"Roper!" Lawrence Larrabee's shout came through even though the phone was nowhere near Jack's ear.

With a sigh Jack put the phone to his ear again. "Mr. Larrabee, *you* called *me.*"

"You're damn right I did. I want to know what's going on."

"I'm doing my job. Keeping an eye on your daughter."

"And?"

"And what? She's fine. Having a ball."

"What do you mean *a ball?*"

"I mean, she seems to be having a great time."

"Doing what?"

"Seeing the sights. Taking in some shows. Gambling a little."

"Gambling?"

"Mr. Larrabee, she hasn't been throwing her money around, I promise you."

"I don't care about the money. It's my *daughter* I'm worried about. She's a very sensitive girl. And if she's developing a gambling problem I—"

"She's not. Forget that."

"All right. But does she seem okay? Emotionally, I mean? And mentally?"

"Look. I'm no mind reader, but she seems fine to me."

"She's recently been put through hell. I don't think I have to tell you—"

"You're right. You don't."

Larrabee had explained all about the two-timing fiancé at the interview. Jack was in no mood to hear it all again. Tonight he'd had to listen to Olivia beg him to forgive her for deceiving him about her last name. He felt like a worm. Jack didn't think he could take it if Larrabee started in again about what some other guy had done to her.

Larrabee was still running his inquisition. "She hasn't hooked up with any suspicious characters, has she?"

Nobody but me, Jack thought but didn't say. He'd yet to explain to Larrabee that *he* was the one Olivia was having a ball with, though he'd had three conversations with the man since he and Olivia had begun spending every waking moment together.

"Well, has she?" Larrabee prodded, since Jack had yet to answer him.

"Hooked up with any suspicious characters?" Jack repeated, begging the question with an obvious stall.

"That's what I asked. Come on, Roper. What do you think I'm paying you for? Give it to me straight."

Jack thought about Olivia. About how all he really wanted was to go on meeting her at noon, wandering this gaudy gambling mecca through the day and into the night together. And not parting until "it was so late, it was practically early."

Or, better yet, not parting at all.

But he knew that what he wanted was impossible.

Unlike Olivia, Jack was a realist. He knew very well that they were on a collision course with emotional disaster.

There was just nowhere this relationship could go. She was a poor little rich girl, who wore her heart on her red velvet sleeve. And he was nobody from nowhere, who'd been duping her from the moment she'd cried out "Wait! Don't go" on the street outside the casino.

And the only way to end it was to cut it clean.

"Roper?" Larrabee's voice was getting agitated.

It was the moment. Time to end this charade.

He made himself do it. "Yeah, she's been seeing a suspicious character, all right. Me."

Larrabee made a sort of wheezing, choking sound. *"What?"*

"I said she's been with me. Since last night—or is it night before last by now?"

The pause before Lawrence Larrabee spoke was a gruesome one.

But at last the older man asked in a voice of equal parts velvet and steel, "What exactly are you telling me, Roper?"

Grimly, Jack explained. "She caught me watching her."

"She *what?*"

"I think you heard me, Mr. Larrabee."

"How could she have caught you? You never get caught. You came highly recommended. You won medals as a cop. You've been in a forced recon team in the jungles of Southeast Asia. You've tracked down men no one else could find and stayed with them for days without them realizing you were watching them. You're the best in the business. I have it in writing from several different sources."

Jack rubbed the bridge of his nose. "I'm just giving you the facts here. She caught me. Twice."

Larrabee repeated the word with frank disbelief. *"Twice?"*

"Yeah, twice."

The truth was that the beer baron's daughter had been the cutest thing Jack had ever seen, sitting there at the blackjack table in that strange red dress, peeking at her cards and biting the edge of her tongue. Jack had forgotten the basic rule of the job: stay invisible.

She'd looked up and caught him gawking like some rank amateur. He'd known then that if she spotted him again, she'd have to put two and two together and realize he was following her. He would be dead meat.

But he'd been sure she would never catch him a second time. No one else ever had.

Wrong again.

Outside, she'd headed off down the street like she knew right where she was going, picking up the hem of that odd dress to keep it from trailing on the sidewalk. Her baby-fine hair, which was an intriguing color, halfway between gold and bronze, had hung in slightly bedraggled ringlets down her back.

He'd thought, *Unreal. Scarlett O'Hara in Las Vegas.*

He'd been amused by her...and he hadn't been on his toes.

She'd chosen that moment to whirl around. She was looking right at him again before he even realized he was had. He explained to Larrabee, "The second time she spotted me, I figured it was over. So I was going to walk away and call you right then, tell you I'd been seen and you'd better find someone else."

"Okay." Larrabee seemed to be speaking through clenched teeth. "And why didn't you do that?"

"Because she'd jumped to a conclusion."

"What conclusion?"

"She assumed I was following her around because I was interested."

"What do you mean, *interested?*"

"I mean *interested*. Attracted. She thought I found her—"

"Never mind. I get the idea. Go on."

"Fine. She thought I was attracted to her, and she was flattered. When I started to walk away, she asked me not to go. We struck up a conversation. I played along. We had dinner together Tuesday. And then from noon

Wednesday, we've been mostly together. I just left her at her room twenty minutes ago."

Lawrence Larrabee allowed another gruesome pause to elapse. Then he softly said, "I don't like this, Roper."

Jack said nothing. What was there to say?

"Have you taken advantage of her?"

Jack groaned. "Oh, come on, Larrabee. I feel enough like a jerk already."

"You've kept hands off?"

"Yeah. I haven't even kissed her. Now, look. I've told you what's happening. And now I'm out of it. I'll send you a bill for the first day, and you can consider Wednesday on me. It was a damn great day as far as I was concerned, anyway. Fair enough?"

"No."

Now Jack was the one speaking softly. "Excuse me?"

"I said, no. It isn't *fair enough,* not by a long shot. I've explained to you that Olivia is in a very shaky emotional state right now. And if what you've described to me, this little *friendship* you two seem to have developed, is really happening—"

"Oh, come off it, Larrabee. Do you actually believe this is something I'd make up?"

Larrabee was silent again. Then he admitted, "No, I do not think you've made it up. Olivia has just had her confidence in her appeal as a woman shattered. Right now, any reasonably attractive man could—"

"Look. Let's not go on and on about this. I'm just a hired hand here, and I want out."

"Well, Mr. Roper, I'm not letting you out."

Jack said something very crude under his breath. Then he carefully inquired, "Was there some specific way you planned to stop me from getting out?"

"As a matter of fact, yes. I'll pay you—"

"Please. There are some things even a P.I. won't do for money."

"What are you saying?"

"Let me draw you a picture. Keep your money."

"Fine. Then think of Olivia."

"Damn it, I *am* thinking of Olivia."

"Roper, you are not. If you were thinking of Olivia, you would know that if you really are her friend now, then the *last* thing you should do is vanish from her life without explanation."

"*Friend* is your word, not mine."

"You're going to have to break this off more gradually, Roper. You know it. And I know it."

"If you're so worried about her, maybe you'd better come here yourself."

"I can't."

"Right. You're so damned *concerned* about her, but you can't spare the time for her."

"That's not it. She doesn't want me there. She's threatened to disappear if I don't leave her alone. Unfortunately I believe her."

Now Jack was the one muttering. "I don't like this."

"Neither do I. But it's happened. And we have to deal with it. You stay with my daughter, Roper. Understand? Keep your hands off and start figuring out a way to tell her goodbye gently. Are we clear?"

Jack swore some more.

"I'll be in touch. Call me here or at Larrabee Enterprises if anything new comes up."

Though Olivia was right on time for breakfast at the poolside café, Jack was there ahead of her.

She saw him before he spotted her, because he already had his nose buried in the morning edition of the *Las Vegas Sun*.

She stood for a moment by the little sign that said Please Wait To Be Seated and let the gladness and gratitude wash over her.

He was here! He hadn't gone away!

All night, or what had remained of it after they'd parted, she'd tossed and turned. She'd been distressingly certain that the strange way he'd behaved before he'd left her at her door had meant the worst: she would never see him again.

Though she'd only spent two evenings and a day with him, and he'd told her nothing about who he really was, Olivia felt that she knew Jack Roper right down to his soul.

He'd never even kissed her, yet in some deep, inchoate way, she knew him intimately.

And she had been certain when he'd left her last night that he had not planned to keep their date this morning. She was also reasonably sure about what had caused his retreat from her.

It was her money. As usual.

Jack was a proud man and, she suspected now, a poor one. He had probably just lost his job or something and had come here to Las Vegas as a place to forget his troubles for a few days before he decided what to do next.

And last night, when he'd learned how wealthy she was, he'd decided it would never work out between them. He'd decided to stop seeing her.

But, thank heaven, sometime in the night he must have changed his mind. And here he was, after all.

"How many?" the hostess asked.

"I'm joining someone." Olivia gestured toward Jack. "That man over there, as a matter of fact."

Just then Jack looked up from his paper. He smiled at her.

"This way, then," the hostess said.

Jack lowered his paper as she approached. His mouth was wary, but his black eyes shone. She knew he was as glad to see her as she was to see him.

Olivia's feet hardly touched the floor. Her happiness allowed her to defy gravity.

He'd met her this morning, after all. And soon enough he would share his secrets. It was only a matter of time.

That day they visited Hoover Dam, where they looked out over the massive spillway onto Lake Mead, rode in an elevator down to the power plant for a guided tour and then watched a movie about the dam's construction. To Olivia it was all great fun to ooh and ah over what the promotional film had declared to be one of the engineering wonders of the United States.

And truthfully, as long as Jack was beside her, it didn't really matter what they did. As far as she was concerned, they could have spent the whole day in the wing chairs by the potted palm.

Jack was attentive and funny and said he was having a good time. And when he looked at her, Olivia knew that at last she'd found someone who wanted her for herself alone.

But she also knew he was troubled. She could see it in the depths of his eyes. And after they had dinner at a place called The Golden Steer, she dared to ask him what was on his mind.

He took her arm. "Let's go for a ride," he said.

She went willingly, praying that the time had come when he would reveal to her the secrets of his heart.

They drove out to the desert, out across the wide, empty flatness in the direction of the gray hump of Mount Charleston, to the northwest.

Out in the middle of nowhere, with only sagebrush and tumbleweed for company, Jack pulled off the road and drove over the cracked and bumpy desert floor until they reached a sign that said: Las Vegas, Where The Fun Never Stops.

He parked beneath the sign and turned off the engine. Behind them was the glow of the city and ahead, the shadow of the mountains. Above, the waning moon gleamed down, and the stars were so thick they all seemed to blend together in the wide, wide sky.

He turned to her, putting his arm across the back of her seat. Even through the darkness, she could see the unhappiness in his eyes.

She gave him an encouraging smile. "What is it, Jack? I've known all day that something is bothering you. Tell me what it is. Maybe I can help."

He shook his head, murmuring her name in a musing way.

And then he cupped her chin.

Olivia went on smiling, though she knew that the smile was a little wobbly. His touch affected her deeply. Her skin burned beneath the light caress of his fingers. Her heartbeat seemed faster and stronger, too.

He longed to kiss her. She could see it in his eyes, in the gentle yet hungry curve of his mouth, which was mere inches from her own. Idly he caressed her jawline, his thumb and fingers softly stroking.

She drew in a breath. It sighed into her lungs. Now her whole body was tingling, though he only touched her chin. She waited for his lips to meet hers.

When it didn't happen, she dared to softly implore, "Kiss me, Jack."

His eyes were so sad. He dropped his hand and sat back in his seat.

Disappointed and slightly mortified, Olivia retreated to her seat as well. For a while they stared out at the wide starry sky. In the distance a coyote howled.

At last Olivia knew something had to be said. "Why didn't you kiss me, Jack? You wanted to, I know you did. I don't understand."

"It would be wrong."

She looked at him. "That doesn't make sense. You said you're not committed to anyone else . . . and neither am I. We're both adults. What could be wrong about us sharing a kiss?"

"A lot."

"But what?"

"Olivia—"

"Is it a money problem, Jack? Are you out of a job or something? If it is, it doesn't matter to me. I swear to you, it doesn't matter at all."

"It's not money."

She wasn't sure she believed him. Still, what else could she do but ask, "Okay, then, what is it?"

"Hell" was all he said. He reached for the keys to start the car.

"Wait." She put her hand on his arm and felt him stiffen in reaction. "Let's not go yet. Please, Jack."

"Olivia, there's no point in staying here."

"Oh, but there is. There really is. We could talk a little, Jack. About ourselves. It doesn't have to be anything too fresh or too painful." She thought of Cameron and realized there was at least one thing in her life that she wouldn't be talking about right now. Around Jack she felt like a beautiful, desirable woman. She wasn't quite ready to have him learn that her ex-fiancé hadn't found her desirable at all.

She rushed on. "It could be anything. Our life stories—at least up to a point. Or maybe what growing up was like for us. I was an only child, myself."

Olivia released Jack's arm and shifted in her seat. She wanted to give him something, to reveal something of who she really was, so that maybe he would feel that he could trust her in return.

She thought of her mother and she felt the old, hollow ache inside.

Olivia had no memory of the woman who had given her life. She knew from pictures that Karyn Larrabee had been pretty, with a heart-shaped face and big blue eyes. And she knew from her father that Karyn had been kind; a gentle woman who laughed easily, who loved cats and roses and movies with Jimmy Stewart in them.

Olivia said, "My mother died when I was just a baby."

Jack looked away. "Olivia, you don't have to—"

"Yes," she said. "I want to. Please listen."

He turned to face her. Then he conceded. "All right."

She twisted her hands together, realized she was doing it and forced them to be still. "My mother was kidnapped," she said softly, "and held for ransom. My father paid. But they killed her anyway.

"It was all over the papers, maybe you heard about it. The kidnappers themselves died in a bloody shootout with the authorities. I was just a baby, way too young to remember any of it." Jack was watching her. She could feel his eyes, though she was staring out the windshield. She made herself look at him. "But sometimes I feel like I remember it, when I look in my Dad's eyes."

"Olivia—"

She put up a hand. "I miss her, you know? Still, to this day. I miss someone I never even knew." She swallowed and took in a breath. "Anyway. About my childhood—remember I suggested that we could talk about our childhoods?"

Jack nodded.

"Well, I was raised by my dad. He was a good dad. He always had time for me. I was fortunate in always having love. My earliest memories are of just the two of us, me and Dad. A family. I had nurses and companions, of course, as I was growing up. But my father was always there to pour my breakfast cereal, to teach me to ride a bike. And to chase away the boogeymen under my bed.

"But he's too protective. I suppose it's because of what happened to my mother. He was always afraid to let me out of his sight. His name is a household word. He even let the ad agency talk him into putting his picture on the bottles when they launched Lawrence Larrabee's Private Reserve five years ago. But he's always been careful to keep me out of the spotlight. I've led a very private, sheltered kind of life. So now I'm twenty-nine years old and still working on making a life of my own, even though I should have done it years ago." She sighed. "Does that make sense?"

"Yeah. It makes sense." Jack's voice was soft. He reached out and touched her hair. It was a touch of understanding, of reassurance. And yet it stirred her body, made her skin feel hot and prickly and her blood pump harder in her veins.

It was odd, Olivia thought, how strongly she was attracted to Jack physically. Until Jack, she'd thought herself pretty much a cold fish when it came to those intimate things that went on between men and women. In fact, *cold fish* were exactly the words Cameron had used at the end, when she'd caught him with Bree Haversham, his executive assistant.

"Oh, get real, Olivia," Cameron had said. *"What do you care if I have a little fun with someone else? You're a cold fish in bed, anyway, and we both know it damn well."*

"Earth to Olivia."

She felt herself blushing.

"Are you all right?"

"Yes. Yes, I'm fine."

Jack gave her a smile that was somehow both encouraging and teasing at the same time. "So. I guess it's my turn, huh? You expect to hear my life story."

Anticipation lightened her heart. Now they were getting somewhere. She squirmed in her seat a little. "Oh, yes. I do, Jack. I want to know everything about you that you're willing to tell me."

He tipped his head, as if he was wondering whether she meant what she was saying. "It's a downer of a story, really."

"Let me judge that for myself, please. You just tell it."

He still looked doubtful, but he agreed. "Okay. You asked for it." He paused, collecting his thoughts, she imagined. Then he said, "I was born in Bakersfield, an only child like you were. Until I was nine, I lived near there on a farm."

"Your parents owned a farm?"

"It was my father's farm."

"What was your father's name?"

"John Roper."

"What was he like?"

Jack rubbed his eyes.

"You're quiet. What does that mean? You had a problem with your father?"

"I guess you could say that. If he even *was* my father."

She was trying to follow this. "He *wasn't* your father?"

"I don't know. John Roper didn't believe he was my father, even though my mother, Alana, always insisted that he was."

"Your father *told* you that he didn't believe you were his son?"

"No. It was a big secret. But every once in a while, when he and my mother would have a fight, he'd let it slip in some sideways remark. And by the time I was seven or eight, I'd figured it out."

Olivia thought of what Jack had said the day before, about his father calling Jack's eyes unusual. "But you don't know for sure, do you, if he was right or not?"

"It doesn't matter." Jack's shrug was unconcerned.

Too unconcerned, Olivia thought. "Jack, come on. It must matter to you."

"Look." Jack's voice was cold. "I agreed to tell you about my childhood. But let's not make a big deal of it, okay? It was a long time ago. And they're both dead now. My father didn't think that he was my father. My mother swore that he was. I don't know which one of them was right. Can we leave it at that." It wasn't a question.

Olivia said softly, "Of course, Jack. Please go on."

"I've forgotten where I was." His tone was curt.

She prompted him. "You said that you lived on the farm until you were nine. What happened then?"

He looked at her for a moment, as if he was considering telling her he didn't want to talk anymore. She was grateful when he went on. "My father died that year, of a massive coronary."

"Your mother sold the farm?"

"Yeah. But the money didn't last long. Eventually Alana went back to what she had been doing before she met him. She was a cocktail waitress and sometime piano player. I lived wherever she lived until I graduated high school and struck out on my own."

"What were you like as a teenager?"

"A borderline delinquent. I managed to avoid getting into any major scrapes with the authorities. But looking back, I don't know how I did it. When I got out of high school, I joined the service. I wanted to see the world. And I saw more than I bargained for. I spent a lot of time in the East. Southeast Asia, to be specific, special maneuvers."

"What are those?"

He shook his head. "Let's just say it was dangerous work, and somehow I survived with all my parts intact."

She thought of the scars she'd seen on his body and asked without thinking, "Is that how you got all those scars? In the service?"

His teeth flashed in a grin. "You noticed my scars."

She was blushing again. "Well. Did you get them in the service?"

"Yeah. Most of them, anyway. I reupped more than once, didn't know what else to do with myself. When I got out, I was twenty-six. So I took the GI bill and went to college for a while."

"What did you study?"

"Police Science. Then I was with the L.A.P.D. for six years, but I decided to get out. It was hell on my liver, I was drinking so much. Four years ago I resigned and started my own business."

"Doing what?"

He had been looking out the windshield. Now he faced her. "Discovery and salvage."

"What's that?"

He let out a long breath.

She knew they were getting to the part he didn't want to talk about. "Oh, all right. You can stop."

He grunted. "Gee. Thanks."

"One more question."

"So you say now."

"You never mentioned a girlfriend or a wife."

"What can I say? I guess they all blur together after a while."

She punched his shoulder. "Very funny. Have you ever been married?"

"No."

"There was never anyone...special?"

"Yeah," he admitted. "There was. Once."

"What was her name?"

"Sandy Chernak. She was a cop, with L.A.P.D. like I was. She was a good woman. And a true friend. We were talking about moving in together. But then she was killed on a domestic call."

"Was that when you started drinking too much?"

"You got it."

"And was it also when you decided to get off the force?"

"Yes."

"What about your mother, Alana? Is she still alive?"

"She died a few years ago. And that was more than one question."

"Oops. Sorry." Olivia attempted to look apologetic, though inside, she was anything but. Though he hadn't exactly been eager to tell her all about himself, he had revealed a thing or two.

She felt she knew him better.

And how she ached for him. For the boy whose father had never claimed him, for the man who'd lost a lover to a violent death. She wondered about his mother. What might Alana have been like? And had she really betrayed John Roper? And if Alana had betrayed her husband, then was there an old man alive somewhere today with eyes like Jack's?

"Earth to Olivia."

She grinned at him. "Just wondering."

"I'll bet. Can we go now?"

She pretended to have to think about it.

He remarked, "You're pushing it, Ms. Larrabee."

She let out an airy sigh. "Oh, all right. We can go."

He started the car and they headed for the road.

Olivia felt wonderful the whole drive back. When they arrived at the hotel, they enjoyed their nightly ritual of sitting in the wing chairs by the trusty potted palm.

At the door to her room, he did it again.

That is, he *didn't* kiss her. But she didn't feel as bad about that as she had the night before. Last night she'd been sure she would never see him again.

But tonight, she had heard the story of most of his life. She understood him better. The kisses would come soon enough, of that she was certain.

And she was learning. She made a date for breakfast before he left and came right out and asked him for his room number, which he gave her with no hesitation at all.

The next day they tried the casinos downtown. They viewed the 100 ten-thousand-dollar bank notes in the glass display at Binion's Horseshoe, played baccarat at The Lucky Lady and yanked the one-armed bandit at The Golden Nugget.

In the afternoon they swam. And in the evening, they went to The Bacchanal in Caesar's Palace, a restaurant that resembled nothing so much as the garden of an Italian villa.

All told, it was another absolutely enchanting day, marred only by the continuing feeling Olivia had that something was bothering Jack.

But whenever she tried to get him to talk about it, she got nowhere.

And the moment came again when they stood at the door of her room to say good-night and she couldn't help wondering how long he would hide his troubles from her—not to mention if she would ever know his kiss.

"Earth to Olivia." Jack was smiling down into her eyes. He touched her hair, a breath of a touch, as if he didn't dare do more.

"Jack." She said his name with great seriousness.

He mimicked her tone. "Olivia."

"Jack, I—"

"Shh." He put his finger to her lips. "It was a great day."

His touch was magic, as usual. She wanted more. So very much more.

But she really had no idea how to *get* more. So all she said was "Good night."

"Tomorrow," he promised. "The poolside café. Noon."

"Yes." And she stood staring dreamily after him until he had disappeared beyond the turn to the elevators.

Then she shook herself and let herself into her suite. Inside, she leaned against the closed door and tried not to feel let down.

She looked around, idly deciding that she really could have invited Jack in without being embarrassed. Things didn't look as bad as they might have, given that she'd been on her own for five entire days. The maids here were kind. They stacked her clothing neatly in the dressing area, so when she came in at night, she didn't trip on her own strewn clothes.

Yes, she could have invited Jack in. But she'd missed the chance. And now it was too late.

Or was it?

Olivia straightened from the door and strode to the love seat.

She sat. Then she cradled her chin in her hand and tapped her heels on the floor, lost in thought. Soon enough, the tapping began to irritate her. So she kicked the shoes across the room and tapped with her nyloned feet.

The more she thought, the more she was positive that they couldn't go on like this. Something simply *had* to be done.

Olivia stood. She swept into the bedroom, headed right for the big walk-in closet and dressing area off the bathroom where her suitcases were. There she began tossing clothes in the air from the maid's neatly stacked pile.

Moments later she let out a triumphant little yelp.

She held up her discovery, shaking it a few times to smooth it out. It was the merest wisp of red satin, with skinny little spaghetti straps and a back that dipped to display more than most women should ever reveal.

Olivia bit her tongue, still thinking. There was a little robe to go with it, she knew there was.

More clothing flew.

And then she crowed again. "Aha!"

With the wisps of satin and lace over her arm, she returned to the bedroom, where she set the lingerie out, with great care, on the bed. Right then, she realized she was going to need something to cover the skimpy outfit when she went to Jack's room. She grinned as she thought of her sable, which Constance always packed for her to take on trips, whether Olivia needed it or not. Tonight, at least, the sinfully expensive fur would come in handy.

That settled, Olivia stared down at the short gown and robe for a time, her tongue caught between her teeth.

She was thinking, *What I am about to do is a conscious act. And I am a responsible woman.*

Though her hand shook a little, she picked up the phone anyway and pressed the button for the concierge.

Twenty minutes later, there was a discreet knock. When she opened the door, a bellman wheeled in a cart bearing champagne on ice. He also handed her a small brown bag, which she quickly set on the cart next to the champagne.

"Shall I open the champagne for you, madam?"

"No, thanks." Olivia shoved an enormous tip at him and ushered him out the door.

Then, right where she was standing, she unzipped the little black number she'd changed into before dinner and dropped it to the floor. Shedding underwear as she went, she marched to the bathroom where the big sunken tub and the scented bath oil were waiting.

On another floor, in a room a good deal smaller than Olivia's suite, Jack was lying on the bed, fully dressed except for his shoes. His hands were laced behind his head. He was staring at the ceiling, thinking exactly what he thought every night lately.

He was a rat. A creep. Lower than the lowest of the low.

He should have found a way to tell Olivia everything by now, so he could do her the biggest favor he would ever do her: get out of her life.

Both yesterday and the day before he'd awakened firm in his purpose: somehow, before they parted for the night, he would tell her who and what he was.

But the moment he'd looked up from his morning paper and had seen her waiting a few feet away, her eyes glowing bright blue at the sight of him, he'd been done for. He'd known he would give anything for one more day.

It was a minor miracle, as far as he was concerned, that he hadn't laid a hand on her.

Or maybe it wasn't. Maybe, though he wanted her to the point of pain, he could bear the pain. As long as he could have one more day at her side.

Somehow, the excuse he'd made for himself that first night had stuck with him. As long as he didn't put his hands on her, the lie he was living remained marginally acceptable.

However, if he ever crossed that line, he would never be able to live with himself.

But he wouldn't cross that line. He knew it. He could control himself—barely.

And she would help him with her shyness and her inexperience. Because she was never going to push the issue, though he knew she felt the same longings he did. She simply wasn't the type of woman to become aggressive about something like sex.

Jack shifted on the bed a little, feeling edgy and aroused. He closed his eyes.

And there she was, on the back of his eyelids, smiling that innocently alluring smile of hers, holding up her lips in the shy hope of a kiss.

He groaned, rolled to his side and tried to call up a few arousal-reducing images. But it did no good. His body, kept so strictly under control every moment he was with her, had to make its needs felt at some point. Now, deep in the night, was the only time.

With a low moan of surrender, he allowed it to happen.

Her image came before him, in the red dress of that first evening. He saw her just as she had looked when they'd stood facing each other on the street, the dress molded against her slim body by the wind; her hair, deep gold and fine as spun silk, blowing around her face, catching on her sweet lips, so that she had to put up a hand and brush it away.

But in his fantasy they didn't stand on a street. They stood in some soft, private place, and the wind was warm, coming from some unknown source. In his fantasy nothing held him back. The last tattered shreds of his mangled integrity no longer clutched at him.

He was free. To touch and to know. To fully possess.

"Jack."

Her voice was soft in his ear as he hovered at the edge of sleep. And the red dress was sliding from her pale shoulders, revealing her slender arms, the soft rise of her breasts, the luminescence of her skin....

"Jack?"

Someone was knocking. Though he hated to leave his sweet fantasy, he opened his eyes.

"Jack?"

Jack lay very still.

"Jack, are you in there?"

It was her. Olivia. Knocking at the door.

"Jack, please."

He sat up and rubbed at his eyes.

"Jack?"

"Coming!"

He rolled off the bed, stumbled to the door and pulled it open.

Only then did he realize the magnitude of his recklessness. Because she really was there. His dream come to life. And his defenses were most definitely down.

All he could do was stare.

Her gold-and-bronze hair was loose on her shoulders. Her pale skin gleamed. She was wrapped in a coat of shining sable that fell to midcalf.

His stunned gaze strayed down the shapely bit of bare leg that could be seen beneath the hem of the fur coat. On her feet were a pair of slippers. Red backless slippers with open toes and high heels. Naughty slippers, designed purely to entice.

He could smell her. A warm, sweet beguiling smell. Like the crushed and purified essence of ten thousand rare and fragrant flowers.

In one hand, with commendable dexterity, she was managing to hold a bottle of champagne and two glasses. In the other hand she clutched a plain brown bag.

Chapter Five

Jack blinked owlishly at her.

Olivia realized she'd caught him napping, though he still had on his clothes. Luckily she'd planned what her first words would be.

"May I come in, darling?"

He muttered something like "Ugh, Olivia."

She decided she'd better take action before she lost her nerve. So, as alluringly as she could, Olivia swept into the room.

"Why don't you close the door?" she asked, low and huskily, just the way she'd practiced it while she was sitting in the tub.

Jack shut the door.

Olivia turned again and took the few remaining steps to the small table and chairs in the corner by the room's one window. There, with great care, she set down the brown bag. That left one hand free to pry the two glasses from her nervously tight fingers. She did this slowly, so as not to drop the champagne. When the glasses were free, she set them on the table not far from the bag.

That left both hands available to deal with the champagne.

Swiftly and masterfully she peeled the foil from the bottle, unwrapped the wire and eased out the cork. It came free with a soft explosion that echoed nicely in the room. A trail of vapor rose into the air.

It was expertly done. She congratulated herself, and her confidence rose a little. Opening champagne was something Olivia had always been good at.

With a flourish she lifted one of the flutes, tipped it slightly and poured. When the glass was full and the bubbles danced upward inside, she held it out.

"Champagne?"

Jack said nothing.

A slight feeling of hysteria rose inside Olivia. She was making a fool of herself.

She cut off the treacherous thought. Trying her best for a seductive sway, she approached him. Then, forcing herself to look provocatively into his eyes, she took his hand and wrapped it around the flute.

Olivia stepped back, keeping eye contact, making her lashes droop a little in a bedroom sort of way. Jack just went on staring.

Panic clutched at her. She was *positive* she was making a fool of herself now.

But it was too late to turn back.

Doing her best to move languidly, Olivia backed up until her knees touched the bed. Very slowly she allowed her sable to drop from her shoulders. She caught it before it hit the floor and tossed it across one of the chairs at the table.

Slowly Jack's gaze traveled from her head to her high-heeled red slippers and back up again. Once he'd looked her over thoroughly, he raised the glass to his lips and took a big gulp of champagne.

Oh, Olivia thought desperately. *This isn't going right at all.*

She said his name nervously. "Jack?"

Jack didn't answer.

Mostly because his throat was so dry it hurt. He took another swig of the champagne.

"Jack?" she asked again. This time her voice cracked.

Jack knew he should do something—say something. *Anything*. But the words just wouldn't come.

He wanted to reach for her.

But he couldn't do that.

If he did, he would never be able to live with himself later.

So what the hell was he going to do?

The answer came. He had to tell her.

Tonight. Right now.

He couldn't live another moment this way, looking at her, wanting her and knowing he could never touch. It was time to bust this thing open, even though he knew it would be the end once she'd heard the truth.

He knocked back the last of the champagne, set the empty glass on the television and forced himself to speak. "Olivia, I..."

Olivia saw the pained look on his face and was certain she knew exactly what it meant.

He *did* think she was ridiculous.

And he was trying to find a way to let her down easy.

Oh, it was all so clear to her now!

The reason he'd never kissed her was the most obvious one. He didn't *want* to kiss her. He wasn't attracted to her at all. Of course he wasn't. Men like Jack were never attracted to wimpy little nothings like she was. He'd enjoyed her company and wanted to be friends. She'd misunderstood his motives from the first.

Her skin, which had felt cold with her nervousness a moment ago, now flooded with mortified heat. And her eyes were burning, filling up with tears of humiliation.

Oh, this was a thousand times worse than finding Cameron and Bree Haversham doing those shocking things on Cameron's cherrywood desk. At least then she'd been calm, dry-eyed and dignified. At least then, she'd been *dressed!*

She glanced down in horror at her bare legs and the little points of her nipples that showed right through the satin and lace of her gown and skimpy robe, and then she glanced up again and into Jack's obsidian eyes.

"Olivia..."

The tears pressed, insistent, unstoppable, against her lower lids.

She had to get out. Now. Before she suffered the final humiliation and sobbed like a baby right here in front of him.

Where she found her voice, she had no idea. But somehow she managed to chirp out in a fractured soprano, "Er, um, excuse me. I see I've made a major error in judgment here. And I really must be on my way."

She grabbed her coat, shoved her arms in it and clutched it close around herself. Then, lowering her head so she wouldn't have to see his face anymore, she aimed herself at the door.

She didn't make it. He caught her arm.

"Damn it, Olivia."

"Let me go." She gave a jerk, but he held on without exerting any effort at all.

"Listen—"

"Please." The tears were rising, pushing to get out.

"Olivia, don't."

The tears started falling. She could feel them, tumbling over the weak dam of her lids and slipping down her cheeks. She bit back a sob just as he pulled her against his hard, warm chest. "Don't cry." His voice was husky against her ear.

She struggled, moaning, as the tears kept falling. She knew they were staining his shirt. Her nose filled up.

She sniffed. "Oh please. I'm so ridiculous. You must let me go."

He didn't. Instead, he made soothing, gentle noises, and he continued to hold her close and sure against his body. "Come on, come on, it's okay."

And suddenly, with a low wail, she was throwing her arms around him, holding him as close as he was holding her. "Oh, I'm such a fool. Such a nothing."

"You're not. Don't say that. There, don't cry." Keeping her close, he took her to the side of the bed. "Come on. Sit down. It's okay. It's really okay."

He sat and gently urged her to sit beside him, which she finally did. Then he reached for the box of tissues on the nightstand and offered them to her. She yanked out several.

"Oh, Jack." She blew her nose. "I'm just not desirable to men."

"That's bull—"

"Don't. Please. Let me finish." It all came tumbling out then, between snorts at the tissues and a hiccup or two. "I thought you found me... that you wanted to, well, you know. But I can see now that it wasn't true. It's like Cameron said—"

"Cameron." He repeated the name in a grim tone.

She explained, "Cameron's my ex-fiancé."

"I see."

"No, you don't. You don't see at all. Because I've been lying to you, by not telling you."

"Telling me what?"

"Oh, Jack."

"Telling me what?" he repeated, relentlessly gentle.

She dragged in a breath. "Telling you the truth."

"And what is the truth?"

She made herself say it. "That the real reason I came here to Las Vegas was because I caught my fiancé—my *ex*-fiancé now—with another woman. In flagrante delicto, or however they say that. Making love. Having sex, you know what I mean?"

Jack made another of those understanding noises. He was stroking her back through the soft fur of her coat.

Olivia sagged against him, resting her head in the hollow of his shoulder. She sighed, swiped at her nose with a tissue again and then forced herself to go on.

"I caught him with his associate, Bree Haversham. On his desk. Can you believe it? His *desk*. And that's when he told me that I was a cold fish when it came to sex and what did I care if he made love with some other woman, since it was obvious that I hadn't any interest or ability in that department, anyway?" She let out a frantic little wail. "He actually said that to me, while Bree was trying to find her panty hose and button up her blouse. He stood there with his, um...not zipped up, and he told me that I was a terrible lover and should go home and think about how if I didn't marry him, what else was I going to do with my pointless little life."

Jack muttered something crude about Cameron under his breath.

"Oh, Jack. It was *horrible*." She cuddled up closer against his side.

He kissed the top of her head and rubbed her back some more. "Is that all?"

She sniffed a little, then confessed, "No, it isn't."

"What else?"

"Well, first of all, Cameron was pretty much right." She could feel him tense beside her and knew he was going to say that wasn't so. "No. Wait. Don't defend me. Let me finish." She gave out a shaky little sigh. "I really am lousy in bed. The two times I made love with Cameron were, well, they were grim, Jack. Really grim."

"That doesn't mean—"

"Shh." She patted his hand, which was wrapped around her shoulder. "Let me get this out. I mean it. I just want to get it all out. Okay?"

He made a low noise of agreement.

She drew in a few breaths and rubbed at her nose with the tissue again. "Thanks. Anyway, I'm lousy in bed. And I was going to marry Cameron, a man I didn't really even love, for exactly the reason he said. Because my life *is* pointless. And I thought that maybe by marrying and settling down with someone dependable, I could make my life more meaningful. Although, as it turned out, Cameron wasn't as dependable as I'd thought."

"Not by a long shot," Jack muttered.

"Oh, Jack. I only ever wanted to do one thing. To cook. I love to cook. I'm a trained chef. But I let my father talk me out of doing what *I* wanted to do. I went to work for him in this stupid figurehead job at Larrabee Brewing that means nothing to me or to the company. It's a pointless job in a pointless life."

Her hand was lying on his thigh. He took it in his, weaving their fingers together, and then lifting it to his lips for a light, comforting kiss. "Anything more?"

"Yes."

"What?" He gave her hand a squeeze, but didn't let go of it.

She held on tight, glad for the contact. "The worst part of all."

"Yeah?"

"My father."

"What about him?"

"What he did, when he heard what had happened with Cameron."

"What did he do?"

"He...he came to my beach house and said he'd fire Cameron. Cameron is president of sales for Larrabee Brewing, and he's the best salesman my father's ever had. But just like that, my father was going to fire him. I didn't want my father firing anyone for my sake, especially not the best salesman he's ever had. And then, right on top of telling me he was firing Cameron, my father said that he'd find me someone new and better in no time."

She pulled away enough to capture Jack's glance. "Can you believe it? My father actually said he'd find me someone *new*. Like a fiancé was a dress or a piece of furniture, something I could return for a refund if I wasn't satisfied. And the scary thing, the really terrifying thing is, it *could* happen. I could live the rest of my life in the house my father gave me, working in the job he made up for me, married to the man he *bought* for me."

Olivia sat a little straighter, pulling out of the circle of Jack's arm and removing her hand from his reassuring clasp. He let her go, sitting a little away himself, as if to give her the space she needed to say whatever else she needed to say.

She rubbed at her burning eyes. Her fingers came away smudged with the makeup she'd so artfully applied before coming to Jack's room. And the smudges reminded her of what a fool she'd just been.

She told him the rest. "I had to get away, Jack. I got in my car and drove all night to get here, to Las Vegas. And I met you. And the way you looked at me, I thought you...wanted me. Just because I was me. I mean, you didn't even know who I was that first night, when you saw me at the blackjack table and followed me out onto the street. And best of all, there was the way I felt when *I* looked at *you*. I thought, well, maybe my life is pointless. But Cameron was wrong. The way I feel about Jack proves I'm not a cold fish after all."

She looked deep into Jack's eyes, which were so very dark and full of things she couldn't understand. "But now I see the truth, Jack. You're a kind man and a good one. You've been nice to me. I don't know why. But I finally get it. You're not interested in me in any romantic way and I—"

Jack loosed a short, crude expletive.

Olivia hiccuped in surprise. "Pardon me?"

"I said, that is baloney."

"I don't think baloney was the word you used."

"Don't cloud the issue. What I'm telling you is, I'm damned interested in you."

"Oh, Jack." She shook her head. Then she stood and looked down at him. "See? That's how you are. Kind. Trying to let me down easy."

"I am *not* kind." His eyes were narrowed. "If I were kind, I would let you believe this garbage you're spouting. I'd hustle you out of here and wish you well with your life—which I'm certain is far from pointless, by the way."

"Oh, Jack. Thanks for trying. But I've already made enough of a fool of myself for one night. I've had a lovely time with you and I—"

He grabbed her hand and yanked her onto his lap.

"Jack!"

"You're going nowhere. Yet." He shifted her around a little, so that she was sitting sideways.

"But Jack, I—"

"Listen." He put his forehead against hers and spoke through gritted teeth. "When I opened the door and found you there just now, I could hardly move. Or speak. And not because I wasn't attracted to you. Get it? But because, when you knocked on the door, I was dreaming of you, in that strange red dress you were wearing that first night I saw you. And in my dream you were taking *off* that red dress. Slowly. Very slowly."

Olivia could hardly breathe. Somehow the surge of hope and pleasure she was feeling had cut off her air. "Oh, Jack. Are you sure you—?"

He stopped her words with a single burning glance. "Yes."

"Well then, why haven't you *kissed* me, Jack? Why haven't you, um . . ."

"Made love with you?"

She looked down at her hands, which were twisting together. "Yes."

"Because I'm not who you think I am."

She lifted her head, looked in his eyes. "What do you mean?"

He dragged in a breath. "I'm a—"

Olivia knew, in a burst of painful understanding, that she didn't want to hear it, not now, not tonight. "No!" She put her hand on his mouth. "I've changed my mind. Don't say it."

"But I—"

"No. Listen." Her voice was strong and steady, a tone so uncharacteristic of her that it shocked them both just a little. "You listen to me."

His eyes searched hers. And at last, with a slow nod, he agreed to her demand. He would not talk until she'd had her say.

For a moment she had no idea how to begin. But then the words came.

"Tonight," she said. "Tonight, right now. This is *our* night, Jack. It's going to happen for us tonight. And nothing, not whatever you're keeping from me, or my fear that you'll find out how really horrible I am in bed— *nothing* is going to stop it from happening. *Nothing*. Do you understand?"

"But—"

"Shh." This time her voice was softer. "Please. You and me, together. In this bed. That's what I want tonight. Is it what you want too, Jack?"

Jack looked away.

She took his chin and guided him back so he had to look at her. "Is it?"

She stared into his eyes, willing him to say the words she longed to hear. "Stop thinking," she commanded. "Do you want me?"

Jack looked at her. He despised himself for what he was about to do.

But he was a starving man. And she'd laid a banquet before him.

To hell with it. He'd take what she offered.

One night of bliss.

"Yes, I want you."

"Then won't you *please* make love with me?"

"Yes." He gave her the answer before she even finished asking the question.

Chapter Six

As soon as she heard his *yes,* Olivia let out a long sigh. Then, smiling, she rested against him.

Jack wrapped both arms around her and cradled her close. She nuzzled his shirt, scenting him and loving the feel of him, the warmth and the strength.

Now that it was truly decided, a shyness came over her. She had no more to say. But he stroked her hair and caressed her back and kissed the crown of her head.

One and then the other, her naughty red slippers dropped to the floor.

"I'm trying to think logically," he murmured against her neck.

"Stop that," she chided. "There's no need for logic now."

His hand, rough, warm and large, was on her thigh, where her coat had fallen away. She looked down at it, saw that the back of it was dusted with shiny gold hair. He began rubbing her thigh, back and forth.

She let her eyes drift closed. And she simply felt his touch. It was lovely.

"Olivia."

"Um?"

"There is a need for logic in one area."

"What?"

"Contraception."

She felt very smug. "Oh, forget that. I've taken care of that."

The rogue dared to chuckle. "What? You're carrying protection around in a pocket of that fancy coat?"

"No. In a brown paper bag." She pointed at the table. "That bag, to be specific."

She could tell by how quiet he was that he was repressing more chuckling. "I see."

"I called the concierge. They sent a box, along with the champagne. A dozen. Will that be enough?"

"Hmm." He thought that over. "I suppose a dozen will just have to do."

"Well." Suddenly she felt shy again. "Good." She buried her face in his chest and found herself wondering if she really was going to be able to go through with this after all.

She'd felt so utterly sure just a moment ago. But now, the more she thought about it . . .

"Shh," he said against her hair. "Don't think. The time for thinking is over."

"Yes." She whispered the word. "I know that. I do."

He stroked her back and shoulders some more with one hand, while the hand on her thigh continued its wonderful massage. Then his fingers strayed.

She murmured his name and then gave a small, excited gasp as his hand slipped inside her coat and touched the red satin there. A little thrill of delight skittered through her as he began slowly to stroke upward.

"I love the feel of you, Olivia." He murmured the words on a ragged breath, gathering her closer, into the heat and hardness of him.

It was then that she felt the bulge of his manhood, pressing at her softness. She shivered a little, both frightened and aroused.

His hand moved between the satin and the lace, up over her rib cage, until it found her breast. She gasped.

He whispered something against her temple. She didn't hear the words. And then his lips tasted her skin. He nibbled a trail over her cheekbone. His mouth sought hers.

And found it.

Olivia let out a small, grateful cry. At last. After four nights of wondering if she would ever know the feel of Jack's lips on hers, it was happening.

They were sharing their first kiss.

And it was everything she'd yearned for. And more.

His mouth played on hers, his teeth lightly nipping, his tongue pressing for entry.

On a soft exhalation, Olivia parted her lips. And his tongue was inside.

Olivia was absolutely stunned. It was wonderful. His mouth tasted hers, his arms held her close.

He broke the kiss. Olivia moaned. His lips moved to her chin, her neck, the little points of bone at the base of her throat.

He gave a low growl. Her coat was in his way. He shoved the soft fur aside, urging her to lift up a little. And then the coat was gone.

The next sound he made was a hungry one as he lowered his head and nibbled starved, hot kisses on her shoulder. As he tasted her skin, he pushed impatiently at the lace robe. He helped her free of the sleeves quickly, ruthlessly. And when the little scrap of robe no longer covered her, he tossed it away, too.

And then, for a moment, he was still.

Olivia felt her heart stop. He seemed to be studying the red satin gown, as if it were the wrapping on a very special package. Experimentally he slid a finger beneath one of the gown's slender straps. Slowly he lifted the strap and let it fall along her arm.

The left side of the gown dropped away, revealing one high, pink-tipped breast. Olivia had to hold back a moan that would also have been a plea. She wanted him to touch her breast.

"What?" he softly inquired.

"I..."

"Yes?"

"I want..."

"What?" He smiled a smile that seemed to know it all. And then his hand was straying again. Moving inexorably downward until, at last, she had her wish.

His hand swept over her breast, sending arrows of pure pleasure down to the feminine heart of her. He brushed back and forth, making her nipple into a hard, hungry nub.

In an ecstasy of sensation, Olivia let her head fall back. Jack cupped her breast, his hand so very warm and encompassing. And then he lowered his head and replaced his hand with his mouth. He licked. And then he sucked.

Olivia let out a groan that was so purely sexual she hardly knew it as her own. She shoved her hands into his hair and clutched him close, as he kissed her in a way that made her cry out for more and more of the same.

He pulled away enough to challenge silkily, "You're trembling."

"I..." Her skin flamed.

"Don't be embarrassed. It's the same for me."

"It is?"

"Don't you know what you do to me?" His hand was on her thigh again, sliding upward, until it disappeared beneath the hem of her short gown. "You turn me inside out."

"Oh, Jack."

"All I want to do is touch you, right here."

She gasped as his finger stroked the little strip of silk that covered her mound. The light teasing touch sent a shaft of liquid heat all through her. Her womanhood seemed to bloom. It was all at once hot and heavy and moist.

He must have felt the heat and moisture through the scrap of silk. He made a male sound of discovery, of satisfaction.

She let out a low moan of pleasure.

Beneath the hem of her gown, his fingers quested, rubbing her more boldly, pressing against the barrier of now-damp cloth. She squirmed and wriggled, pushing herself against his hand. And he seemed to know exactly what her body wanted, because he stretched her panties out of the way.

And then he was touching her, in her most secret place. His fingers found her and parted her.

She cried out. He muttered something low and knowing. She moved, frantic and needful, against his stroking hand.

And then it happened. Like a flower made of moist fire, she felt herself opening, expanding, pulsing out to set the rest of her aflame. She called out something that wasn't a word, but was nonetheless utterly triumphant and totally free. And then she went limp in Jack's strong arms.

"Olivia," he whispered, after several moments had gone by.

"Um?"

"Come on." Proprietarily he smoothed the strap of her gown back in place over her shoulder, covering her breast again. "Lie down."

"Um," she said again. It was the only thing she could manage right then. She felt so contented. So peaceful. Like a little boat drifting on a still summer sea.

She grumbled a bit in protest when he slid her off his lap and onto the bed. But he ignored her murmurs of complaint, as he stood and then bent to raise her feet onto the mattress and to urge her to lie with her head among the pillows.

When she was comfortable, he straightened and looked down at her. "Feel good?"

"Um." She stretched a little, pointing her toes, thoroughly enjoying the way his gaze swept over her, hot and possessive. She held up her arms.

But he didn't come down to her.

He took one of her hands and lightly kissed it. Then he went quickly to the table and returned with the brown bag. From it he took the box of condoms, which he set on the nightstand.

After that he undressed. He did it swiftly, tossing each item of clothing onto the corner chair as he removed it.

Most of his body was already familiar to her. They had shared more than one swim at the roof pool, after all. But still, to see him standing before her completely naked made the heat start to curl in her belly all over again.

She gazed on the fine musculature of his shoulders and arms, wondering again at the scars that here and there marred the bronze perfection of his skin. She let her gaze wander, following the T of golden hair that whorled around his nipples, trailed down his solar plexus and over the rock-hard planes of his abdomen. The hair grew darker near the juncture of his thighs. He was fully ready for lovemaking. She blushed a little at the sight.

With the swift and easy grace so characteristic of him, he stretched out beside her. He pressed himself along the length of her. She found herself assailed by a thousand sensations.

There was the heat of him and that manly scent that was only his. There was the corded strength of him. And the rough kiss of his body hair.

He clasped her waist. His hand slid upward. He took the straps of her gown and peeled them down, one at a time, revealing both of her round, pale breasts. He bent over her, gently, and kissed each one in turn. She gasped a little, and she felt his smile against her skin.

"Sit up."

She did as he bade. He gathered the hem of the flimsy gown.

"Raise your arms."

She did. And the gown was gone.

All that was left was her silky panties. But not for long. He whisked them away, too.

And then he urged her to stretch out again. She lay back down, compliant and brimming all through with a strange, peaceful, utterly perfect desire.

In a distant sort of way, she thought of Cameron. And the bleak experience that making love with him had been. But that all seemed very far away now. And so terribly simple.

Cameron had been the wrong man. That was all. And though her foolish mind had kept trying to tell her that she and Cameron would somehow make things work, her body had refused to be fooled.

"What is going through that mind of yours?" Jack asked.

It didn't even occur to her to dissemble. "I was just thinking that Cameron was the wrong man." She brazenly wrapped her hand around Jack's nape and pulled him closer. "And you're the right one."

His eyes clouded. He opened his mouth to speak.

She shook her head against the pillow. "Shh. No more doubts. No more hesitations, remember? Not tonight."

He lowered his head even closer to hers and nibbled her lower lip. "I remember." He nibbled some more. And then, with a low, hungry moan, he opened his mouth on hers.

Olivia gave a long, delighted sigh as her lips parted. Their tongues played together. And as he kissed her, his hand found her center once more. She lifted her body toward him.

He muttered, "You're ready. I want you. Can't wait." He was kissing a path down her exposed neck to her breast. And then he captured that breast in his mouth and began to suck.

"Yes, yes, yes," she chanted, as she held his head close.

But he would not stay there. He kissed his way down, over her ribs to her quivering belly and then lower still.

Then his lips were there, in her most private place. And she wanted them there. She felt his mouth opening, his tongue delving, and she gave herself up to this most stunning of intimacies.

She felt her body rising, building toward fulfillment once again. And she clutched at his hard shoulders, thinking to pull him up, so he could enter her and join her this time.

But the sensations were too overwhelming. And those intimate kisses went on and on. And the hot flower of her womanhood was blooming again, opening, spreading to encompass the whole world.

Lost to everything but Jack's secret kiss, Olivia tossed her head on the pillows and found her release.

And just when the tremors began to subside, he was rising above her. She moaned and clutched at him. Swiftly, impatiently, he grappled with one of the condoms. And then it was on.

She looked up at him, into his midnight eyes, as he covered her body with his. He positioned himself. Then slowly, inexorably, he found his way home.

Oh, she thought, as her body took him in. She had been empty, empty all this time.

And now, at last, she was filled. With him. She opened wider, he pressed deeper.

"I knew," he muttered on a torn breath. "Yeah. I knew. Like silk, Olivia. You're like silk."

At last he filled her completely. There was no emptiness left. Only him.

And still he held her eyes.

Experimentally, he pulled back. She gave a low cry. And he returned. He did it again, only to come back again.

And soon enough she was pulling back and returning with him. He lowered himself fully upon her. She clutched his broad back and held on tight.

He picked up the rhythm. She followed without missing a single beat. They moved faster and faster, toward a white-hot center of absolute bliss. She lifted her legs and wrapped them around him, holding on for dear life and for their mutual ecstasy.

Again fulfillment approached, like a huge wave breaking over her, consuming her, towing her down. She welcomed it, writhing and whimpering like a wild thing.

And then she felt Jack stiffen. He cried out.

As he spilled into her, her consummation came, more powerful and complete than the two that Jack had given her before. Her cries echoed his cries. The world spun away.

Oh, how had she lived, she wondered inchoately, until this moment? Her life had been gray until this moment. And now it was a rainbow. A technicolor dream.

They lay entwined for the longest time. And then Jack rolled them both to their sides, so that they faced each other. Idly he smoothed her hair and then edged even closer to place a light kiss on her nose. Then he left her to rid himself of the condom.

He was back in no time, stretching out beside her once more.

She dared to reach out and touch his chest, to feel the hair there that was wiry over his nipples and became silky where it began its inviting trail down his abdomen. She felt one of the scars, jagged as a lightning bolt, that started in the curve of his shoulder and traveled down to his left nipple.

"Where did this come from?"

"An encounter with an angry barbwire fence, I think."

"And this one?"

"Hell, who knows?"

"The one on your leg, that curls around your calf?"

"In a bar on Alvarado Street, when I was still a cop. I tried to break up a knife fight. Two mean drunks. I got a hold of one of them and was reading him his Miranda rights, when the other one, who was supposed to be passed out on the floor, crawled up and grabbed my leg and started—"

"Never mind. I get the idea." She kissed the jagged scar he'd said he'd acquired on a barbwire fence. Then she snuggled into his shoulder with a sigh. "Maybe we could just lie here like this forever."

She could hear his smile in his voice. "Not a bad idea."

His arm was wrapped around her, his hand tracing a heart on her upper arm. Then in one long stroke, his hand slid down her arm and over the gentle curve of her hip. Her belly jumped when he caressed the little cove between her pelvic bone and her abdomen.

"Hey."

She lifted her head. He snared her glance. She watched the heat kindle in his eyes.

He touched her, opening her. She looked down, watched his hand, even as she felt the magic beginning all over again. Olivia surrendered to it utterly, wishing the night would never end.

Her wish was not granted. Though for a few enchanted hours Olivia was sure that the wonder and power of their passion could hold back the dawn.

Still, the moment came when, through the open curtains of the window, the rising sun began painting the desert sky in iridescent strokes of orange and magenta.

Olivia buried her head against Jack's chest. "It's morning," she whispered. And then she yawned.

Jack lifted up a little and looked past her shoulder at the clock, which sat on the nightstand next to the phone.

"Yeah." He shook his head when he saw the time. He lay back down and she snuggled against him as he tucked the blankets more comfortably around them.

She kissed his chin and closed her eyes. She felt herself drifting toward sleep and smiled. "Good night. Or should I say, good morning?"

"Does it matter?"

"No. Doesn't matter. Doesn't matter at all."

She felt his hand, smoothing the hair back from her neck. She felt his lips on her forehead, right between her brows, in the most tender of kisses.

With a soft sigh Olivia let sleep have its way with her.

The phone by her bed was ringing.

Olivia reached out and grabbed it from its cradle just as it shrilled out a second ring, before she remembered that it was not her phone at all, but Jack's.

"'Lo?" She murmured the word without thinking how drowsy and contented she must sound.

"Olivia?" She recognized her father's shocked voice. "Olivia, my God, is that you?"

Chapter Seven

Olivia dragged herself to a sitting position.

"Olivia, are you there? Olivia!"

She looked at Jack. He was sitting up, too, by then. He stared back at her. His face was very strange, very still. His eyes were so deep. They told her nothing.

On the phone her father kept talking to her, saying her name. But she knew that he had not called to speak with her.

It was Jack he had called for. So she held out the phone. Jack took it.

"Yeah?" he said warily into the mouthpiece.

Her father started shouting at Jack. He shouted loud enough that Olivia could make out a few of the words. Her father called Jack a bastard. And she heard him say the word *fired*.

"Fine," was all Jack said. Then he held out the phone to Olivia. "He wants to talk to you."

Olivia took the phone. Very carefully she put it to her ear.

"Livvy?" her father asked. She could hear his fear for her and his love, but she felt no response to it. She felt numb, anesthetized.

"I told you that you had to leave me alone, Dad." She spoke slowly and precisely.

"Livvy, please, I—"

"Goodbye, Dad."

"Olivia, wait! Don't—"

Olivia quietly hung up the phone.

Sitting there in the silence of harsh morning, in the bed where she had known such tender ecstasy only hours before, she stared at Jack. He stared back.

And then the phone started ringing again.

Olivia turned to it, picked it up and found the plug where the cord was connected. She pulled it out.

"There," she said calmly as the ringing stopped. She tugged the sheet up to cover her breasts and then folded her hands in her lap. "Now. I think you owe me an explanation, Jack."

Jack looked at her, at the grim set to her pretty chin and the flat deadness in her eyes. He realized that it had all happened just as he'd feared it would.

He'd done it. Tossed away his last shred of self-respect. Made love to the sweetest, most innocent woman on earth without telling her the truth about himself first.

"I'm waiting, Jack." Her voice was as dead as her expression.

There was nothing to do now but one thing. Tell her. Time, as he had always known it would, had run out.

"I'm a private investigator," he said. "Your father hired me to keep an eye on you while you were in Las Vegas."

She stared at him. "I see."

He made himself continue. "It was a simple surveillance gig, or that was all it was supposed to be."

"But then I caught you watching me."

"Right. You caught me twice. And I knew it was either give up the job or make a move."

"You made a move."

He nodded.

"So this was all a job to you."

"Olivia—"

She put up a hand. "No. Never mind. Don't explain any more. I've heard enough. More than enough." She raked her hair back from her face and stared blankly at the bedspread. Then she lifted her head and looked at him, a vacant look. "I have to go now."

And with that she tossed back the covers and swung her feet to the floor. For a moment she hovered there, on the edge of the mattress, her slim back slumped, her head hung low.

Jack's gut clenched. He hated himself. "God. Olivia." He reached out.

"Don't." There was steel in her soft voice. Her shoulders straightened. "Don't touch me. Ever again."

His insides twisted at her words. He withdrew his hand.

She bent and slid on the red slippers. Then she stood.

He watched her, wanting to stop her, knowing he wouldn't.

He remembered how young she had seemed—was it only last night? Right now she didn't seem young at all.

Her pale, slim body gleamed in the morning light. She was beautiful, the way a statue can be beautiful. He felt that if he did touch her now—which he wasn't going to do—her skin would be cold and smooth as marble under his hand.

She strode to the table, where her coat hung over a chair. He watched her round, tight buttocks, only vaguely aware that he was clutching the sheet in a death grip to keep from rising and preventing her escape.

She scooped up the coat and wrapped herself in its thick folds. She walked to the door.

She turned back to him before she went out. "Don't follow me anymore, Jack. If you do—" Her voice broke then. He saw the lost little girl inside of her. A pain shot through him, sharp and terrible. He had to look away. "If you do," she began again as he made himself face her once more, "I'll call the police."

She turned and went through the door, closing it softly behind her.

After she had gone, Jack didn't move for a while.

He was trying to convince himself that he should respect her wishes and give her what she wanted. He should leave her alone.

But then he knew he couldn't do that. After what he'd done to her, he couldn't just leave her alone out there in the big bad world. At the mercy of suspicious characters like himself.

He looked at the clock. It was seven minutes since she'd left. In her mental state she might do anything. She could just keep on walking, to the elevator, down to the lobby and right out the door.

"Please, God, don't let her do that," Jack muttered at the ceiling. He was not a religious man, but he was willing to try anything right then.

He threw back the covers, strode to his own suitcase and grabbed a pair of jeans and a sport shirt. He was packed and out the door in five minutes flat.

He needn't have hurried.

Olivia was in bad shape, but not so bad that she'd stroll out onto the Las Vegas Strip, wearing nothing but her sable and a pair of red high-heeled slippers.

She returned to her room.

When she let herself in, the phone was ringing. It would be her father, of course. She walked to the table by the love seat and unplugged it. When the extension in the bedroom kept on ringing, she marched in there and unplugged that one, too.

Then, when it was finally quiet, she sank to the side of the bed and rubbed her eyes. She looked at the clock. It wasn't even nine yet. She'd had about an hour and a half of sleep.

She felt terrible, all shaky and bewildered. But she knew that if she stretched out on the bed, the comfort of sleep would elude her. And even if she did manage to doze off for a while, she would still feel awful when she woke up.

Besides, there was her father to consider. He would be on his way here, she had no doubt. In a few hours he'd be pounding on the door.

She wasn't going to be here when Lawrence Larrabee arrived. He had meddled in her life one time too many. This thing with Jack was the last straw.

Jack.

Olivia hunched her shoulders, clutching her middle. Just thinking his name made her double over with pain. She had to stop thinking of him. She must forget him. Completely.

She made herself sit straight.

Then, shoulders back, she got to her feet and let the sable drop to the floor. She walked out of the red slippers. She went to the bathroom and stood under the shower, trying to clear her mind a little.

It didn't do much good. She got out and dried herself and tossed some more clothes on the floor, until she found some pink slacks and the big pink shirt that went with them. There was a cat's face embroidered on the shirt, a winking cat's face. It was a silly outfit, really. A silly outfit for a silly woman with a pointless life. She even found the pink flats that completed the ensemble. She'd be totally color coordinated as she ran off to Lord-knew-where.

When she was all dressed, she packed. Or she tried to pack. But she had no clue how to get her clothes back into all the suitcases and garment bags. Constance, who usually went with her whenever she traveled, always packed for her.

Finally she stuffed a few things into one of the smaller suitcases. Then she transferred her wallet and other essentials back to her shoulder bag from the evening purse she'd used last night. Slinging the shoulder bag in place, she grabbed the suitcase and her makeup case and headed for the door.

In the room she left a fortune in designer clothing, not to mention her sable. But what did she need with all those things, anyway? She was nobody, headed for nowhere. Starting fresh and traveling light.

She took State Route 95 because, when she got out on the highway, her car ended up on that road. It wasn't really important which road she took, though. As long as she wasn't headed back to L.A., any direction was fine with her.

State Route 95, as it happened, took her north and slightly west, through the high desert. She saw a lot of tall mesas and more sagebrush than she ever wanted to see again. She drove with single-minded concentration, stopping only when she had no choice, either for gas or to answer nature's call.

As morning faded into noon and noon moved along toward evening, she drove by high, stark peaks and past towns named Indian Springs, Beatty, Tonopah and Coaldale. It was nearing five and the sun was sinking toward the horizon when State Route 95 met up with

Highway 80. At that interchange she switched directions a little and found herself heading straight for Reno.

Olivia reached Reno at six o'clock and left the highway briefly. Looking around in the gathering twilight, she decided that Reno was a lot like Las Vegas, only smaller. Also, it had pine trees instead of sagebrush.

She considered checking into a hotel for the night, especially since the air had the moist chill of a coming storm in it, and big dark clouds had rolled in, obscuring the early-evening sky.

But then she decided that she still wasn't ready to be cooped up inside four walls with only her own thoughts for company.

Better to keep moving.

She got back on the highway and went west, crossing into California. But then she kept seeing signs that said how far it was to Los Angeles. And she wasn't going to Los Angeles. She was going *away* from Los Angeles.

She turned off the main highway the next chance she got. By then, twilight had settled over the world. It was almost full dark. Then the rain started.

At first the rain was light. Olivia turned her wipers on low and had no problem. Occasionally a flash of lightning would bleach the angry darkness and make the tall trees on either side of the road seem to loom threateningly at the car. Then the thunder would roll.

Olivia drove on as the gathering darkness became true night, turning randomly each time she came to a crossroads. Soon enough, as the rain increased and each new road grew narrower and more twisted, she realized that she really had no idea at all where she was. Not that it mattered. She'd been headed for nowhere when she left Las Vegas, after all. And these tiny, rutted roads she was driving on made her more and more sure she was getting there.

Once she came to a crossroads that she was certain she'd been at before. The sign had the same unfamiliar places listed on it as the one she'd just seen a while back.

It came to her that she was probably driving in circles. A small shiver of uneasiness went through her. She tried to ignore it.

But the storm was becoming a little frightening. The rain grew progressively worse. It began beating at the windshield, heavy and thick. And now it was freezing a little, becoming slushy, half snow. She had to crane her head forward and squint her eyes to see the narrow road, even with the wipers on high.

Once or twice, far behind her, she caught a glimpse of the beams of another car's headlights when the road would straighten out for a little. But ahead there was only darkness. Sometimes she thought she saw the lights of cabins or houses tucked among the trees off the road, but by the time she spotted them, she'd be rounding another bend and the reassuring glimmer of brightness would be lost to her.

She began to feel very much on her own. More than once she found herself looking in her rearview mirror for a sign of that other vehicle behind her, to prove to herself that she wasn't completely alone on an unknown road.

She tried not to give in to anxiety. She told herself not to be foolish. Of course she would find her way out of this maze sooner or later. Actually it had barely been an hour since she'd turned off the highway. It only *seemed* like the middle of the night.

She would be okay. She would be just fine. She was in charge of her life and affairs.

Right then her cute little foreign car made two small coughing noises and stopped running.

It took Olivia a moment to realize that she was slowing down and that pressing the gas pedal had no effect.

As soon as she accepted that the car wasn't working, she steered to the shoulder, a maneuver made possible by the fact that she was on a slight downhill grade at the time.

It was after she'd come to a full stop that she glanced at the gas gauge. It was as far to the bottom of the reserve space as it could get. And the little red signal light was on. Obviously it had been on for quite some time now.

With a tired groan, Olivia leaned her head on the steering wheel.

Oh, why hadn't she remembered to fill up in Reno? Her mind was simply not working very well.

She was fatigued from lack of sleep. She'd been driving for eleven hours, and she was using every ounce of willpower she had at every moment not to think of Jack.

Jack.

There, she'd done it.

With a moan that was half exhaustion and half wounded grief, she let her head drop back against the seat.

Jack.

Rain beat on the car. Lightning flashed, thunder boomed and rolled away.

Jack had betrayed her. He'd done worse than betray her. He'd deceived her. The Jack she'd thought she knew didn't even exist. He'd been her father's man all along.

She had thought that what had happened with Cameron was bad.

But that was *nothing* next to this.

Jack's deception was a lance, turning in the deepest part of her.

Making love with Jack had been the one bold and dangerous thing she'd ever done in her life. And it had all been a lie.

Jack was her father's employee. He had made love to her in the line of duty. Everything they'd shared had been a sham. As Olivia herself was a sham.

A poor little rich girl.

And *girl* was the right word. There was no point in kidding herself. In all the ways that mattered she was still a girl at twenty-nine. A girl no man would want without the added attraction of her daddy's millions.

Olivia looked up. The furious rain still beat on the windshield. And a pair of high beams shone in the rear window at her.

She was about to be rescued by some kindly traveler. The car was pulling to a stop behind her.

Olivia sat up straight in the seat and raked her hair back with both hands. She felt marginally better, now that help had arrived. She might have made a mess of everything, but at least she wouldn't be stuck here alone in the freezing rain all night.

In fact, now that she thought about it, it was probably rude of her to just sit here and let her rescuer get all wet. If anyone got drenched it should be her, a girl who didn't even have enough sense to put gas in her car before leaving the main highway in a thunderstorm.

Olivia shoved open her door and stepped out into the driving, icy rain. She was soaked to the skin in ten seconds, the time it took her to close her door and turn with a grateful, if somewhat forced, smile for her deliverer.

But the smile froze into a sneer.

Because her rescuer was Jack.

Chapter Eight

Jack emerged from his car, which he'd left running, and came straight for her.

Olivia watched him approach, his tall, broad-shouldered body silhouetted in the beams from his headlights. The rain pelted her, plastering her hair to her head, gluing her silly pink outfit to her body. She felt only minimal satisfaction in noting that he was getting just as wet as she was.

"What's the problem?" he asked, when he was close enough that she could hear him without his having to shout. His breath came out as freezing mist.

She clenched her fists at her sides to keep them from scratching his eyes out. "I told you not to follow me."

"I suppose you're out of gas."

"I told you to leave me alone."

"Pop the trunk. I'll get your things."

"I don't want your help."

"Olivia, it's damn wet out here." He reached for the door latch.

She slid to the side and blocked him with her body. The rain truly was very cold. She was starting to shiver. She wrapped her arms around herself. "I won't take your help."

Lightning forked across the sky. Thunder boomed.

Jack spoke with great patience. "You don't have any choice." Water ran off his hawklike nose and over the beard stubble on his cheeks.

He hadn't shaved that morning, she realized. He must have been in a big hurry to chase after her. Her father must really be paying him a lot.

"Come on, Olivia." He sounded tired. "Get in my car and turn up the heater. I'll get your things."

"No." She shivered harder, hunching her shoulders to hoard her body's warmth, pressing herself back against the door.

He shrugged. And before she could yell at him to get his hands off her, he took her by the shoulders and moved her out of his way.

Then he pulled open her door. She watched as he yanked the keys from the ignition, popped the trunk latch and scooped up her purse, all in one fluid movement. He was very efficient, she decided. But then, her father only hired the best.

He slammed the door. "Get in my car. Now."

"No."

They looked at each other through the thick veil of the rain. Even with water running down his nose, she thought, he was the best looking, most purely masculine man she'd ever seen.

She hated him.

But hatred wasn't all of it.

Her traitorous body yearned for him.

Last night he had taught her what she was capable of feeling. It was a lesson that would be engraved on her nerve endings for the rest of her life. And right now it was fresh as a new wound.

She tore her gaze away from his, but it did no good. She only ended up slowly perusing the rest of him. His black knit shirt was stuck to the hard muscles of his torso. His jeans were shiny, slick with the rain, clinging to the strong shape of his legs. He looked good in denim, she decided. More dangerous, more elemental, even more rawly masculine than he did in his suits or his sports clothes.

"Olivia." His voice was rough and husky. It seemed to ignite her already-taut nerves. She realized what she was doing, looking him over with blatant sensual intent. Her head snapped up.

And she was staring right into his eyes again. She read the message in those eyes. She saw that he was thinking exactly what she was thinking.

About last night. About the two of them. About their separate bodies joined and moving as one.

Another javelin of lightning blazed across the sky. The thunder that came after was like giant sheets snapping in a gale-force wind.

"Jack." She barely mouthed his name. She was captured, held by his eyes. All she wanted right then was to throw herself against him, feel his arms close around her and lift her mouth for his kiss.

Her own desire shocked her. She wanted him. Right now. Here, in this wild, unknown place in the driving rain. Even after what he had done, after the way he had betrayed her. Next to the physical need she was feeling, his deception suddenly seemed a paltry thing.

"No." Her voice was low and husky, not convincing at all.

"Olivia."

"No." With a sharp cry she broke the seductive hold of his gaze. She spun on her heel and began walking away, down the narrow road between the tall rows of evergreens, not caring that there was really nowhere to go, only knowing that if she stayed near him for one second longer, she would be begging for his kiss.

Behind her she heard him swear. She waited for him to catch up to her, to dare to touch her. Because she was going to fight him. She was going to kick and scratch and bite to get away from him. He had no right to touch her now. And she would show him that was so.

But he didn't follow. Instead, after a moment or two, she heard her trunk slam. She kept walking, fast as she could, head down, clutching her middle, trying to press her teeth together hard enough that they would stop chattering. Her pink flats were full of water. They squished disgustingly with every step.

But she doggedly put one foot in front of the other, even after she realized that Jack had climbed back in his car and pulled out onto the road again. At first she thought he was going to leave her there, do exactly what she'd ordered him to do. And right at that moment she was glad he was going, even though she had no idea what she would do once his car had disappeared around the next bend.

But she never had to confront that problem. She saw soon enough that he wasn't going anywhere. He only eased in alongside her and drove at a snail's pace to keep even with her.

She walked faster, shivering so hard she almost felt nauseous. But walking faster was a silly and ineffectual gesture, of course. Because he only sped up from three miles an hour to four and stayed with her.

The road took an uphill turn. Head into the wind, she began climbing. The rain beat at her unmercifully. She slogged along.

In ten minutes or so she reached the top of that grade. Ahead of her, by the light of Jack's high beams, she could see that the road twisted down and then vanished around a bend into the trees.

She bent her head again, which kept the worst of the rain off her face, and started down.

She got about five steps before the futility of it all came crashing in on her. She stopped there, on the side of the road, next to a yellow sign with a picture of a leaping deer on it.

Jack, riding slowly and patiently at her side, stopped as well. He leaned across the seat and pushed the passenger door open. With a sigh of resignation she slid into the seat.

She pulled the door closed, her body immediately grateful for the warmth of the heater that was blasting around her freezing bare ankles.

"Here." Jack reached over the seat. "Wrap this around you." It was a thick plaid blanket. She took it from him without comment, wrapping herself in its heavy folds and then huddling against the door.

She closed her eyes as Jack backed the car onto the shoulder and skillfully turned it around. Once they were pointed back the way they'd come, he smoothly depressed the accelerator, and the car picked up speed.

She stayed hugging the door in grim dread. She was sure that once they were really moving, he would start talking. Lecturing her for being a fool. Or perhaps taunting her for the way he knew she felt about him. But he didn't. He was a cipher behind the wheel.

And she was grateful. She wasn't in the mood to listen to a single word from him.

She wasn't in the mood for anything but wallowing in her own despondency. She'd thought she'd hit rock bottom back in Las Vegas. But this was a new low altogether.

Slowly her spasmodic shivers faded. Her hair was still sopping wet, and her clothes clung, damp and uncomfortable, to her body. Her pink shoes felt like wet cardboard against her toes, and she seemed to be enveloped in a musty, humid smell, like wet wool. But at least she didn't feel like she was going to throw up from being so cold.

They reached Highway 80 again in less than twenty minutes. Olivia's depression deepened when she saw how ridiculously close she had been to civilization all the time. She *had* been driving in circles.

And Jack, who had been following her, knew that she'd managed to get herself lost just a few miles from the freeway. It was one more humiliation on top of all the others.

She was leaning against the passenger door pondering this most recent disgrace when Jack spoke. "We'll stop there and get a room." She glanced his way in time to see the sign he was gesturing at.

Gas Food Lodging
TRUCK PLAZA
NEXT RIGHT

"You need to get out of those wet clothes," he added, sounding defensive. "And I want to change, too. And a good night's sleep wouldn't hurt either of us."

She didn't answer, only looked out the windshield at the pounding sheets of slushy rain.

"Olivia, you'll feel better in the morning. Then you can decide what you want to do next."

She leaned against the door again and closed her eyes. She knew very well what would happen in the morning. He would inform her that now that she was rested, she was ready to go back to Daddy where she belonged.

"Olivia." He swore, low and feelingly. "Okay, I'll take your silence for agreement." He turned the wheel toward the off ramp.

When he pulled to a stop, she sat up and looked around. They were parked before the lobby doors of the Highway Haven Motel. Out the windshield she could see the coffee shop and truck stop, which branched off the motel in an L. Out her side window she spied a few cars and pickups, looking small and lost in the pouring rain. Beyond the cars and pickups loomed a row of big rigs.

"I'll be able to see you from inside the lobby," Jack said.

She let out a tired breath of air. "What's that supposed to mean?"

"It means if you get any more crazy ideas about running off, I'll see you go."

She leaned her elbow on the door and rested her head on her hand. "Jack, this may come as a shock to you, but I'm a grown adult. And this is the United States of America. You have no right to stop me from going anywhere I want to go."

"I didn't say I'd stop you. I won't stop you. But I won't let you wander off alone, either."

"You mean you'd follow me."

"You got it. So stay here."

She shook her head.

"What does that mean?" he demanded.

She slanted him a look. "It means I'm too tired to fight with you right now."

"You'll stay here, then?"

She made a low noise of disgust. "Sure."

"Do I have your word?"

She made the same noise again. "Sure." She gave him a direct look. "I promise I'll stay here."

He stared at her for a moment. Then he seemed to decide her word was something he could trust.

"Good," he said. "I'll be right back." He got out of the car and went in through the glass doors. He glanced at her once before turning his back to her and enlisting the night clerk to check him into a room.

Olivia watched him, sitting very still. After thirty seconds it was clear that he'd decided she was too beaten and dejected to try any more crazy stunts tonight.

Good, she thought grimly. Because she wasn't quite as beaten as she'd led Jack to believe. And right then he should have known that her word could not be trusted.

She knew she didn't have much time. A minute or two at the most, before he either turned around again or finished at the check-in desk.

She looked around for her purse, but it wasn't on the front seat. He'd either put it in the back seat or tossed it in his trunk.

Well, too bad. She'd do without it. This was a point of honor as far as Olivia was concerned. She had to get away before Jack returned her to her father as if she were some naughty, runaway little girl with no power at all over her own destiny.

Olivia tossed the blanket off her shoulders, leaned on her door and swung her feet to the pavement. Hunched over, not daring the slightest glance back, she shoved the door closed and made a beeline through the rain for the row of huge trucks that stood so tall and proud at the edge of the lot.

She slipped between them. Then she crouched against the nearest one, the rain pelting her. She was listening for Jack's pursuit. But what she heard instead was the sound of a truck's powerful engine starting up. It wasn't the one she crouched against, but the one right next to it, a shiny maroon affair with a huge picture of a pretty blond woman painted on the trailer. She was just staring into the wide brown eyes of the bigger-than-life-size blonde when she saw and heard the driver's door of the maroon rig swing open.

Her own swiftness astounded her. She was around the back of the maroon rig before its driver jumped to the pavement. She bent down and watched the man's booted feet under the truck as they went the way she had come. As he moved toward the back, she inched forward, past another giant-size rendering of the same pretty blonde that adorned the other side of the trailer. She found herself at the front of the truck just as its driver reached the back. She heard him fool with something back there, probably checking to see that the big doors were firmly shut.

The driver's door was still open, the engine still running at a low, smooth idle. Not daring a glance at the motel, where Jack was probably discovering right now that she wasn't where she was supposed to be, Olivia darted past the nose of the truck and reached the driver's side. With a low grunt she hoisted herself up and into the cab. Then she saw the curtains behind the seat and knew they must lead to that little area behind the cab where the truck driver could sleep during long-distance rides.

Praying the driver wouldn't notice the extra water in his truck, since he himself was probably pretty wet by now, she slithered up over the seat and through the curtains.

She found herself on a bed that was surprisingly comfortable. Swiftly she scooted around to make sure the curtains were in place. Then she froze, hardly daring to breathe, as she heard the driver climb back into the cab.

The cab door slammed. The driver turned on the radio, and country music played. She heard the massive gears shifting. And the truck was moving.

She couldn't believe it. They were driving away. She had actually escaped from Jack.

She closed her eyes, feeling a lovely surge of self-righteous triumph. And then the triumph faded.

Now what was she going to do with herself?

And, now that she had a minute to think about it, what about Jack? Leaving him in his room at a Las Vegas hotel had been one thing. But escaping him here, at a truck stop on Highway 80 after dark, was something else altogether.

He would be worried sick. Even if he'd made love to her under false pretenses, she knew he still felt responsible for her. And her disappearing like this would not be easy for him to take.

Olivia rolled over on the bed and contemplated the nearby ceiling. Oh, what was the matter with her? That Jack Roper might experience a little emotional distress when he found she was gone was the least of her problems right now.

And, anyway, what else could she have done? She wasn't about to return to her father. Never again. Not until she was a grown woman in more than just years.

Olivia realized she was shivering again. Now that the adrenaline rush of running from Jack had passed, her whole body ached and shook with cold. Luckily the bed had blankets.

In fact, now that her eyes were adjusted to the dimness, she could see that this cozy sleeping place was quite nicely appointed. There was a little square of floor, a narrow door that would allow exit without going over the seat of the cab, some cupboards and even a microwave. She gave a little sigh and knew she could have done much worse than having to spend a few hours in this snug portable room.

If she was lucky, she might even manage to slip out when the truck stopped, without the driver even knowing she'd been there. It would be one less embarrassing moment that she'd have to live through.

Gently she slid off her soggy flats and set them in the corner by the pillow, against the cab, where they wouldn't fall off onto the tiny floor and alert the driver that he wasn't traveling alone. She slipped under the blankets and pulled them gratefully up around her chin.

The bed was comfortable, really comfortable, she decided. Her eyes drooped closed.

Sleep came like stepping off a cliff, a quick drop into the waiting arms of oblivion.

"All right, Mr. Roper, we've got the description. We can keep an eye out for her."

"In case she turns up dead in a ditch, you mean," Jack supplied grimly.

The deputy gave him a wounded look. "There's only so much we can do. You gotta know that. Without signs of a struggle or any evidence of foul play, all we've got is an adult female who decided she didn't want to stay where she was."

Jack knew the deputy was right. He stood. "Fine. Well, you have the description. I'll be at the Highway Haven Motel until morning. And I'll call here before I move on."

"Sounds good. Sorry we can't do more."

"Yeah, I know. Thanks, anyway." Jack turned with a wave and left the sheriff's small station.

Outside, the rain was still coming down heavily. He stood in the shelter of the overhanging portico and stared out at the darkness and the storm.

He'd been a damned idiot, just as he'd always been when it came to the beer baron's daughter. He'd been sure she was finished, too worn-out to try any more funny stuff. And he'd taken her word that she would stay where he'd left her. He'd turned his back on her for two full minutes. And she'd used that time to get away.

She'd vanished into nowhere.

God. Where was she now? Please, let her be all right.

He'd checked every inch of the damn parking lot, gone through the coffee shop from end to end, including both rest rooms. She was nowhere to be found. Then he'd driven up and down the frontage road. Nothing.

He even took the ramp onto the highway and headed for the next exit, at which he'd turned around and gone back the other way, making a loop in both directions for a distance of fifteen miles.

Now, he was reasonably certain she'd managed to hitch a ride during that crucial two minutes when he'd been signing into the room. She hadn't even taken her purse with her, the little fool. What did she think she was going to do with herself without even a quarter for a phone call, wandering around in a freezing rainstorm wearing only a pair of cotton slacks and a big pink shirt with a cat's face on it?

He prayed that whoever had picked her up was a decent human being. And he swore that when he found her, he would wring her pretty white neck.

Because he would find her. There was no question of that. He'd found more than one person who'd tried to disappear. That was what he was best at: hunting down the missing, whether they wanted to be found or not.

Something wasn't the same.

Slowly Olivia opened her eyes. She saw the ceiling, close enough to touch.

Where was she?

She remembered. The big truck with the woman's face painted on the side. She'd crawled into the sleeping compartment, and the truck had driven away from the Highway Haven Motel. And from Jack.

But she wasn't going to think about Jack. Not right now.

She had to figure out what wasn't the same.

Then it came to her. The truck had stopped.

Olivia lay very still, listening for sounds that would tell her the driver was still in the cab. She heard nothing but the steady drone of rain on the roof.

Cautiously she pushed the warm cocoon of covers back and dared a peek into the cab. There was no one there.

Shy as a turtle she withdrew her head from between the curtains. She groped for her shoes, found them and slid them on, though they felt as sodden and squishy as water-logged newspaper.

She slid off the edge of the bed onto the floor. The sudden movement caused a mild bout of dizziness. She paused a moment for the dizziness to pass. Once her equilibrium had returned, she patted at her damp, tangled hair and pressed the pads of her fingers against her eyes. She straightened her soggy pink slacks and smoothed her wrinkled shirt.

Then she drew in a deep breath and grasped the latch of the little door. It swung out. She jumped to the ground, right into a huge puddle.

Dejected, she looked down at herself. Now she was not only wrinkled and soggy, she was splattered with mud. The rain, steady and hard as it had been for what must have been hours now, poured down on her head, soaking her damp hair all over again.

Olivia shoved the door of the sleeper shut. It looked as if the truck was parked on the street of some small town or other. She was only a few steps from an old-fashioned covered sidewalk, so she took those steps.

She was out of the rain. And that was good. She was also standing by some sort of quaint store. The window by the door was painted with a rainbow. Over the rainbow, it said, Santino's BB & V. Below the rainbow, in smaller letters there was the explanation: Barber, Beauty And Variety: For All Your Household Needs.

Olivia walked on, shivering, wrapping her arms around herself, to the next door up, which belonged to Lily's Café. The sign said Homemade Eats. Breakfast Served All Day.

Both businesses were closed. She turned, now that the big truck no longer blocked the view, and looked up at the heavens. They were gray and angry and showed no stars or moon. In the distance a rim of hills touched the sky. The hills were covered with the dark, spiked shadows of evergreen trees.

Shivering harder, she turned and began walking the other way, down the street, past the café and the store called Santino's and another store that was named Fletcher Gold Sales. She was looking for a light or some sign that someone in this place was awake. As she walked, though she despised herself for doing it, she longed for Jack. She also wished that she could just crawl into a hole and pull the hole in after her.

The minute she cleared the big rig on the other end, she saw a business that was still open. It was the town tavern, across and a few doors down the street. The lights were on there. Music and laughter came from inside.

Even through the heavy numbness of her misery, she was drawn to the light and the voices like a hungry animal to the smell of food. She slogged out into the rain and trudged across the street.

The name of the place was written in lariat script on the window and over the door: The Hole in the Wall.

Olivia shivered even harder when she saw that. She was feeling so strange and dizzy, and she had wished for a hole to crawl into. And here it was.

Maybe she was dreaming. Maybe none of this was real. Maybe, in a few moments, she would wake beside Jack in his room in Las Vegas. He would wrap his arms around her and kiss her on the tip of her nose, and she would be so grateful because none of the awful things that had happened since this morning would have been true. It would all have been one long, distressingly vivid bad dream.

She could tell her crazy dream to Jack, and Jack would hold her close and rub her back and say she mustn't worry. It was only a nightmare. And now it was over. He would tip her chin up and look deeply into her eyes and she would sigh and offer her mouth eagerly for his kiss.

Olivia closed her eyes. She shook her head. She waited for the nightmare to end.

But when she opened her eyes again, she was still standing on the strange small-town street in front of a bar called the Hole in the Wall.

With a little moan she moved forward onto the sidewalk. Then she took the few steps to the double doors. She reached out both hands and pushed the doors open, slipping between them before they swung shut again. The moment she was inside, she shrank back into the shadows to the side of the doors.

Warmth. And smoke. And music and laughter.

There were a lot of people in this place. And they seemed to be having some kind of a party. Crepe paper streamers hung from the light fixtures, and there were balloons everywhere. There was a banner over the bar that read Happy Seventy-Seventh, Oggie.

In the center of the room an old man with his back to her was sitting in front of a cake. A very pregnant woman with strawberry hair bent near, lighting the candles, *a lot* of candles.

"Hey, Jared. 'Nother round down here," a voice called from the other end of the long bar to her left.

"Coming right up."

Olivia glanced toward the bartender when she heard his voice. He was a tall, dark man dressed all in black. His body was hard looking and lean, like Jack's, and he—

Olivia gasped as the man turned in her direction and she got a good look at his face. Oh, Lord. He looked like Jack. So much like Jack it was frightening.

The bartender must have heard her gasp. His eyes found her in the shadows. His eyes were gray eyes, not Jack's eyes at all. Olivia's heart slowed down a little.

"Can I help you, miss?" the bartender asked.

"I, uh..."

All at once everyone began to sing "Happy Birthday" to Oggie. There was much stomping and whistling and several catcalls.

"Settle down, you hooligans," the old man groused. "I got a lot of candles here. This is going to be some job." Slowly the old man pushed himself to his feet.

"Miss?" the bartender asked again.

Olivia hardly heard him. Absently she waved away his question. She was noticing more individual faces now. And there were several in the circle closest to the old man that reminded her of Jack. And there was a blond woman. A blond woman who looked just like the painting on the side of the truck that had brought Olivia to this unknown place.

Olivia trembled. Her heart raced. Could she be hallucinating? It was surely possible after all she'd been through.

The old man drew in a huge breath and blew. He got half the candles. He blew again. "That does it," he declared. "Cut the damn thing, will you, Eden?"

"Miss?" It was the bartender again. Somehow he'd come around the bar and was at her side without her even noticing that he'd moved. "Are you all right?"

She waved him away again and began to move, like a sleepwalker, toward the people and the cake and the old man.

"Get her a stiff one, Jared," a man's voice wryly suggested. "She looks like she needs it."

The tall, pregnant redhead looked up then from cutting the first slice of birthday cake. She drew in a sharp breath.

"Oh, my God." The pregnant woman set down her knife. "Jared, she's drenched. Get a blanket from the back room. Now." The pregnant woman moved then, pushing through the press of people. She had a beautiful, kind face with a wide mouth and big dark eyes.

Olivia watched the pregnant woman coming, until a movement from the old man distracted her. She blinked and shifted her gaze to him as he slowly turned to look her way.

Olivia heard a tiny, mewling cry and didn't even know it was coming from her own mouth.

It wasn't possible. It must be a dream. But the old man's eyes—small, beady eyes—reminded her quite forcefully of Jack. It made no sense. They weren't like Jack's eyes at all. Except for the color.

Obsidian.

Yes, obsidian eyes. And the set of the old man's jaw, the shape of his mouth. So much about him. Like Jack.

It was too much for Olivia. Slowly, and then faster and faster, the room began to spin.

Suddenly all the people were converging on her. Their concerned expressions and exclamations of surprise overwhelmed her.

She sank into unconsciousness, her last awareness that of strong, unseen arms catching her before she hit the floor.

Chapter Nine

"There. She's coming around," a man's voice said.

Cautiously Olivia opened her eyes. A man was bending over her. "Can you hear me?" the man asked.

Olivia managed a nod as she became aware that someone had put a pillow under her head and tucked a warm blanket around her body. "What happened?"

"You fainted." The man smiled. "I'm Will Bacon. I run the local medical clinic. We were just trying to decide whether to call for the ambulance or not."

Olivia struggled to sit up. Gently the man eased her back down. "Relax. Don't push yourself."

Olivia blinked and shifted her glance from the man's kind face. She drew in a sharp breath when she saw that there were people all around, looking down at her.

"Step back everyone," Will Bacon said. "Don't crowd her."

The ring of faces receded a little.

"Find out who she is," another man whispered.

"Let's not worry about that now," a woman said. Olivia sought the voice. It was the pregnant redhead from her strange dream—the dream that seemed not to have ended, after all. "She appears to be thoroughly exhausted more than anything. What do you think, Will?"

"Yes, I'd say that's exactly her problem," Will Bacon agreed. "What she probably needs most right now is a good night's sleep in a warm, dry place."

"Sam and I have plenty of room," a small, voluptuous black-haired woman offered. "She can spend the night with us."

Olivia stared at the black-haired woman. She was one of the people who resembled Jack.

"Well, what do you say?" Will asked. "We can call the ambulance, if you want. Or you can spend the night at Delilah's house."

Olivia looked around at all the curious and concerned faces. She felt an instinctive trust for these people. Even if half of them did look like Jack.

Or perhaps *because* half of them looked like Jack.

"It's up to you," Will prompted softly. "Would you like to go to the hospital, or stay at Sam and Delilah's?"

"Sam and Delilah's, please," Olivia said.

"Good enough." Will looked up. "Patrick, why don't you carry her out to your four-by-four?"

"Sure."

A man came and bent beside her. His hair was brown and his eyes were blue. But he had Jack's chin. Olivia closed her eyes.

With great care, the man, Patrick, slid his arms beneath her and hoisted her, still wrapped in the warm blanket, against his chest. Then Patrick stood and carried her out into the rain and the darkness and gently slid her into the front seat of a vehicle.

The drive to Sam and Delilah's house was a short one. To Olivia it seemed that they'd barely started and they were there. The man named Patrick carried her in the front door. Inside, the black-haired woman, Delilah, took charge.

"This way, carefully." Delilah led the way up a flight of stairs. "I have the bed turned down."

They took her into a large, blue room and eased her onto a firm double bed.

In the doorway the old man with the obsidian eyes was watching, leaning on a cane. "Hell. She's a cute little thing, ain't she?"

"Forget it, Father," Delilah said. "You're out of sons to match her up with. And you and Patrick may go. We want to get her out of those wet things."

Grumbling, the old man turned and stumped off down the hall. Patrick followed. Olivia was left with four women: Delilah, a fine-boned brunette, the pregnant red-haired woman and the blonde whose likeness had been painted on the side of the truck.

The brunette was at Olivia's feet, sliding off her soggy shoes. "Your feet are like ice." Her warm, soft hands rubbed them in a wonderful massage.

Olivia sighed in pleasure as her poor toes grew warmer at last.

"Can you sit up?" the blonde asked. "We've got to get these wet clothes off."

"Come on," the redhead clucked. "We'll be gentle." They eased Olivia to a sitting position and carefully helped her to remove her mud-stained clothes.

"Here we go." Delilah held out a white cotton night-gown. "Lift up your arms."

Feeling like a child with four tender mothers, Olivia obediently held her hands high. The soft fabric whispered over her head and was smoothed down her tired body by gentle hands.

"Now, her hair." The brunette was ready with a big, fluffy towel. She dried Olivia's hair with the towel, and then the blonde appeared with a brush. Olivia received a hundred strokes.

"Now you can lie down," the redhead said.

Olivia gratefully stretched out once more.

Delilah tucked the covers snugly around her.

"Rest now," the brunette murmured, smoothing Olivia's hair back as if she were a child.

"Thank you."

"You are most welcome."

Olivia watched as the women went to the door. "Good night," she said.

They whispered four good-nights in turn and then they left her, switching off the light and closing the door very softly behind them.

Once she was alone, Olivia stared at the closed door through the darkness for a long while as a lovely feeling of peace stole over her. A smile took form on her lips.

She'd made a terrible mess of things, she knew. And yet, some deep instinct told her that all was not lost.

She'd divested herself of all her worldly possessions save the clothes on her back. She'd wandered, lost and alone in a rainstorm until she reached the end of nowhere.

And the people there had taken her in. She had the peculiar sense that she was exactly where she belonged at last. Simple human kindness surrounded her. It did a lot to heal her wounded heart.

Thinking of her heart, she thought of Jack.

Oddly enough, her thoughts were tender.

She was beginning to forgive him, she realized. Now, safe in a warm bed, due to the kindness of strangers, she could let herself remember the real concern on his face when he picked her up on that deserted road. She could allow herself to recall that she'd heard her father fire him on the phone, which meant that when Jack came after her, he'd most likely done it on his own.

Poor Jack. The more she thought about him, the guiltier she felt. He was probably going out of his mind with worry. And her father. Oh, Lord. Olivia couldn't even bear to *think* about what her father was doing now.

Yes, she'd made a mess of things, all right. She had no idea at all how she was going to go about righting all the wrong she'd done.

But she would work it out. Somehow tomorrow she would deal with it all. But for now she was simply too worn-out.

Olivia turned on her side and rested her cheek on her hand. Her eyelids drooped closed. With a sigh, she surrendered to her tired body's need for sleep.

Jack wasn't so lucky.

He sat on his bed in his room at the Highway Haven and watched the blinking of the motel sign reflected in the windshield of a truck across the parking lot.

He was thinking of forget-me-not eyes. And the dusting of freckles across a certain pert nose.

He was *willing* Olivia to be all right.

With a low, crude oath, he looked at his watch. Past eleven.

He thought of Lawrence Larrabee, who was probably in Las Vegas by now. And going insane with worry over Olivia, just as Jack was.

It would only be asking for more abuse to call the man and tell him what was going on. It was the last thing Jack should do.

But still, he picked up the phone and got the number of the Vegas hotel where he and Olivia had stayed. He punched up the number, calling himself a fool after each digit.

When the hotel operator answered, he asked for Lawrence Larrabee's room.

"I'll connect you," the operator said.

Larrabee picked up before the first ring had stopped. "Hello, this is Lawrence Larrabee."

Jack dragged in a breath. "This is Jack Roper."

A barrage of heated epithets erupted from the phone. Jack waited until they petered out a little, then asked, "Do you want to know what's going on or not?"

"Of course I do, you lowlife. How is she? Where is she? Is she all right?"

"Settle down, Lawrence." Jack waited.

After a moment, in a very controlled voice, Larrabee said, "All right. I'm calm. Tell me everything. From this morning on."

"Okay. She left the hotel there at 9:30 a.m."

"You followed?"

"Yeah. I tailed her up through Tonopah and Reno. Then she crossed back into California. She got off the main highway and drove in circles on side roads until she ran out of gas. I picked her up. That was around seven-thirty tonight." He digressed enough to tell Larrabee exactly where they'd left Olivia's car.

Larrabee said he'd have the car taken care of. "What happened next?"

"I brought her back here."

"Where's *here?*"

Jack gave the general location of the Highway Haven, but nothing specific. The last thing he wanted was Lawrence Larrabee showing up there. "We were both beat. I was planning that we'd spend the night here and probably head for L.A. tomorrow."

"So she's with you now."

"Well—"

"Let me talk to her."

Now came the unpleasant part. Jack confessed, "That isn't possible."

Larrabee was silent again, as if keeping himself carefully reined. Then he inquired, "Why not?"

"She isn't here."

"What?"

"She disappeared when I went to get the room. I've been to the police, and I've combed the area. Nothing. So far."

There was another lengthy silence. Larrabee talked to someone on his end. Then he asked, "Are you saying that my daughter has vanished into the Northern California woods somewhere?"

"For now, yes."

Jack heard a woman's voice from Larrabee's end. Probably the girlfriend, Mindy Long. The voice was making those soothing sounds women make when their men are about to go through the roof.

Larrabee said, "Consider yourself fired, Roper."

Jack gave a wry chuckle. "Get current, Lawrence. You already fired me this morning, remember?"

Larrabee sputtered and huffed a little, then he asked, "Well then, why are you still out there, if you know you're not getting paid?"

"None of your damn business," Jack said. "But I'm on my own time with this, and if I tell you what's going on, it's only because I think that somewhere in that pompous, overly possessive heart of yours, you love your daughter and want the best for her."

"Well, of course I love my daughter, you—"

"Save it, Lawrence. I'll call you when I've got more to tell you."

Jack found it very satisfying to hang up on Larrabee for a change.

And after that, not knowing what else to do, he kicked off his shoes, stretched out on the bed and grimly waited for sleep.

Near dawn, Jack sat bolt upright.

He'd dreamed of the motel sign, blinking in the windshield of a big truck. In his dream the truck had pulled out and driven away. He'd watched it go.

It was a fancy rig, glossy maroon in color, with a giant painting of a big-eyed blonde on the trailer. A rig just like the one that had been pulling out of the lot when Jack turned around and saw that Olivia was no longer in his car.

"Damn," Jack muttered under his breath. It was a long shot. But right about now, it was the only shot he had.

He got up and pulled on his clothes.

Then he went to the coffee shop and ordered breakfast.

There, for five long hours, he made a complete nuisance of himself, asking question after question of anyone who would talk to him.

Finally, around eleven in the morning, after he'd drunk so much coffee his molars felt as if they were floating, he described the maroon rig to a trucker, who answered, "You must mean the Sweet Amy."

Jack's heart, already speeding from all the caffeine, raced a little faster. But he tried to keep his voice calm. "The truck has a name?"

"It sure does. The owner, Brendan, named it after his wife."

"Brendan who?"

Now the trucker became wary. "Brendan's a good man. I wouldn't want to be sendin' no trouble his way."

"Look." Jack did his best to make his expression sincere. "I don't even know the man. And this has nothing to do with him, really. It's only that I think he might have picked up a hitchhiker here last night."

"You're after the hitcher?"

"Yeah."

"Woman or man?"

"Woman."

"Yours?"

Jack made a quick decision to play this for sympathy. He nodded. And then he looked away.

The trucker, as Jack had suspected from a certain sensitivity in his bleary eyes, had a soft heart. "Hey. You'll work it out. Me and my wife, we have our battles. But we come back around. We get through it."

Jack stared at the dusty plastic flower in the bud vase at the end of the table, as if he couldn't trust his own emotions. And then, as if he had to force himself to do it, he looked the trucker in the eye. "I have to *find* her first. Before we can work this out."

"Hell." The other man took a swig from his coffee mug. "Okay. The trucker you're lookin' for is Brendan Jones. Out of North Magdalene. That's about twenty miles above Nevada City on Highway 49."

When she woke, it took Olivia a moment to remember where she was.

And then it came to her. The blue room. In the home of some people named Sam and Delilah.

Though the room was dim, she could see that it was sunny outside. There was a rim of bright light around the shades.

Olivia pulled herself to a sitting position and was just rearranging the covers a little when the door opened a crack.

"Ah. I see you're awake at last." Delilah bustled in. She went to the window and ran up the shades.

Bright midday sun poured into the room. Olivia squinted and looked away. But her eyes adjusted swiftly to the light, and then she turned back to look out the window. She could see the top of a maple tree, whose leaves had turned the browns and oranges of fall. The sky was a clear, pristine blue.

"The rain," Delilah said, gazing out the window. "It does wonders. Makes everything seem new." She turned to Olivia, a smile on her rather exotic face. "Last night it seemed more important to get you warm and dry and rested than to make introductions. I never told you my name."

Olivia gave the other woman a shy smile. "Your name was mentioned though, I think. Delilah, right?"

Delilah nodded. "Delilah Fletcher. I'm a teacher. My husband, Sam, owns Fletcher Gold Sales on Main Street." Delilah came and sat on the edge of the bed.

Olivia knew Delilah was waiting for her to introduce herself. Instead, she asked, "What town is this?"

"North Magdalene."

"In California?"

"Yes."

"And what time is it?"

Delilah shrugged. "After noon. How are you feeling?"

"Much better."

Right then the brunette from the night before appeared in the doorway. She was carrying a tray.

"Here's your breakfast," Delilah said and stood so that the brunette could set the tray across Olivia's legs.

Olivia looked down at raisin toast, two nicely poached eggs and a mug of coffee. The coffee smelled wonderful. "I'm starving. Thank you."

"You're welcome," the brunette said. "What do you take in your coffee?"

"Black is fine."

The brunette stood, backing up until she was beside Delilah. The two of them watched, smiling, as Olivia sipped her coffee and started to work on the eggs. After a moment the brunette volunteered, "I'm Regina Jones." She gestured at Delilah. "Delilah's brother, Patrick, is my husband."

Olivia nodded. "I remember Patrick drove me here last night." She took a bite of toast. The simple food tasted like heaven. It occurred to her that she hadn't eaten at all yesterday.

Right then the doorbell rang.

"That'll be Amy or Eden," Delilah said, and left to answer.

"They're both here," Delilah announced a few moments later. She introduced the blonde as Amy. And the redhead was named Eden. They were the Jones women, Regina explained with a wry grin. Except for Delilah, who'd been born a Jones, each of them had married one of the Jones men. The old man whose birthday party she'd interrupted was named Oggie Jones. He lived here with Delilah and Sam—in the back bedroom downstairs. He was the patriarch of the Jones clan.

Now they'd introduced themselves, the four women looked at Olivia expectantly.

Finally Regina pointed out in her gentle voice, "You haven't told us *your* name yet."

Olivia looked from one face to the next. She had no idea why she was holding back. These people had been so kind to her. She certainly owed them an explanation.

She swallowed the last bite of egg and said, "I'm Olivia Larrabee. As in Larrabee Brewing?"

"The beer company?" Amy asked.

"Yes. That's my father's company."

The women nodded.

"Ah."

"Yes."

"We see."

"But what brings you here, to North Magdalene?" Regina wondered.

Olivia confessed. "I'm on the run."

The women nodded and clucked among themselves some more.

Then Delilah asked, "From whom?"

"From everything."

"Everything?" Regina repeated.

"Yes, everything."

"What is *everything*, specifically?" Amy asked.

"Everything," Olivia said once more with an expansive gesture. "Everything includes my father, who loves me a lot but won't let me lead my own life. And my father's money, which I never earned. And also my completely pointless life. And last but not least, a man named Jack."

"Ah." The women nodded to each other.

"A man."

"Yes."

"Of course, a man."

"Look." Olivia pushed the tray away. "Can we talk?"

"Certainly." Regina took the tray and set it on the dresser by the door.

"Talk," Delilah said.

Amy added, "Please do."

And Eden chimed in. "Get it all out."

Which is precisely what Olivia did.

For well over an hour she talked.

She poured her heart out. She told them everything, from her overbearing father's loving domination to her unfulfilled dream of becoming a chef, to her ex-fiancé's betrayal, to the sad and tender story of her brief, heartbreaking affair with Jack.

The women listened and clucked their tongues. They nodded and shook their heads at all the right places. Olivia felt that for the first time in her life she was fully understood.

And when at last she said, "So that's how I ended up at Oggie Jones's seventy-seventh birthday party last night." Her heart seemed to be purified and her soul felt cleansed.

For a few minutes, once the story was told, everyone was quiet. Amy patted Olivia's hand and Regina gave her a sympathetic smile. And then Eden looked at Amy, who glanced at Regina, who gave a nod to Delilah.

Delilah said gently, "Well, then. I suppose that the question you have to ask yourself next is..."

"Yes?" Olivia wondered eagerly.

"What are you going to do now?"

Chapter Ten

An hour and a half after the trucker told him where to look for Brendan Jones, Jack parked his car on Main Street in front of Lily's Café.

Experience had taught him that the best places to go for information were bars and coffee shops. In North Magdalene, he found one of each. He'd passed the bar just a moment ago. It was across and down the street right next to a restaurant called the Mercantile Grill. He would try asking questions there as soon as he was through in the café.

He got out of the car and stretched a little, working out the kinks from the drive. Then he headed for the café.

He was just about to pull the door open when it opened from inside. Two older women came out. Both were tall. One was very thin and the other was big boned and deep breasted. They wore dark-colored dresses with little white collars and looked like what they probably were: two good Christian ladies who'd just enjoyed a leisurely Sunday lunch after spending a pious morning in church.

They came out chattering together. And then they saw Jack.

They both snapped their mouths shut and stared. It would have been comical, Jack thought, if it wasn't so strange.

The thin one muttered, "Oh no. Linda Lou, it can't be. Not *another* one."

And then the big one seemed to shake herself. "Come along, Nellie," she intoned. "The resemblance is only coincidental, I'm sure. And it's rude to stare." She took the skinny one's hand and pulled her off down the street.

Jack watched them go, wondering what the hell *that* was all about. Then he shrugged and went inside.

He took a seat at the counter, ignoring the sudden hush that seemed to settle over the room as one and then another of the customers glanced his way.

"Do you want to see a menu?" the young waitress asked. Jack looked in her eyes and wondered where he'd seen her before. There was something vaguely familiar about her. "Coffee?" she prompted.

He shook his head. She seemed to be studying him, looking him over closely. He sensed that she found him familiar, too.

Well, so what? He had to find Olivia. Whether or not he and this waitress had met before was unimportant.

"I'm looking for a man," he said. "A trucker, name of Brendan Jones. You know him?"

The waitress turned and set down the coffeepot on a burner. Then she faced him again. "I'm Heather. But folks call me Sunshine. Who are you?"

In the second before Jack replied, the café was eerily silent. Jack felt as if all the eyes in the place were focused on his back, as if they all waited, holding their breaths, to hear who he was.

He told them. "My name's Roper. Jack Roper."

Was it only his imagination, or did he hear them all start breathing once again?

The waitress took the pencil from behind her ear, looked at it and then stuck it back in. "I've never heard of you."

Jack shrugged and kept to his objective. "How about Brendan Jones? Have you heard of him?"

The waitress didn't answer. She just looked at him, eye to eye. Then she said, "Wait a minute. I'll be right back."

She disappeared through a door at the end of the counter—to make a phone call, he assumed. It was a long five minutes before she returned.

When she marched over and faced him again, he took the initiative. "Well? *Now* do you know Brendan Jones?"

The waitress gave him a bright smile. "Yes. He's my uncle." Before he could demand to know more, she instructed, "You go on over to the Hole in the Wall. That's the bar, down the street and on the other side. Ask for Oggie Jones."

"What about *Brendan* Jones?"

"You ask Oggie. He'll tell you what you need to know."

The Hole in the Wall was dark and cool and very well kept.

The same thing happened there as had happened at the café. The few customers at the bar all turned and stared when Jack pushed through the double doors.

"Hell," one man muttered. "If that ain't a Jones, then I'll swear off drinkin'."

"Don't make promises you'll never keep, Rocky," the handsome young bartender advised with a show of even white teeth.

Jack decided to ignore the remarks. He wasn't going to get sidetracked from his goal.

"Oggie Jones?" he asked the bartender.

The bartender flipped a thumb over his shoulder toward a curtain that was strung across one wall. "Through there."

When he went through the curtain, Jack found himself in a windowless alcove, the bar's back room. There was a round table, covered with a green felt cloth, and a number of bentwood chairs. The light came from a cone-shaded light bulb suspended from the ceiling.

At the table sat an old man. He was idly shuffling a deck of cards.

The old guy looked up.

And that weird feeling came over Jack again, that feeling of familiarity, the same as with the waitress at the café. Jack had never seen the old guy before. He was sure of it. And yet there was something about him that made Jack positive they'd met in the past.

And Jack could have sworn that the old fellow was thinking just the same about him—only more so. The man looked as if he'd seen a ghost.

But then the shock in the beady eyes passed. "I'm Oggie," the old man said in a voice of gravel and dust. "Park your butt right there, son." He pointed at a chair.

Jack gave a brief shake of his head. "No, thanks. I'll stand."

"Suit yourself." Oggie Jones pushed the deck of cards to the center of the table and sat back. "What can I do for you?"

"I'm looking for a trucker named Brendan Jones."

"So I've been told. What d'you want with my boy?"

"This Brendan's your son?"

"Yep." Oggie pulled a cigar from his breast pocket. "Smoke, Mr....?"

"Roper. No, thanks."

"Ah, yes. Roper. That's right. Sunshine told me the name. But I'm seventy-seven yesterday. The memory fails."

Looking into the crafty dark eyes, Jack didn't believe the memory had failed one bit. He explained, "I think your son may have taken on a hitchhiker at a truck stop up near Donner Summit last night."

"What makes you think that?"

"Timing. I turned my back and this person disappeared. Right at that moment your son's truck was pulling out of the parking lot where it happened."

"This person. Is it a man?"

"No, a woman. A woman named Olivia Larrabee." Jack took out the snapshot Larrabee had given him when Jack took the job of tailing Olivia. It showed Olivia in front of a Malibu restaurant with Cameron Cain. Jack handed the picture to the old man.

Oggie studied it closely. When he looked up again, his road map of a face revealed nothing. "She your woman?"

The word "Yeah" was out of Jack's mouth before he even stopped to remind himself that he was getting out of Olivia's life just as soon as he made sure she was okay.

Oggie took a moment to bite the end off his cigar and light up. Then he asked, "She a good woman?"

Jack didn't like the direction of this. "What do you mean, a good woman?"

The old coot did some puffing. At last he elaborated, "I mean the kind of woman a man wants to hang on to. A woman of heart and intestinal fortitude."

Jack grunted. "Intestinal—?"

"Has she got guts, son? Guts."

Jack thought of Olivia, of how fanciful and frail she was. Not someone a man would describe as having "guts," not by a long shot. But even if she didn't have "intestinal fortitude," she *was* good. "Yeah," he said, ruing the slight huskiness that crept into his voice, a huskiness that the shrewd old man would be sure to note. "She's a good woman."

Oggie looked at the snapshot again. "The fellow in this picture don't look like you."

"It isn't."

"Hmm." Oggie returned the photograph, then sat back in his chair and fiddled with the grimy suspenders he wore. He pondered aloud, "It ain't you in the picture."

"So what?"

"So, you *say* she's your woman."

"She is."

"You say she's a *good* woman."

"She's that, too."

"But somehow, you let her get away from you."

Jack felt his patience slipping dangerously. "Where the hell are you going with this, old man?"

Oggie Jones let out a nerve-flaying cackle of laughter. "Well, I gotta tell ya, son. For a man to lose a good woman is the worst kind of carelessness. A good woman is what it's all about. Ask any of my boys, they'll tell you about the importance of a woman who can—"

Jack chopped the air with his hand, a short gesture of starkly controlled violence. Oggie, who was not a fool, fell silent.

"Look," Jack said very quietly. "When can I talk to Brendan Jones?"

"A week, maybe two."

Jack stared. "What the hell do you mean?"

"I mean he's on a cross-country run. Left early this morning. Won't be back for a while."

Jack murmured the crudest phrase he could think of. But then he realized what the old man had just said. "He left *here* early this morning?"

"Yep."

"Then I take it he did come back here last night?"

"Yep." The old man grinned a crafty grin and puffed on his cigar. "He came in special, for his old man's birthday party."

"So you saw him last night?"

"Damn straight. It was *my* party I'm talkin' about."

Jack slapped the photograph with the back of his hand. "Was the woman in this picture with him?"

Oggie seemed to ponder deeply. "No, son. I can't say as she was."

Impatience curled like a fist in Jack's stomach. He quelled it and pressed on. "Did he say anything about picking up a hitchhiker?"

"No, he didn't say a thing about a hitchhiker as far as I can recall."

The old man was so transparent, it was an insult. He was holding something back, and he didn't care if Jack knew it. Jack asked very carefully, pointing to the picture, "Have you seen this woman?"

Oggie scrunched up his wrinkled face. He looked from the picture to Jack and back again. "Son—"

"Stop calling me son."

"Sorry, er, Mr. Roper."

"Answer my question. Have you seen this woman?"

Oggie looked torn. But at last he said, "I just can't see my way clear to answerin' that question right now."

"So you *have* seen her."

"I ain't sayin' that. I ain't sayin' anything."

"Do you know where she is?"

With some stiffness, Oggie Jones got to his feet. "For right now, Mr. Roper, I'm through talkin' to you." He turned to collect the cane that was leaning against the wall. "But I'm sure we'll be communicatin' in the future."

Jack's hands itched to close around the old rogue's wattled neck. "You're damn right we will. I'm not leaving this town until I find her."

The old rascal let out another of those ugly-sounding cackles. "I ain't surprised. When a man is damn fool enough to lose a good woman, the least he can do is give it all he's got to get her back."

Jack, who'd always prided himself on his iron control, felt that control slipping. "Who the hell do you think you are, old man?"

Oggie cackled again. "I don't believe you really want to know—at least not right now, anyway."

Jack almost asked *What the hell is that supposed to mean?* But he stopped himself. The old man was right. He *didn't* want to know. He had more important things to think about, like finding Olivia and making sure she was all right.

He reiterated, "I won't leave this town until I find her."

Oggie gave a nod. "You told me that. Gotta go." He sidled around Jack.

Jack held himself back, though the urge to violence was a hot, clawing thing inside him. He wanted to grab the old coot and shake him until the truth fell out. But he didn't. Mostly because he knew it would do no good. Oggie Jones was tough as old boots, that much was obvious. Jack knew he would get nothing out of him that he didn't want to reveal. So Jack watched, still and silent, as Oggie pushed the curtain aside and hobbled through it, vanishing from sight.

When she heard the shouting from downstairs, Olivia was in the guest bathroom enjoying a long soak in the tub.

"Where is that gal? I gotta see her right away." The voice was unmistakable: the old man, Oggie Jones.

Faintly, Olivia heard a chorus of feminine voices raised in protest, though she couldn't quite make out the words that the women said.

Oggie's reply, however, came through loud and clear. "It can't wait. I gotta talk to her now."

"But, Father—"

Olivia heard the sound of stomping on the stairs.

And then more feminine protestations, one voice after another. "Give her a few minutes."

"She's relaxing in a nice, hot bath."

"You can't—"

"Watch me." Oggie sounded resolute.

"She's been through so much, she needs a little peace."

"Peace?" Oggie snorted. "She wanted peace, she never shoulda showed up around here."

Olivia sat up straight in the tub as Oggie began pounding on the door. "I gotta talk to you, gal. Get decent and get out here."

"All right," she called back. "Give me five minutes."

"You got 'em. But no more."

Olivia heard the sound of retreating footsteps, the stumping of Oggie and his cane, followed by the lighter tread of the Jones women. Quickly she reached for a towel.

Four and a half minutes later, she emerged from the bathroom dressed in clothes borrowed from Delilah. At the bottom of the stairs, Delilah was waiting.

"He's in the study." Delilah pointed to a room right off the entrance foyer. "Be careful."

Olivia shot her a puzzled look. "What do you mean?"

"Just what I said. I don't know what he's up to. Watch your step with him. He comes up with these schemes sometimes. You have to watch him, that's all."

"What kind of schemes?"

Delilah rolled her eyes and shook her head. "Got a month? I'll tell you a few of them. You'll understand, the longer you know him. But for right now, just watch yourself. And watch him."

"Okay."

"Now go on. He's waiting."

Cautiously Olivia approached the open door of the study. She peered around the doorframe and saw Oggie, sitting in a leather swivel chair, an unlit cigar clamped between his teeth.

"It's about time. Come in. And shut the damn door."

Olivia did as she was told.

"Sit down."

She sat.

Oggie chewed on his cigar, then took it out of his mouth and looked at it. He stuck it back between his teeth unlit. "You're feeling better, I see."

Olivia cleared her throat. "Um. Yes. Much. Thank you."

"My whole damn family's taken a real shine to you."

"I'm glad. I feel the same about them."

"Yeah. It's odd, ain't it? I mean, you show up here outta nowhere, and all the women want to mother you and the men want to protect you."

"Your family is kind."

"It's more than that."

"What do you mean?"

"I think you know." His eyes bored through her. Then he shrugged and explained, "It's you, gal. They all sense your need, sense the rightness of your being here. It was the same for me. I was thirty-five when I first came here. And the minute I set foot on Main Street, I knew I was home. I met the woman I would marry that first day, and I knew she was the one. And she knew it, too. And so did her people, the Rileys. I believe you're like me. And like Eden and Sam, too."

"Eden and Sam?"

"Yeah. They came here seekin' their place. And they stayed. You been lookin', ain't you?"

"Looking?"

"For your place." The rough voice was a little impatient now. "For the place where you belong. And now you're beginnin' to realize that North Magdalene might be it. Am I right?"

Olivia didn't know quite what to say. This whole conversation was exceedingly odd, especially considering the decisions she'd just made with the help of the Jones women.

"Well?" The old man's eyes were full of secrets. "Am I right?"

"Yes." Olivia swallowed. "As a matter of fact, you are."

"'Course I am." Oggie sat back in his chair and fiddled with his suspenders a little, chortling to himself. Then he craned forward once more. "Now, I got some news for you."

"You do?"

"You bet. Your man's tracked you down."

Olivia blinked. "Excuse me?"

"Your man. Jack Roper. He's in town."

Olivia's mouth dropped open. Deep in her heart she'd always known he'd find her. But she'd imagined it would take a little longer than this. "Already? But that's impossible. How could he have found out where I went?"

Oggie waved a gnarled hand. "I ain't got a clue how. All I'm tellin' you is, he's here. He's flashin' a picture of you and askin' a lot of questions."

"You've talked to him?"

"I have."

"Did you tell him—?"

"Nothin'."

"Oh." Olivia forced herself to take a few deep breaths. A thousand emotions warred within her. Apprehension. Fear. Defiance. Anticipation. And longing.

"In this town," Oggie said, "he'll find you soon enough. We got a lot of real talkative types around here, folks that can't keep a secret even if you staple their lips shut."

Olivia pondered this information and realized that it didn't upset her as much as it probably should have.

Now that she'd enjoyed a long sleep and a good heart-to-heart talk with four sympathetic women, she felt much more able to cope. And she'd made a few plans now. She knew she wasn't going to be running anymore. She fully intended to call her father as soon as this impromptu interview with Oggie Jones was concluded. She was going to tell Lawrence Larrabee of the new plans she'd made, and she was going to carry out those plans, no matter what her father said.

Facing Jack would be harder. But she'd do it, somehow.

"It's okay," she told Oggie.

Oggie was studying her. "What do you mean, 'It's okay'?"

She drew in a breath. "I mean, you've all been wonderful. But I'm not hiding. At least not anymore. If Jack asks you again where I am, you just tell him. All right?"

Oggie looked doubtful. "That man is one tough character. And he ain't in a good mood. You know what I'm sayin'?"

Olivia sighed. "Yes. I'm afraid I do. And thanks for the warning. But I mean it. Just tell him where I am. I'll talk to him. I'll straighten things out."

"If you say so."

"I do." Olivia stood. "And now, if that's all, I'm going to call my father and—"

"Sit back down, gal."

"What?"

"It ain't all." The old man's voice was flat.

Olivia sank slowly back into the chair. "What? What's the matter?"

The old man looked at her, a piercing look. Then he turned his gaze out the window at a birch tree there. He watched the little gold leaves flicker in the gentle wind. A few blew off and floated to the ground before he admitted, "This is the hard part. And I'm at a damn loss."

Olivia said nothing. She had a feeling that being at a loss was a rare thing for Oggie Jones.

"You seen my oldest son, Jared?" Oggie asked, suddenly. "He's Eden's man. He was tendin' the bar last night."

Olivia recalled the tall, gray-eyed bartender. The one who had looked so much like a dark-haired version of Jack that she'd imagined she was hallucinating when she saw him. "Yes. I remember him."

"Jared looks just like my own father." Oggie spoke in a musing tone. "Got that tall, lean, hungry look. You know the look I mean?"

Olivia knew. It was the same look Jack had. She nodded.

"My father wasn't much of a man, to tell you true. Oh, he was tough enough and mean enough. But he had no heart. He died in a brawl when I was thirteen years old. That was back in Mission, Kansas. A long time ago."

Oggie chewed on his unlit cigar a little. His eyes were faraway. Olivia had a pretty good idea what was coming. Anticipation made her shiver a little, but she knew enough not to try to rush the old man over something as important as this.

Oggie continued. "My father had strong blood, though. His look is in all my kids. And in their kids. Some more than others." Oggie turned his beady black eyes on Olivia now. She felt he could see into her mind. "It's the look of your man, Jack. Did you notice?"

"Yes. I noticed." Olivia's voice was barely a whisper.

"You know your man's history?"

"Some of it."

"You know his mama's name?"

"Yes."

There was a long silence. The old man sighed deeply. Then he said, "I want to tell you a little story, gal."

"Yes. I want to hear it."

"But you got to promise me—"

"Anything."

"You won't go pushin' the truth on that man. You'll let him come to it in his own time."

"What?"

"You heard what I said."

She'd heard, all right. But she didn't like it. She tried to protest. "But the truth is important. He should know it."

The old man waved her argument away. "He doesn't want to know it right now. You gotta let him find his way to it in his own time."

Olivia captured her tongue between her teeth, the way she always did when she was pondering heavily.

"Well?" Oggie prompted.

"But I—"

"No buts. You keep your mouth shut, or this little talk stops now."

Olivia mustered up a glare and aimed it at the old man. "I think he should know."

"He will know. When *he's* ready." Oggie folded his hands over his paunch. "I'm waiting."

"This isn't fair."

"You're damn right."

Olivia threw up her hands. "Oh, all right. I won't say a word."

The old man beamed. "Attagirl."

"Now tell me." Olivia leaned forward eagerly. "Tell me all of it."

Oggie glanced at the door to see that it was firmly shut. Then, in a low, intense voice, he began to tell his story.

Chapter Eleven

Less than an hour after he'd confronted Oggie Jones at the Hole in the Wall, Jack found one of those people who couldn't keep a secret if you stapled their lips together.

His name was Ben Quail and he was eighty-three—or so he told Jack. His lined face was wide and his false teeth clicked together when he talked. He had two gray wisps of hair on his head, which he'd combed carefully over his crown. Jack found him sitting on a bench in front of the North Magdalene Grocery.

The first thing Ben said was, "You look like a Jones to me." The second was, "You hear about the big commotion over at the Hole in the Wall last night? Some woman came in out of the rain just when Oggie was blowing out the candles. It was Oggie Jones's birthday, see? Anyway, this woman was soaked to the skin. She took a look around the place and fainted dead away."

"No kidding. What happened next?"

"She came to, soon enough. And they took her over to Delilah's for the night."

"And where does Delilah live?"

"With her husband, Sam. Down Bullfinch Lane. Big, new house on the left, near the end. Can't miss it."

"Thank you, Ben."

"Don't mention it—you sure you aren't a Jones?"

In less than ten minutes Jack was ringing the doorbell at the house Ben Quail had described. It was opened by a petite dark-eyed woman with large breasts, a stubborn chin and a lot of glossy black hair around her face.

Jack and the woman stared at each other for a moment before either spoke. Once again, with another stranger, he had to fight down that disorienting feeling of familiarity.

"Yes?" The woman eyed him as warily as he was eyeing her.

"Hell." It was Oggie Jones's voice. "It's him. Better let him in."

Jack looked beyond the woman's shoulder and through the small foyer into the living room. He spied the old coot, stretched out in a fat easy chair, his feet propped on an ottoman.

"Where is she?" Jack demanded of the old man.

"Now, just a minute here," the gypsy-haired woman warned.

Oggie waved a hand. "Let him in, Delilah."

"I don't like his attitude."

"Delilah. Let him in."

Delilah turned enough to look over her shoulder at Oggie. They glared at each other for a moment. Then she turned back to Jack and stepped aside. "All right. Come in."

"Thank you," Jack replied, laying on the sarcasm.

He walked right by Delilah and into the living room, which was a very pleasant room with high ceilings, filled with books and comfortable-looking furniture. He saw Oggie and a big man with red gold hair combed back into a short ponytail.

But he didn't see Olivia.

"Where is she?" he demanded again.

Oggie chortled. "Allow me to introduce you folks. This is my daughter, Delilah, and her husband, Sam Fletcher. Sam and Delilah, meet Jack Roper."

"Where is she?"

"You got a one-track mind, there, son."

"Don't call me—"

"Jack."

Jack turned at the sweet sound of her voice.

She was standing on the landing at the top of the stairway, to his right. Her tawny hair was a halo around her pale face, and her eyes were soft and wide. She was wearing jeans that were a little too short for her and a shirt that was made for more generous curves. Her tender mouth trembled a little, but she appeared neither ill nor injured. She was the most adorable sight he had ever beheld in his life.

And she was all right. Every cell in his body screamed with relief.

"Olivia." He said her name, and that was all he could say. Something had temporarily cut off his air. His heart was doing the most disturbing things inside his chest.

"Oh, Jack . . ."

"Damn it, Olivia. You scared me to death."

In his easy chair, Oggie cackled.

Delilah said, "You don't have to deal with him now, Olivia, if you're not up to it."

Sam grunted. "Stay out of it, Lilah."

"But, Sam . . ." Delilah's voice trailed off. A quick glance in their direction showed Jack that Sam had put his arm around his wife. The couple shared a look that managed to be both mutual challenge—and agreement.

Jack decided he had a lot of respect for Sam Fletcher, to be able to silence the bossy Delilah with a few words and a look.

Sam volunteered, "You two can go in the study, if you need some privacy."

"Thanks, Sam." Olivia was smiling, a wistful little smile that had Jack's heart acting up all over again. "But I think Jack and I will go for a walk." She gave Jack a questioning glance. "All right, Jack?"

"Fine." He made his voice flat, in order to reveal none of the jarring tumble of emotions that roiled inside of him.

She came down the stairs. He stepped back when she reached the bottom. Right then he didn't trust himself to be too close to her.

"I'll be back soon," she told the others as she turned toward the door. "Let's go, Jack." She led the way out. He followed, keeping back.

Behind them, Oggie couldn't resist a parting shot. "You give a holler, gal, if he bothers you!"

Jack shut the door before Olivia could answer the old scoundrel.

When they reached the street, she turned to him. "I think there's a river that way." She pointed the opposite direction from the way he had come. "I saw it from one of the upstairs windows."

"So?" He felt edgy. He wanted to touch her—to pull her against him and breathe in the scent of her. But of course, he wasn't going to do that. He wasn't going to do that ever again. He was here to see that she was all right. And that was all.

"So, shall we walk that way?"

He shrugged. "Fine."

She started off down the street. He fell in beside her, but not too close. Within minutes the paved road ended, and they walked on a rutted road of red dirt lightly blanketed with pine needles. The red dirt was soft and muddy, and the ruts were full of water after last night's rain. To avoid the puddles, Jack fell in behind Olivia, who seemed quite sure of where she was going. He tried not to watch the taut curve of her buttocks as she walked. He looked up, around, anywhere but at her slim back.

From the trees a blue jay scolded them. Some distance off he could hear the honking of geese. The sky overhead, which he could glimpse through the lacy fanwork of the pine branches, was a pure blue, like Olivia's eyes.

Soon enough the needle-blanketed road came to a dead end. Olivia didn't hesitate. She walked on to where the ground dropped off. Jack followed and saw the path she'd found that cut downward to the river's edge.

They descended. When they reached the bottom, the river lay crystalline in the afternoon sun. A little to the right of the trail was a rocky point, splashed with sunlight. Olivia went out and sat on it.

Jack stood in the shadow of a big, gnarled oak for a moment, watching the way the sun glinted on her hair. And then, with a low curse, he went to her and crouched a few feet away.

He looked out over the moving water, because he couldn't quite trust himself to look at her. He was fighting that urge to touch her again.

Hell, he always wanted to touch her. He feared he would be longing to touch her when they laid him in his grave.

And he wanted to shout at her that he hadn't slept more than an hour last night for worrying about her, for picturing her lost and injured or the victim of some unsavory character or other.

Instead he made his voice level and spoke of practical matters. "I've talked to your father."

She surprised him. "So have I. Just a few minute ago."

"You called him, in Vegas?"

"Yes." She lifted her chin. The fine curve of her white throat taunted him.

He looked away. "Did you tell him where you were?"

"Yes, I did."

He shook his head. "So he's on his way here now, I suppose."

"No. He's not coming here now."

He shot her a glance. "You seem pretty sure of that."

"I am." Her voice was so calm, so assured. He realized he believed her. "It's finally happened, Jack."

"What?"

"I've finally managed to convince my father that I have to lead my own life." She shifted a little on the rock and drew her legs up, hugging them. "I guess I really scared him last night. He says he stayed up all night, talking to Mindy—you know who Mindy is?"

"Yeah."

"Well, the two of them talked all night. And he's decided to let me alone for a while. I mean *really* alone. He won't be sending anyone to, um, track me down, this time."

"Good." He edged a little closer, though he knew he should stay back. "You don't seem so angry at me anymore."

She looked at him, her expression gentle and unbearably sweet. Then she curled her legs to the side and leaned his way. "I'm not, Jack. I've had a little time to think it all over. I realize now that you were as trapped by the whole situation as I was."

Conflicting emotions warred inside him. "You're too forgiving."

"Not in this case."

"I should have walked away the second time you caught me watching you, out in front of the casino, that first night."

"My father would only have sent someone else."

"Someone who wouldn't have hurt you."

She made a soft little sound in her throat. "You never wanted to hurt me, Jack. I know that." He looked at her freckles and her slightly parted lips.

He was leaning toward her, just as she leaned toward him. He knew he should get back. But he didn't get back.

He was thinking that if he leaned forward just a little bit more, his lips could brush hers. And now he was close enough that he picked up her scent. A warm, sweet, fresh-scrubbed scent.

"I should have walked away," he repeated and leaned closer still.

Her lips now curved in the most tender of smiles. "I'm glad you didn't. If you had walked away, our beautiful time together never would have happened." She blushed a little. He watched the warm color pinken the skin beneath her freckles. It was a thoroughly enchanting sight.

"Olivia." He said her name and nothing more. It was as if her name was the only word he knew.

"Yes?" She tilted her head a bit, lifting her mouth, offering it up to him, like she'd done all those nights in Vegas when he'd left her at her door.

But the difference between those nights and now was that now he knew what her lips felt like. He knew the honeyed taste of her. And he craved more.

He leaned that crucial fraction closer.

Like the brush of a butterfly's silken wing, her lips grazed his.

That did it.

With a low oath, he shot to his feet.

He heard her disappointed little sigh but ignored it.

He stared out over the sun-shimmered water and waited for the embarrassing physical signs of his arousal to fade.

When he thought he could trust himself to look at her, he turned and met her eyes. Her expression was quite calm, which irked him to no end.

"It was all a mistake between us," he said gruffly.

"No." Her voice was firm.

"I never should have made love with you."

"Please don't say that."

"It's the truth."

"No, it's not."

"It's over." He spoke through gritted teeth. "It never should have happened in the first place, and it will never happen again. You'll go back to your life, and I'll go back to mine. Understand?"

She said nothing. For the first time since he'd met her, he found he couldn't read her thoughts in her eyes.

As they looked at each other, a slight wind came up. The trees sighed, a sad, whispering sound. Olivia shivered a little in her thin, borrowed shirt.

Jack decided he should get on with this, so he broke the silence between them by offering, "Listen. I suppose you'll be ready to go home pretty soon. I'll be glad to drive you there. Or to take you to the airport in Sacramento so you can catch a flight."

She smiled up at him. It was an enigmatic smile, one he didn't think he liked. "No, Jack. I'm going nowhere. I'm staying right here. My father's going to have Constance, my housekeeper, close up the beach house. Then she'll go and work for him. Zelda, my father's housekeeper, is retiring next spring, and so it'll all work out just fine."

Jack wondered what she was babbling about. "You're what?"

"I said I'm not returning to Malibu. I'm staying here."

He stared at her, trying to fathom what in the world she was up to now. "What for?"

"I'm going to live here."

"But why?"

"I like it here. And Eden—one of Oggie's daughters-in-law?—has offered me a job."

Jack mentally counted to ten before asking quietly, "A job doing what?"

"Cooking. I told you I could cook, didn't I?"

This was getting worse and worse. "Cooking where?"

"At the Mercantile Grill, the restaurant adjacent to the Hole in the Wall saloon."

"You're going to be a cook . . . at a *restaurant?*"

"Yes, Jack. I am. I told you, if you'll only remember, that cooking is what I've wanted to do all my life. And I am trained as a chef, after all."

"But this is insane. You work for your father."

"I *worked* for my father. Past tense." In one graceful motion, she stood. "Now I work for Eden Jones." She brushed off the back of her borrowed jeans.

"You don't even know these people. You can't just—"

She put up a hand. "Yes, I can, Jack." Her expression was utterly composed. "And I *do* know these people. I know this place. I know it in my heart." She touched her breast and looked up at him, her eyes bright as stars. "This is the place and these are the people I've been seeking all my life."

Jack looked at her and shook his head. It all was becoming painfully clear to him now. After all, he'd studied psychology in college.

She had not recovered from the series of crushing emotional blows that Cameron Cain, her father and then Jack himself had inflicted on her. She was mentally disturbed. There was no other word for it.

She'd driven out of Vegas going nowhere and ended up in this bend-in-the-road burg. And then, in a desperate attempt to create some kind of order in the chaos of her life, she'd convinced herself that fate had brought her here. And now she was unwilling to leave.

Which meant, of course, that he wasn't going to be able to leave, either. He felt too responsible.

He made himself ask in a reasonable tone, "You plan to live with the Fletchers, is that it?"

"No." For a woman who was mentally unbalanced, she sounded annoyingly decisive. "Delilah owns another house, over on Rambling Lane. She lived there until she married Sam. It's vacant now and fully furnished. She's going to rent it to me."

Jack looked at her, trying to push down his feeling of irritation with her, trying not to grab her and kiss her, trying to remember that she was mentally a few cards short of a full deck and thus deserved to be treated with careful consideration.

But for all his good intentions, when he spoke, his exasperation came through loud and clear. "You sure as hell have got everything worked out in a damn short period of time."

Olivia lifted her chin proudly, a Mona Lisa smile curving her sweet mouth. "That's how it is, when fate takes a hand."

Jack felt his blood pressure rising. He wanted to grab her and shake her and make her confront the hard truth right now, this very moment. He wanted to force her to admit that there was no such thing as fate, to compel her to see that she'd slipped into some netherworld of delusion.

But somehow he controlled himself. He kept his mouth shut and his hands to himself. He didn't have the right to make her face anything. He'd done way too much to her already.

It was a time for patience, he knew. He must wait. Eventually she'd be willing to look at the harsh realities that were what life was really about. She'd give up her crazy fantasy that there was something special about these infuriating people and this nowhere town.

"Oh, Jack." She was looking at him so sympathetically, as if he were the one who required patience and understanding. For a moment, that spurred his irritation. But when she went on gazing at him so tenderly, his exasperation melted.

Damn. She was one of a kind, even in her deluded state. After all he'd done to her, she could look at him with tenderness.

Though he knew he shouldn't, he touched the side of her face. It was like silk, as he'd known it would be, only warmer. "Olivia, I..."

"Yes, Jack?"

Suddenly he felt as tongue-tied as a boy with a big crush. "I'm sorry, about everything."

She caught his hand and kissed the knuckles one by one. His skin burned where her lips touched. Then she held his hand to her cheek and met his eyes. "Oh, no, Jack. You mustn't be sorry. It's all working out just as it should."

God, he thought, she's really lost it.

And yet her appeal for him, even in her state of mental confusion, was as strong as ever. It took every shred of willpower he possessed not to hook his hand around her nape and ravage her mouth with his. Hell, it was worse than ever now, with the memory of their one night branded forever in his brain.

Swiftly, before he could do the unpardonable, he stepped back from her and pulled his hand free of her tender grasp. "Look. I'll be in town for a while."

Her face showed frank delight. "Oh. I'm so glad."

He had to clear his throat before continuing. "Yeah, well..." He collected his thoughts. "I passed a motel at the foot of Main Street. Swan's, I think it's called. I'll check in there. If you need me, just call me."

"All right." That Mona Lisa smile was on her mouth again. "If you say so."

"Yeah." He was backing up. Because he knew that if he didn't back up, he'd be moving toward her. She was like a human magnet for him. He had to get far enough back to get out of her force field. "Listen, let's go. I'll walk you back to the Fletchers' house."

Still smiling, she shook her head. "It's beautiful here. I think I'll stay a while." She looked at him from under her lashes. "You could stay, too."

"No. I have to check in at the motel."

She gave a little wave. "All right, then. See you later."

"Yeah. See you later." He kept backing up, until he stumbled against the old oak tree. Then he turned and forged up the path away from her, not daring to look back.

If he had, he would have seen that she was still smiling that enigmatic smile.

Chapter Twelve

Swan's Motel sat at the foot of Main Street, the first sight to greet the weary traveler when he or she arrived in town. It consisted of two box-shaped buildings that faced each other across a tarred parking lot.

The office was paneled in knotty pine and furnished in overstuffed plaid. Above the plaid couch to the side of the check-in desk was a nicely framed colored-chalk drawing of a very pretty blonde. The blonde was looking over her shoulder and smiling a come-hither smile.

"I'd like a room," Jack said to the man behind the counter.

The man, who was reading a magazine, looked up and gasped. A fiftyish fellow, he bore a faint resemblance to the coy blonde in the drawing over the couch.

"What the hell?" the man exclaimed.

"A room," Jack said slowly. "I'd like a room."

The man backed toward the far wall, his hands up as if Jack held a gun on him. "Look. I don't want any trouble."

"Neither do I. Just a room. That's all."

"Fine. Fine." The man smoothed his thinning hair. "For how long?"

A nameplate nearby read Chuck Swan. Jack said, "One night at a time, Chuck."

Chuck coughed, then ventured, "You get a better rate if you pay for a week."

"One night at a time."

"Sure, sure." Chuck's hands were up again. "Whatever you say."

"Have you got a room at the back, on the second floor, away from traffic?"

"You bet." Chuck gestured over his shoulder at a pegboard with the room keys on it. "Room 203 or 206 is what you're after."

"Either one, then."

"Great." Chuck spun the registration book around and pointed at a blank line. "Sign here. Address, phone and license plate number, too."

Jack handed him a credit card and filled in the blanks in the book. He'd barely finished when Chuck twirled the register back around and peered at what he'd written. Chuck looked up. "Roper? I never heard of you. I thought you were one of the—"

Jack didn't want to hear the name Jones. He cut in. "I never heard of you, either, Chuck. Would you give me my key... and my credit card, too?"

"Yeah. Sure. Right." Chuck quickly took an impression of Jack's card and handed it over. Then he turned, grabbed the key to 203 off the pegboard and tossed it in the air.

Jack caught it neatly. "Thanks."

"Sure. All right. No problem."

Over the pegboard there was a stuffed deer head. The deer had big brown glass eyes and a wide rack of antlers. Somebody had stuck a cigarette between its lips. Jack saluted the deer and went out to get his bag from the car.

When he opened the trunk, he saw the bags he'd taken from Olivia's car last night. Damn. He'd forgotten all about them. Jack stood for a moment staring into the trunk, remembering Olivia in her ill-fitting borrowed clothes. The nice thing to do would be to drive back over to the Fletchers' house right now and deliver her bags to her.

But Jack Roper wasn't nice.

And he didn't feel like dealing with Olivia again right this minute. He'd had enough for one day. She might be the most adorable woman on earth, but she was also disturbed and refused to admit it. In fact, she acted as if she thought *he* was the one with the problem.

And besides, she knew where he was. If she needed her things right away, she could get in touch with him. Otherwise, he'd get them to her when he was damn good and ready to play delivery boy.

That decided, he shouldered his own bag and went to his room, which he discovered had been done up just like the office—in knotty pine and plaid, but minus the deer head and the flirty blonde. He put his bag on the rack in the tiny closet. Then he stripped down and showered, after which he stretched out on the bed.

When he woke it was growing dark outside and he was hungry.

In a town the size of North Magdalene, his options for dining were limited. He could choose between the Mercantile Grill and Lily's Café.

It wasn't much of a choice. Both places would no doubt be infested with people named Jones, or at the very least, crawling with people who were related to people named Jones. Right then, he didn't care much for Joneses.

After a few minutes of consideration, he decided he'd eat his dinner at Lily's.

However, when he got to the café, he saw that they closed at five on Sundays. He was too late.

Grimly he turned for the Mercantile Grill.

The first thing he heard when he entered the restaurant was Olivia's laughter. It was only a short trill of sound, but he recognized it, muffled by the wall that divided the kitchen from the main part of the restaurant. He deduced that she'd started right in at her new job.

He asked for a secluded table and got one. For a few moments after he was seated, he kept listening to hear Olivia's laugh again. But then he realized what he was doing.

He was here to fill his growling stomach, not to moon over a woman that he was soon going to have to learn to forget. To take his mind off her, he concentrated on his surroundings.

The restaurant, surprisingly, was a nice one. The walls were warm looking, exposed brick, the carpet a deep forest green. He ordered steak, potatoes and a salad.

The food was good. He ate undisturbed. By the time he got to that final cup of coffee, he was actually beginning to imagine he might get fed and get out without having to talk to anyone named Jones.

But then, just as he was signing his credit card slip, Oggie Jones hobbled in from the Hole in the Wall next door.

"Well, what have we here?"

Jack stood. "I was just leaving."

"No, you don't. Not so fast."

"Listen—"

"You play poker?"

Jack looked at the old man, a chilling look, and didn't answer.

Oggie blithely continued. "You come on next door. They got a good game going. It's just a friendly game. They never play for big stakes. Ask anyone." The old fool chortled to himself, as if he'd told some hugely funny joke.

"No."

"Aw, come on. What else you gonna do with yourself tonight? This here's North Magdalene. We ain't got a movie house, there's no place to go dancin' and the only stage show we get around here is when the school puts on *Arsenic and Old Lace*. That's comin' up in a month or so." There was more chortling. "But not tonight."

Jack couldn't believe this. The old man refused to get the message. "Look. No, thanks. I've got to—"

"You gotta nothin'. Come with me."

The old geezer had a hold of his arm. Jack couldn't shake him loose without being rough about it. And he didn't really feel like being rough.

What the hell, he thought. Tonight the old man didn't seem much worse than cordial. There were no strange looks or cryptic remarks.

What harm could it do to go next door and have a beer or two? Especially when the alternative was four knotty-pine-paneled walls and a lumpy bed. He'd end up there soon enough.

Oggie started pulling him toward an interior door, which Jack assumed led to the Hole in the Wall. Jack shrugged and went along.

Four hours later and two hundred dollars richer, Jack headed for Swan's Motel. He was weaving a little as he went. He'd had a beer or two more than he should have.

But all told, he felt pretty good. The night air had a real bite to it; it cleared his foggy mind a little. He stood beneath a street lamp and looked up at the sky and the rim of mountains all around and decided that this was a pretty nice little town, after all. He wondered woozily what it would be like to live in a place like this, where everyone knew everyone, and as a general rule people were open and friendly, willing to give a stranger a chance.

Even a nobody from nowhere. A professional hunter of other people's lost loved ones, with no loved ones of his own and no place to call home.

Jack leaned against the lamppost and chuckled at himself. Nothing like a few too many beers to give a man an excuse for a little self-pity.

He hugged the lamppost for a while, pondering the friendliness of people in small towns, reaching no particular conclusion. Then with a grunt he straightened, aimed himself at the motel and started moving. He didn't stop until he reached his room.

He was snoring before his head hit the pillow.

The next morning, after swallowing a couple of aspirin for his mild hangover, he had breakfast at Lily's. The waitress called Sunshine wouldn't give him his coffee until he drank his tomato juice. He grumbled that where he came from, waitresses didn't tell their customers what to eat.

She only beamed. "Aren't you glad you're *here,* then?" Next, she breezily informed him that his girlfriend was moving into her new house today. "You'll be there to help, I guess."

He wanted to ask her where she'd heard that Olivia was his girlfriend—and what help Olivia could possibly need moving into a furnished house with nothing but the borrowed clothes on her back to take with her? But he didn't. He knew he'd only be asking for more bright smiles and another volley of impertinent questions.

With breakfast over, Jack began to spare a thought or two for his business in L.A.

Roper, Inc., was a very simple operation. It consisted of Jack and an answering machine. He hooked up with clients through an ad in the yellow pages and, more frequently, by referral.

Jack returned to his room. He intended to pick up his messages from the machine at his apartment and then call back any potential clients to explain that he was currently tied up. It was a chore he didn't relish. While Lawrence Larrabee had been paying him big money for a simple job, it had made sense to put any other work on hold. But now he was on his own time. Being unavailable was throwing money away, pure and simple.

However, there was no sense crying over it. What was left of his common decency demanded that he stay here until Olivia emerged from her mental fog and agreed to return home.

He saw he had a problem when he got back to the room. Swan's Motel was a long way from the cutting edge when it came to the amenities. Not only was the mattress lumpy, the phone was an old rotary model—and he had no doubt all the calls would have to be channeled through Chuck out front, anyway. He needed a touch tone and a direct line to get through to his answering machine.

He ended up standing at the kiosk by the grocery store, scribbling his messages on a notepad while Ben Quail sat nearby and pretended he wasn't listening. Before Jack hung up, he taped a referral to Swan's Motel into his message, thinking that it might be somewhat appeasing to impatient clients if they had another number to call.

That done, he decided he'd go back to his room and phone the few prospects who'd left messages with the news that he wasn't available right now. Then he'd sign on for another day's lodging at Swan's Motel. And after that he'd take Olivia her suitcases, a chore he didn't relish, but which had to be done sooner or later.

He asked Ben Quail where the house on Rambling Lane was, the one Delilah Fletcher had lived in before she got married. Obliging as ever, Ben told Jack what the house looked like and how to get there.

The house was a tidy little clapboard structure. White with green trim, it had a small, sloping lawn and rose bushes in front of the porch.

Jack could hear a vacuum cleaner going, which meant Olivia was probably inside. No doubt Delilah, the dragon lady, would be there, too.

Grimly he pounded on the door. But the vacuum cleaner kept running. He rang the bell. No one came and the vacuum cleaner went on roaring.

He turned the door handle, and the door swung inward. He stepped beyond the threshold, calling out, "Hello?"

The house was as neat and simple inside as out. The front door opened directly into the living room. Right on the other side of the living room, through an arch, was the kitchen. To his right, a cheery fire burned in a potbellied stove. Beyond the stove was another arch. The roaring of the vacuum cleaner came through there. Hesitantly he followed the sound.

In one of the two bedrooms he found Olivia. She wore the same clothes she'd worn yesterday. Her hair was tied back with a scarf and her tongue was caught between her teeth. She was pushing a big, ancient-looking, upright vacuum cleaner back and forth on the small strip of beige carpet between a low, mirrored dresser and a double bed.

The sight was so appealing that Jack leaned on the doorjamb and watched.

Since she was thoroughly absorbed in her task, it took Olivia several seconds to realize she had a visitor. But when she at last noticed him, her face lit up in a delighted smile. Jack couldn't help but smile back.

With more than a little maneuvering, she managed to switch off the machine and snap it into an upright position. "Jack. Hello." She gestured at the vacuum cleaner, her smile turning proud. "Just cleaning up a little." She blushed charmingly. "It's my first time."

He gave her a questioning look.

"With a vacuum cleaner," she explained. "I found it in the closet. I've never used one before."

He bit the inside of his mouth to keep from chuckling.

"Don't you dare laugh."

"I wasn't."

"Right." She wrinkled her nose at him, then stepped around the vacuum cleaner. "Come on. I'll give you a tour of my new house. It won't take long, I guarantee." She spread her arms. "This is the master bedroom."

He made a great show of looking around. "Very nice."

"I think so. Step this way." She edged around him at the door. He caught the smell of her, just a taunting whiff of soap and sweetness, and she was past him.

"This is the bath." She stood in the tiny hall and pointed at the pink-tiled room.

"The master bath?" he teased.

"The only bath."

He pretended to think deeply. "Very efficient."

"My sentiments exactly. This way to the back bedroom." She turned around and pointed.

He looked in. "Charming."

"Thank you." She gestured some more. "Here's a storage closet, and there are the stairs to the attic. It's a real attic, complete with spiderwebs, a few spare bed frames and a dusty dollhouse."

"Fascinating."

"This house belonged to Delilah's mother."

"I see. Speaking of Delilah," he wryly remarked, "where is she?"

"At work. She's a teacher, you know. And it's a school day."

He was still suspicious. "Then where are the rest of them?"

"The rest of them?"

"The Joneses. I expected to find them all here, helping you to get settled in."

She shrugged and held out her arms to encompass the whole small, neat house. "What's to settle? There's a little bit of dust, but I need the practice wiping it up myself. Otherwise, the place is ready to use."

She went on to explain. "When Delilah and Sam combined their households, they took the best stuff to his house, where they live. Everything else they store here. They let visiting, out-of-town relatives stay here sometimes. Very tidy relatives, from the way the place looks. So there's nothing to do but buy food."

"I see." He was leaning against the doorjamb of the back bedroom now, thinking that he loved to watch her talk, to watch the different expressions flit across her face, to see the way her hands moved when she wanted to punctuate a thought.

"Jack?"

"Yeah?"

"Would you like to go into the living room and sit down?"

The minute the words were out of her mouth, he wondered what the hell was wrong with him. The sight of her pushing that vacuum cleaner had disarmed him. He'd been behaving as if this were a social call.

He straightened from the doorjamb. "No." He made his voice flat. "I brought your things."

She looked away, the movement a transparent masking of her disappointment that he wouldn't stay. When she looked back, she was smiling again. "Of course. I was going to call you about that. Thanks for bringing them."

"It's nothing. I'll get them."

When he returned with the small suitcase, the makeup case and the shoulder purse, she was waiting in the living room.

"You can just put them down there."

He did as she instructed. Then he backed away. It was time to go.

"Listen, Jack . . ." Nervously she licked her lips.

"Yeah?"

"I do hate to impose on you any more than I already have, but I—"

His heart rose, though he denied the sensation. After all, if she needed something, what else could he do but help? "What? Ask."

"I haven't decided what to do yet about getting a car."

"Yeah?"

"And I wonder—"

"What?"

"I need to shop for food. And from what I understand, the local grocery store is a little limited in what it can provide. Delilah says that for major shopping most people in town drive down to Grass Valley to one of the supermarkets there and—"

"You want me to take you."

"Yes. Would you?"

"When?"

She hesitated. "Well, now would be fine. If you don't have other plans."

"I don't."

"You mean you will?"

"Yeah. Let's go."

"Well, gee." She was all smiles again. "That's great." She pulled off the scarf that held back her hair and tossed it onto a chair. Then she shook her head, so the honey gold curls fell, vibrant and silky, around her shoulders. She grabbed her purse. "Can you wait just a second and let me at least put on some lipstick?"

"You don't need lipstick." He despised the huskiness that he heard in his voice.

She laughed, a light, happy sound that caused a flaring of heat in his belly. "Oh, Jack. Of course I don't need lipstick. Anymore than I need to wear clothes. But I feel a lot better if I have it on."

"Hell."

"Please?"

"Make it quick."

"I will." She started to turn. Then she seemed to remember something. "Oh, one thing."

"What?"

"Let me cook you dinner tonight, since you're doing this for me."

The idea held definite appeal. Too much appeal. "Don't you have to work?"

"No. It's Monday. The Grill and the Hole in the Wall are both closed Mondays."

He said nothing for a moment, thinking that he should say no. Yet he couldn't help imagining the evening he'd have instead—a sandwich at the café and then off to his room and his lumpy bed. Maybe he'd stop in at the grocery store and buy a magazine to read. Or perhaps there'd be an old Western movie on the late show.

"Please, Jack." Her eyes were full of sweet appeal. "Let me do this for you. After all you've done for me."

"All I've done for you?" His voice was harsher than he meant it to be. "I've brought you nothing but grief, and you damn well know it."

She shook her head. Her eyes were shining. "That's not true, Jack. You brought me the most joy I've ever known. You know you did."

Swiftly he turned away. "Go put on your lipstick."

"What about dinner, Jack?"

"All right." He growled the words, still turned away. "Now get a move on."

At the big supermarket on Sutton Way, they filled three carts with staples and produce and all the sundry articles Olivia needed to set up housekeeping. When they reached the check-out line, Olivia flipped out a credit card to pay for everything.

After they'd loaded the groceries into the car and were started on the half-hour drive back to North Magdalene, she gave Jack a sheepish look.

"Today, Eden asked me if I had enough cash."

"Who's Eden?"

"She's my new boss at the Mercantile Grill, remember? Oggie's daughter-in-law."

"Oh. Right." Jack shot her a swift glance and then took his gaze back to the road. "So Eden asked you if you had enough cash?"

"Yes."

"And what did you say?"

"We had a long talk. I explained how I was thinking maybe I should make a totally new start here, that I should refuse to spend any money I hadn't earned from my new job."

"What did Eden say to that?"

"She laughed. She said if I was rich, I should learn to live with it. But on my own terms. She said money was only a tool, anyway.

"She's really something, you know? When she came here a year and a half ago, the Mercantile Grill was nothing but an empty building and the Hole in the Wall was a rundown saloon where brawls broke out every other night. Eden changed all that. She's worked in bars and restaurants since she was in her teens. She really knows her stuff. People come from all over to eat at the Grill, did you know that?"

He grunted, thinking of the good meal he'd had last night. "I can believe it. So what are you telling me? That you were considering throwing all your money away, but now you've changed your mind?"

"Yes. That's exactly it. I'm going to use it frugally. I'll buy only what I need to be comfortable. Soon enough I'll be able to live on what I make at the Grill. And then eventually I plan to use the money I've inherited in places where it's needed. I don't know exactly where, yet. But I will know, when the time comes."

Jack paid strict attention to the road. This sounded a little like what she'd told him yesterday, all that weird talk about "fate" and what was "meant to be." But it also made a strange kind of sense.

And that disturbed him. Because it led to an obvious question. Could it be that his poor little rich girl really was coming to grips with her life, after all?

If that was so, then he was holing up at Swan's Motel amid the plaid and knotty pine for no reason at all, while at home his phone kept ringing with job offers he could ill afford to pass up.

"Jack?"

"What?"

"Are you all right?"

He reminded himself that it was way too soon to know for sure what was going on with her. He needed to keep an eye on her for a while.

"Jack?"

"Huh?"

"I asked if you're all right?"

"Me? Yeah. I'm fine. Just fine."

He was amazed at the meal she cooked him. There were little lamb chops that she'd marinated and then charred in a cast-iron skillet, new potatoes with parsley and butter, greens that had been steamed in some kind of tart broth, hot bread and a salad with more strange types of lettuce in it than he'd ever seen before.

She'd threatened to serve him Brussels sprouts and he'd almost believed her when he'd seen her buy them at the supermarket. But in the end she hadn't done it.

Instead, it was all perfection, right down to the candles and the Bordeaux. And yet she made it seem so easy.

As she cooked and served him the meal, he saw a whole new side of her. In the kitchen she was utterly at home and completely self-assured. Her bags still sat in the living room, waiting to be unpacked. But all the groceries and cooking utensils she'd bought were put away.

She kept the talk light and companionable. When they'd finished eating and were sharing more wine, she explained all about her new job.

"I'll start out doing mostly prep work," she said, "and that's fine with me. I can chop, slice and dice with the best of them. But Eden says I can run things Tuesday and Wednesday nights if I work out. And by the time the busy season starts next summer, well, who knows what might happen."

"Yeah," he muttered wryly, "who knows?"

"You know Eden's pregnant, don't you?" She laughed. He watched her, thinking that her skin had a soft radiance to it in the light from the candles that flickered between them. "I mean, it's pretty hard to miss, if you've seen her. She's due in a few weeks."

He finished off his fourth glass of wine and confessed he'd yet to meet the wondrous Eden.

"Well, you'll know her when you see her. Tall and gorgeous, with strawberry hair and a stomach out to here." She held her hand away from her body to show what she meant.

"Sounds memorable."

"Oh, she is. She is." Olivia leaned in a little and pitched her voice to a volume suitable for sharing secrets. "But the real story is that Regina's pregnant, too."

"Who's Regina?" Jack helped himself to more wine.

"She's Patrick's wife. Patrick is Oggie's second son. Regina and Patrick have been married about three months and she's only two months along. So they're kind of keeping it just in the family, for now."

Jack sat back in his chair, thinking that the wine and the good food had produced a pleasant glow. He should probably be leaving soon, but he was reluctant to break the mellow mood.

Olivia picked up her wineglass and sipped from it. "So tell me, how are the accommodations at Swan's Motel?"

He gave her a patient look.

"What?" She batted her eyelashes. "Not deluxe?"

"No. Not deluxe." He realized she didn't have his room number. "By the way, I'm in room 203. Just in case."

She repeated it. "Room 203. Thanks." They stared at each other for a few moments. Then he remembered himself and looked away.

Brightly she asked, "You know about Chloe Swan, don't you?"

He glanced at her once more. "Who's Chloe Swan?"

She fiddled with her glass. "She's the town scandal."

"Well fine, but who is she?" He raised his own wineglass to his lips.

"She used to run the motel where you're staying. But now she's going to prison. So her uncle, Chuck Swan, has taken over."

"I've met Chuck. But why is this Chloe Swan going to prison?" Jack drained his wineglass once more.

"Well, Chloe always loved Patrick—you know, Regina's husband, Oggie's middle son?"

"Got it." Jack set down his glass.

Olivia filled Jack's glass for him. "Chloe's very beautiful, I understand. She's got pale blond hair and a terrific figure and men really go for her."

Jack remembered the drawing of the come-hither blonde over the couch in the motel office and realized who she probably was.

Olivia was still talking. "But Chloe's always been obsessed with Patrick. And then, this summer, Patrick married Regina. And Chloe went over the edge."

"You mean she went crazy?"

"Exactly. She lost it. Completely." Olivia went on to tell a long, involved story that ended with Patrick Jones being shot.

When she finished, Jack refilled his wineglass again and asked, "Is this for real?"

Olivia solemnly crossed her heart. "It's the truth, I swear. And now Chloe will be doing time. And her poor Uncle Chuck has to run the motel, which he's been doing for over a year, anyway, because Chloe had run off with a stranger previously and been gone for fourteen months."

"Who told you all this?"

"Eden and Amy, mostly. Amy's Brendan's wife. Brendan's the one who—"

"I remember who Brendan is."

She chattered on. "And I've talked a lot with Regina and Delilah, too. Do you know Delilah grew up despising her brothers and her father?"

"That I can understand."

Olivia clucked her tongue. "Oh come on, the Jones men are great."

"Right. They're great. Just great." He toasted her with his wineglass, drank and set it down.

She put her hand over his. "Oh, Jack. You'd like the Joneses if you gave them half a chance."

Jack watched her mouth move. Suddenly he was having trouble making out her words. Right then all he could think about was the feel of her soft palm on the back of his hand.

Her touch was light. She probably meant it as no more than a companionable gesture.

But for Jack her touch could never be merely companionable. Not when a bolt of heat shot up his arm and his heart started thudding a deep, needful rhythm inside his chest. Not when forbidden memories assailed him, and his defenses were down from too much wine.

"Jack?"

He couldn't speak.

"Jack?"

He wanted her closer.

Slowly he turned his hand over and captured her wrist. He gave a tug.

She rose, pliant and so sweetly willing, and dropped into his lap almost before he realized she was on her way.

The soft weight of her was a miracle. She smelled of wine and coffee and that fresh, indefinable something that was only hers.

"You're so damn cute." The mundane words seemed ripped up from the depths of him.

She looked at him, her eyes luminous as the twin candles in the center of the table.

What was it she did to him? It was the strangest thing that had ever happened to him. It was desire, and yet so much more. In her sky-colored eyes he seemed to see a fresh chance. She made the world new again.

It was only a fantasy; he knew it. But when he looked at her it seemed real. With her, somehow, he could almost believe he would find what he was missing.

Even with Sandy Chernak, the policewoman who had loved him and been good to him and whose death had nearly broken him, he'd been more careful, more guarded, more a prisoner inside himself.

But Olivia was different. He had known it from the first—when she'd looked up from that blackjack table and their eyes had met and locked.

Olivia cracked him wide open. She looked right down into his soul.

And he let her do that. He *liked* it when she did that.

She lifted her arms and set them on his shoulders. "Kiss me, Jack."

It was agony, this need he had for her.

"Kiss me, please."

With a low, urgent moan he captured her sweet mouth.

Chapter Thirteen

He was like a starving man.

And Olivia was utterly content to ease his hunger. A joyful groan escaped her. She pressed herself against him, opening her lips for him, so his tongue could enter and have its way with hers. She clutched his shoulders, loving the good, hard feel of them, kissing him back with everything that was in her.

His mouth wandered. He kissed a searing trail down her throat. She held him close.

"Oh, Jack." The words she'd longed to say were on her lips. She let them take form. "I love you so."

And that was when he froze, became a statue in her arms.

"Oh, no. Oh, Jack." She clutched at him, begging him with all of herself not to pull away.

But he only took her hands and held them, craning back from her, staring hard into her eyes. Soon enough, beneath his harsh regard, she stilled. Then, very gently, he lifted her and set her on her feet.

He stood. "Thank you for the dinner. There's no doubt about it. You can cook."

And then he turned and headed for the door. She watched him go, out of the kitchen and across the living room.

"Jack."

He stopped with his hand on the doorknob, his big shoulders held stiffly, as if whatever she might say next would be a knife in the back.

She moved swiftly into the living room, halting just a few feet from him.

"I meant what I said, Jack. I love you."

He flinched. "You don't. You're confused."

"No, Jack. I'm not the one who's confused."

He pulled open the door. Outside, the night was cold and the sky was full of stars. "Good night, Olivia."

She stood in the doorway and watched him go.

After that, Jack didn't trust himself to get too close to Olivia. Though he watched over her, as he'd sworn to do, he also kept his distance.

He heard from Ben Quail that she'd had her phone hooked up. Ben's grandson was the technician who'd done the job. He also learned from Sunshine that Olivia was doing just fine at the Mercantile Grill, catching on quickly and already beginning to make useful suggestions.

Sunshine knew all about Olivia's progress in her new job because Sunshine was Jared Jones's daughter by a previous marriage, which made Eden Jones her stepmother. Every time Jack went to Lily's Café for a meal, Sunshine was ready to make him eat his vegetables and to fill him in on how Olivia was faring at the Grill.

Nights generally found him at the Hole in the Wall. It was a good place to keep an eye on Olivia. And what else was he going to do with himself in a town this size, anyway?

The only real drawback to visiting the Hole in the Wall was that Oggie Jones hung around there, too. Once or twice, Jack caught Oggie staring at him. It was a watchful look, a waiting look. A look that sent cold fingers of dread slithering up Jack's spine. Jack would turn away.

And when he would glance over again, the old coot would be cackling with his cronies over some traveling salesman joke, paying no attention to Jack at all.

It wasn't a big deal, Jack decided. The old codger could send him all the significant looks he wanted. Jack would simply ignore him.

Beyond ignoring Oggie, Jack monitored his own alcohol consumption. He was careful to nurse one or two beers through the evening. The last thing he needed was to end every night drunk.

As one day faded into another, he found he began honestly looking forward to his evenings at the bar. The people were always friendly. The regulars—like Rocky Collins, Tim Brown and Owen Beardsly—could usually be talked into a game of pool or poker, which Jack sometimes won and sometimes lost. In the end he figured he just about broke even.

Even Jared Jones, who tended the bar most nights, was okay. Once Jack overcame that spooky feeling that he experienced with all the Joneses—that feeling of having known them before—he found he actually liked Jared. There was a sense of inner peace about Jared Jones that Jack couldn't help but respect.

On the bench in front of the grocery store one afternoon, when Jack had been in town almost a week, Ben Quail tried to tell Jack that until Jared Jones married Eden Parker, he'd been the worst brawler and troublemaker of the whole Jones gang, a man with a chip the size of Alaska on his shoulder.

"I don't believe it," Jack said flatly.

"Believe it or not, it's the absolute, unvarnished truth."

Right then, two little boys came running at them from across the street. Breathless, they asked Jack if he'd buy a few candy bars to help them raise money for their soccer team. Jack forked over ten bucks while Ben looked on disapprovingly.

"What're you gonna do with ten candy bars?" Ben wanted to know.

"It's not your problem. Have an Almond Delight." Jack handed the old man one of the candy bars in his lap.

"You're getting a reputation." Ben began peeling off the wrapper.

"As what?"

"An easy mark." Ben took a big bite. False teeth clicking, he inquired as he chewed, "How many candy bars and gift subscriptions have you bought in the six days you've been here?"

"That's my business." Jack looked up the street, away from Ben. Maybe he had bought more from the local kids than he should have. But the little suckers were damned hard to resist. Most of them were polite and enthusiastic. He liked to see that in kids. He liked to see kids with dreams still shining in their eyes.

"So tell me, Jack. You on vacation, or what?"

"You're a nosy man, Ben."

"Never said I wasn't. And I've been wondering what you're doing around here. Not that I don't like your company. I do. But this isn't tourist season. Don't you have a job you should be going to?"

"Yeah. I've got a job. But I've got a . . . responsibility, too."

Ben snorted. "We're talking about that new woman in town, am I right?"

Jack didn't reply.

Ben lifted his stooped shoulders in a shrug. "Hey. We all know she's your woman."

"Who's *we?*"

"The whole town. Get used to it. Around here the word *privacy* doesn't exist. What do you do for a living, anyway, Jack?"

"Is this any of your business?"

"Of course not." Ben grinned broadly, displaying those huge artificial teeth. "But tell me, anyway."

Jack stood. "See you later, Ben."

Ben called after him. "You might as well tell me yourself. I'll only ask around. I'll know by tomorrow, you see if I don't."

Jack avoided the old meddler for two days. But when he sat down beside him the following Monday morning, shortly after breakfast, the first words out of Ben's mouth were, "Well, if it isn't our local private eye."

Jack said nothing, only shook his head.

"Gal, we gotta talk." Leaning on his cane, Oggie stood on Olivia's porch. Behind him on the street, the old Cadillac he drove sat like a galleon at anchor. "Can I come in?"

"Of course."

As Oggie hobbled over the threshold, Olivia ran around the room, grabbing up various articles of clothing that Delilah and Eden had loaned her. Somehow she was always forgetting to hang up her clothes. She was working hard to be a better housekeeper. But Rome wasn't built in a day, after all.

"Have a seat." Her arms full of outerwear, Olivia gestured awkwardly at the couch.

"Don't mind if I do."

Oggie stumped over to the most comfortable chair and dropped into it as Olivia darted to the back bedroom, tossed the sweaters and scarves inside and shut the door.

"Can I get you anything?" Olivia asked politely, when she joined Oggie once more.

"Cup of coffee, four sugars. And an ashtray." Oggie waved one of his cigars.

"Fine. I'll be right back." Olivia hurried into the kitchen, poured the coffee, ladled sugar into it and found a cracked saucer that would have to pass as an ashtray. She quickly returned to the living room with her offerings.

Oggie was already puffing away. He tossed his match in the makeshift ashtray almost before Olivia could set the thing beside him.

She handed him the coffee. "Here you go."

He took it and sipped. "Ah. That's good." He set the mug down beside the cracked saucer. "Eden tells me your father's coming for a visit."

Olivia smiled. "News travels fast around here."

"That it does, that it does."

Olivia had called her father and invited him and Mindy only that morning, and she'd spoken to Eden just an hour before.

"I want to have a special dinner, while my father's here. I hope you'll come."

"Gal, you couldn't keep me away if you locked me in the county jail and swallowed the key."

"Good. Then I'll plan on you."

There was a silence. Then Oggie asked, "Now. You got any clue why I'm here?"

Olivia sighed. "It has something to do with Jack, I imagine."

"Damn right. He ain't comin' around, is he?"

She shook her head sadly. "No. He isn't."

"But then again, he ain't left town, either. So there's hope."

"I'm glad you think so." Olivia tried not to sound as discouraged as she had begun to feel.

Oggie slurped up some coffee and then spoke quite gently. "He's been avoiding you, ain't he?"

Olivia felt ashamed, as if she was letting everyone down somehow. "Yes."

"You can't let that go on."

She threw up her hands. "What am I supposed to do? I've already been completely shameless. You have no idea."

The old man cackled.

Olivia blushed. From the Jones women, she'd heard a lot about Oggie and the things he'd done in his life. "Okay, maybe you do have an idea."

Oggie did some more cackling. "Maybe I do, maybe I do."

Olivia stared at the old man for a moment, considering. She remembered Delilah's warning, to watch out for Oggie's schemes. But she was starting to feel desperate. She would take any help she could get. She prompted, "Really, Oggie. What should I do?"

Oggie looked pleased. "Well, I am flattered you've asked me. I truly am. Even though if you hadn't, I'd have told you, anyway. But you didn't doubt that, did you?"

"No. Now tell me."

"All right, all right." Oggie sat back. He drank from his coffee and puffed on his cigar. Then he sagely announced, "You need more time with him."

Olivia groaned. "Well, I know that."

"But you ain't makin' it happen, are you?"

"It's pretty hard to spend more time with a man who won't come near me."

"You got to *make* him come near you."

"I know that. But how?"

"Well, let's see." Oggie rubbed his gray-stubbled chin. "What we need to do is to give him a reason to get closer, to be around you more."

"What kind of reason?"

"Maybe something to protect you from."

"But what?"

"Don't rush me, gal. I'm thinkin'. I'm thinkin'...."

The next morning Sunshine was waiting for Jack when he took his seat at the counter at Lily's. There was a worried look on her smooth young face. "Have you heard about the mountain lion?"

"What mountain lion?"

"The one Olivia saw last night."

"When?"

"Near the cabin my father owns."

"Your father is Jared Jones?" Jack was still having trouble keeping all the relationships straight. Everybody seemed to be related to everyone else.

Sunshine looked pained. "Right. Jared Jones is my dad."

"Fine. So Olivia met a mountain lion near the cabin—"

"Where my father and Eden live. Olivia was over there for dinner, since it was the night they all have off. She left late and decided to take a shortcut back to her place. She met the lion on the trail she found that cut across to Main Street."

"She met it? It introduced itself?"

Sunshine rolled her eyes. "You want to hear about this or not?"

"I want to hear."

"Good. Then don't get sarcastic."

"All right. Tell me."

"Fine. She wasn't hurt. The mountain lion only appeared on the path in front of her, growled at her and then walked off into the trees." Sunshine turned and poured Jack a tomato juice, which she then set before him. "Grandpa Oggie doesn't like it. He says the cougars are taking over, now a man can't shoot them anymore." She set out a napkin for Jack and put flatware on top of it. "My father and Sam Fletcher are talking about seeing if they can get a depredation permit so they can track it down and get rid of it. But it'll never happen. Not unless the cougar actually kills somebody's dog or attacks a kid or something." She looked up. "You want the usual, right?"

Jack was already turning for the street.

"Hey, what about your breakfast?" Sunshine called after him.

He gave her a wave and said nothing. He had more important things to deal with than bacon and eggs.

Since Olivia had been reasonably sure Jack would be paying her a visit, she should have been prepared for the sight of him. But she wasn't.

When she pulled open the door and saw him standing on her porch, her heart seemed to stop for a moment. She had to remind herself to speak.

"Jack! How nice to see you. Come in."

He stayed where he was. "I heard about the cougar."

"You did?"

"Yeah. I don't like it."

"Yes, it was pretty frightening, but I—"

"When are you getting a car?"

She blinked. This was not how she'd imagined this conversation would go. She did her best to keep up with him. "A car?"

"Yeah. When are you getting one?"

"Well, as a matter of fact, I'm doing all right without one so far." The truth was that as soon as she had a vehicle, she'd no longer have a reason to ask Jack to drive her anywhere.

"You can't go on without a car forever. When will you buy one?"

"Oh, I don't know. My father and Mindy are coming for a visit next weekend. Maybe I'll think about finding a car then. My father said he would help me choose one."

Jack looked at her measuringly. "So your father's coming, huh?"

"Yes."

"You think you're ready to see him?"

"Yes. I think I am."

He studied her, his midnight eyes unreadable. "Well, good for you," he said at last. There was honest admiration in his voice.

Olivia should have been pleased. But she wasn't. Her heart sank to her toes.

She really was ready to see her father. She'd come a long way in a short time. But she sensed that what kept Jack in town was his feeling of responsibility for her. Thus, each new proof that she was dealing with her problems brought Jack that much closer to deciding she was fully capable of taking care of herself. She knew what would happen then. He would walk out of her life forever.

He demanded, "Now, what about the car?"

She tried again. "Jack? Won't you come in?"

"No. Answer me about the car."

She sighed. "Well, as I said, maybe I'll take care of getting transportation when my father comes. He's mentioned that we could drive down to Auburn together and look for something."

"Good. Do it. Until then, stay out of the woods. And until you do get a car, I'll meet you at the Mercantile Grill after your shift every night, to drive you home."

One of the many bits of advice Oggie had given her was that she should put up enough resistance to Jack's plans that he wouldn't become suspicious of a setup. So she argued. "But I like walking home. It's not very far and I—"

"Fine. As long as the weather's good, I'll walk you home."

She allowed herself to smile again. "Well, all right. That would be very nice."

"And I mean it. Don't go wandering around the woods alone."

"Jack, this is the mountains. There are wild animals in the mountains. That's the way it is." Since there had been no cougar, except in Oggie's imagination, this was easy for her to say.

Jack was not impressed with her fearlessness. "Fine. Stay out of the woods. Do you work tonight?"

"Yes. Every night but Sunday and Monday."

"I'll be there when you get off."

"All right."

He turned to leave.

She remembered another bit of advice from Oggie: "Don't you miss a single opportunity to be near that man, understand?"

"Wait. Jack?"

He faced her again. His expression was not encouraging. "What?"

"I'm sorry to impose on you any more than I already have. I really am. But I'm out of food and I wonder if—"

"No problem. I'll get myself some breakfast and come back for you. About an hour. Good enough?"

"Thanks. But listen. I was just ready to fix my own breakfast and it would be no problem to fix some for you, too."

She knew he was remembering what had happened the last time she'd cooked for him. She could see it in his eyes.

"No, thanks. One hour. Be ready."

"But—"

He turned and ran down the steps away from her so fast that an uninformed observer might have wondered what was chasing him.

Chapter Fourteen

The trip to Grass Valley got Olivia the groceries she needed and that was all.

With Jack she got nowhere. He sat behind the wheel, not speaking unless spoken to, his face a stern mask. He pushed the cart for her in the supermarket, never cracking so much as a smile.

When they drove up in front of her house at a little after one in the afternoon, he helped her lug the bags of food and sundries into the house.

"What time are you off tonight?" he asked when all the bags were inside.

"I'll be through by ten-thirty."

"Fine. I'll be waiting for you."

Before she could even thank him for his help with the groceries, he was out the door.

It was the same that night. He met her as he'd said he would, walked beside her to her house and then stood on the sidewalk and watched to see that she was safely inside.

The next night was no different. Olivia began to wonder if she would ever break through the wall of silence he'd thrown up to keep her at a distance.

On the third night, Thursday, the situation improved a little. But only because a pretty little calico cat that Olivia had recently befriended was waiting on the porch when they arrived.

"What is that?" Jack surprised her by breaking the silence between them. "You've got a cat now?"

She jumped at the chance to exchange a few sentences. "No, not really. She's the neighbors' cat. But she comes over sometimes. Just to visit. She's a very social cat."

He grunted. She could see in his eyes that he was on the verge of leaving again. She cast about frantically for some way to extend this pitiful attempt at conversation.

"I'll bet you're worried about..." She groped for the name of the tomcat he'd once said hung around the apartment where he lived. It came to her. "Buzz. I'll bet you miss Buzz."

He actually chuckled at that, though the sound held no humor. "No, Olivia. I do not miss Buzz. And I'll lay you a dime to a dollar that when I get back, Buzz will be long gone."

"How can you be so sure?"

"Buzz is an alley cat. He's used to taking life as he finds it. He's not one of those domesticated animals who'll hang around, sad and forlorn, waiting for some human to return."

Olivia looked at him through the darkness, wondering if he was talking about more than just a cat. "I don't agree," she said. "I have faith in Buzz."

"You don't even know Buzz." He looked away. "And besides, it's just a cat."

She dared a knowing grin. "I'll bet he's there waiting at your apartment for you to return."

Jack made a low, scoffing sound. "It would be a fool's bet. You'd lose."

Her grin widened. "Fifty bucks says he's there right now."

Jack groaned. "And how are you going to prove this?"

She considered. "I'll ask my father to find out. Will you take my father's word?"

"Olivia, this is stupid. I'm telling you, that cat is history."

"Fifty bucks, Jack."

"No."

"See? You know you'll lose."

"What do you mean? I'm saving you money."

"What for? I'm rich, remember?"

"It's a stupid bet."

"Then take it. Make an easy fifty."

"You're asking for it."

"Good." She lifted her chin. "So give it to me."

There was a silence. A lengthy one, while all that was unspoken—and forbidden—arced in the cold night air between them.

"Fine," Jack said at last. "You're on."

"You'll have to tell me your address."

He looked at her suspiciously, but then muttered, "Got a pen?"

She dug one out of her purse and gave it to him. He took a business card from his pocket and scribbled on it, then handed the card and the pen to her. At the bottom, he'd written an address.

Olivia met Jack's eyes once more. "Good. I'll call my father tomorrow and ask him to check. He'll be here on Saturday. Is that early enough to find out who wins the fifty?"

"How long will your father be staying?"

"Till Monday."

"Then we can settle this harebrained bet Tuesday, when I meet you after work."

"Tuesday it is, then." She stuck out her hand. He hesitated, but at last he reached out and took it. His grip was warm and firm. Longing filled her. He gave her hand one pump and then dropped it.

"Good night, Olivia."

"Good night, Jack."

The next night she told him that she wouldn't be working Saturday.

"Eden's given me the night off, since my father and Mindy will be here. So you won't need to walk me home."

"Fine."

As always, lately, she tried to keep the meager conversation limping along. "I'm looking forward to showing them around."

He grunted. "And introducing them to all the Joneses, too, I'll bet."

She nodded. "That, too. Jack?"

"What?"

"Tomorrow night, I'm cooking a big dinner. For Mindy and my father and Oggie and Delilah and Sam and Delilah's brothers and their wives. It'll be quite a squeeze in my little house. But Delilah's arranged for me to borrow a couple of folding tables and some chairs from the community church. I'm going to seat everyone in the living room and I, well, I'd really like it if you would come, too."

His dark eyes were fathoms deep. And very sad. She knew he wanted to go. And that he wouldn't go.

"No."

"But Jack..."

"Thanks for the invitation. But no." He turned and left her there, by her front walk.

She knew she should call him back and ask him to drive her to Grass Valley again early tomorrow morning to buy the food for the dinner that night. After all, she was not supposed to waste any opportunity to be near him. But she just didn't have the heart to do it, to make him drive her around to get everything for a party he wouldn't be attending. One of the Joneses would take her or lend her a vehicle. All she had to do was ask.

With a dejected little sigh, she headed for her door.

Lawrence Larrabee and Mindy Long arrived at eleven Saturday morning, just after Olivia had returned from Grass Valley with the groceries for that night's feast.

Olivia saw the rental car drive up and jumped from the chair at the window where she'd been watching. She ran out the door and down the front steps with her arms spread wide.

Her father emerged from behind the wheel. Olivia flung herself against his tall, stooped body. He hugged her tight. She breathed in the reassuring scents that for her had always meant security, the smells of spicy aftershave and wool and the wintergreen mints he favored.

"It's good to see you, Dad," she whispered into his jacket.

"Good to be here, Livvy," he whispered back. "Good to be here."

After a moment she stepped back and wiped her eyes with the heel of her hand. And then she turned to Mindy for another hello hug.

"And what's this?" Olivia asked when she and Mindy broke apart. She lifted Mindy's left hand, on which an engagement diamond gleamed. "It's beautiful." She smiled into Mindy's hazel eyes. "I'm so glad."

"So are we," her father said, and put his arm around his wife-to-be.

"When's the big day?"

"At Christmastime." Mindy smiled fondly up at Lawrence. "Probably during the week before Christmas Day. And then we're flying to Gstaad for an extended stay." Mindy turned to Olivia. "You'll come for the ceremony, won't you?"

"I wouldn't miss it for anything."

"Wonderful."

The two women beamed at each other, then Olivia remembered her manners. "But let's not stand out here all day. Let's get your bags and go on inside."

Olivia turned to the rental car. A long, pitiful wail came at her from the back seat.

She saw the animal carrier and stepped back. "Oh, I don't believe it. You *found* him!"

"Aside from being half-wild, that cat is not a happy traveler," her father remarked rather grimly. "He yowled through the entire flight. We were smart to take the Cessna. We probably would have been thrown off a commercial flight."

Olivia was already yanking the door wide so she could peek inside the carrier and see what Buzz looked like.

A pair of crossed amber eyes stared back at her.

"Hello, Buzz."

The cat made a sound that was not quite a growl, but almost.

"It's so nice to meet you."

The cat made another unfriendly little noise.

"Oh, come on, you're going to love it here."

The cat glared at her and even dared a warning hiss. Olivia shrugged and looked him over.

He was not an impressive sight. His hair was short and mottled gray. There was so little of it on his head that he really did look like someone had given him a flattop haircut. His face was scarred, one side of his mouth cut so he showed the world a grisly grin. One ear was split, no doubt torn in some long-ago fight. He was scrawny to the point of emaciation.

"He's the ugliest damn thing I've ever seen," Lawrence remarked from behind her.

"Shh." Olivia turned and shot her father a chiding frown. "You'll hurt his feelings."

Lawrence grunted. Buzz let out another long yowl.

"Let's get the cat—and everything else—inside, shall we?" Mindy suggested.

Olivia reached for the carrier while her father went around to collect the bags from the trunk.

They left Buzz in the living room, still in the carrier, while Olivia showed her guests the spare room. She didn't miss the glance they exchanged over the narrowness of the twin beds, but nothing was said. She left them to freshen up.

While Mindy and Lawrence took turns in the bathroom, Olivia found the bags of cat supplies they had bought and set about making a place for Buzz on the back service porch. Then she took the carrier out there and opened the door. Buzz pressed himself back into the rear of the carrier and hissed.

"Fine," she told him. "When you're ready, you come on out. But you'll have to stay in the house for a few days, I'm afraid. Until you become acclimated."

The cat glared at her, a silly-looking glare, since his eyes were crossed. Olivia left him there on the service porch, closing the door to the main part of the house to contain him.

Once they were settled in, Olivia led her guests on a tour of the town, which took no time at all, since North Magdalene's population was less than two hundred and fifty, and almost every building of note was on Main

Street. They had lunch at Lily's Café after the tour and then went back to the house where Olivia began preparations for the dinner party that night.

All things considered, the party was a great success, though Olivia didn't miss the frantic looks that darted between her father and Mindy when they were first introduced to Oggie Jones. But Olivia had been prepared for that. She kept the champagne flowing.

By the end of the evening, her father and Oggie had discovered their mutual affection for the verses of Robert Service. They took turns reciting *The Cremation of Sam McGee*, toasting each other after every line.

When the party broke up around midnight, Lawrence, who had never been much of a drinker, staggered in and fell across his narrow bed. Mindy helped Olivia to clean up the house.

Once the dishes were put away, Olivia went out to the service porch to check on Buzz. He wasn't there. She had no idea how he might have escaped, but he was not behind the washer or the dryer, and there was no place else in the small space for him to hide. She and Mindy searched the house, to no avail.

Then Olivia went outside and called for a while. But there was no sign of the tom. At last she gave up and went in, feeling terrible and trying not to think about mountain lions and bears, doing her best to reassure herself that he would turn up tomorrow.

The next morning the first thing Olivia did was go outside and call, "Here, kitty, kitty, here Buzz," over and over again.

But if Buzz heard, he chose not to respond. After fifteen minutes of cat calling, she gave up and turned for the house.

She was in the kitchen sipping a solitary cup of coffee, castigating herself for shanghaiing poor Buzz from the alleys he called home and dragging him off to the woods where he didn't know his way around, when the phone rang.

Before she even had time to say hello, Jack's deep voice was grumbling in her ear. "I said your father could check and see if the damn cat was still at my place. I did *not* say he could bring the cat up here."

Warmth flooded through her at the sound of his voice...and at what his words meant. "Oh, Jack. You mean Buzz? Buzz is all right?"

"As all right as a cockeyed cat with a bad attitude can ever be."

"He got away from me last night. I was so worried."

"You can stop worrying. Just come and get him."

She almost agreed, but then reconsidered. "Jack. It's pretty obvious he wants to be with you."

"Great." Jack muttered something low and uncouth.

"Give Chuck Swan a little something extra, and I'm sure he'll let you keep Buzz in your room."

"I don't *want* Buzz in my room."

"Oh, stop fighting it, Jack. Buzz has chosen you. Accept your fate."

"I hate that word."

"I've got a litter box and lots of cat food here, if you want to drop by and pick it up."

"I'm making do."

"Well, it's all here if you want it."

"Thanks."

She sensed he was about to hang up, so she quickly added, "We missed you last night."

"I'll bet."

"Everyone said the food was superb. And the company was...interesting."

"I have no doubts about the food."

"Thank you. Oh, and don't forget. You owe me fifty dollars."

"*Minus* whatever I have to fork over to Chuck to keep a cat in my room."

She pretended to have to think that over. "Well. All right. You can deduct Buzz's expenses, but nothing else."

"I'm so grateful."

"Good."

"You have a nice time with your father," he muttered darkly.

"Thank you. I will."

She heard the click from his end before she could find something else to say to keep him on the line. She sighed. And then she hugged the receiver and stared dreamily out the window over the breakfast table. All right, it hadn't exactly been a tender tête-à-tête, but at least he had called.

About then her father stumbled in wanting to know where she kept the aspirin. She was forced to hang up the phone and hunt down the pain reliever.

Olivia made German pancakes for breakfast. Later she and her guests walked the wooded paths near the house together. They talked of ordinary things. Her father asked her if perhaps she'd like to go shopping for that four-by-four she'd mentioned she needed. Olivia thanked him but refused.

That night she took her guests to dinner at the Mercantile Grill. They complimented the food and the service, and she knew they meant what they said. The Grill was a fine place to eat. Later, back at the house, they played Hearts with a deck of cards that Olivia had found in the hall closet.

Monday it rained. But still Mindy decided to borrow one of the umbrellas Olivia had found in the attic and walk over to Main Street. Olivia and Lawrence were left alone in the house, sitting in the two easy chairs in the living room by the cozy fire in the stove.

Olivia knew what was coming. Mindy had been transparent in her efforts to give father and daughter some time alone.

"What happened to the cat?" her father asked, after a few moments of companionable silence had passed. He was staring at the friendly flames through the little window in the stove.

"He went looking for Jack."

"And found him?"

"Yes."

"Is that good?"

"I think so."

Her father shifted in his chair a little. "Is this serious, then, between you and Roper?"

Olivia spoke with quiet conviction. "Yes, it is. Very serious. It's also momentous, wonderful, scary and sad."

Her father let out a long breath. "Whew. That about says it all."

"Yes."

"You love this man?"

"Yes."

"You know, you never told me you loved Cameron."

Olivia only looked at him and then looked away.

"I didn't fire him," her father said softly.

"You mean Cameron? I'm glad."

"He quit. He said he felt the working conditions would be too difficult, after what had happened. He's found something else already, of course."

"I'm not surprised. He's a great salesman."

Her father took out one of his wintergreen mints, but didn't unwrap it. "Livvy, I..."

Olivia waited, giving him time to frame his words.

"Are you happy, Livvy?"

She thought before answering, taking time to tuck her legs up beside her and lean on the armrest of her chair. "In most everything, yes. This town is just the place for me. And you know I always wanted to cook for a living. I feel that I'm just where I should be, doing just what I should be doing."

"But?"

Olivia picked at a worn place on the chair arm and then stopped herself. She decided she didn't want to talk about Jack right then. She said gently, "It's my problem, Dad."

Her father looked out the window. Olivia watched his Adam's apple work as he swallowed. "You were always such a sensitive girl. I wanted to protect you from the world, from all the cruel things out there."

"I know."

"I still want to protect you."

"But you can't."

He hung his head. "I know. At last, I know. I was terrified when you disappeared. It reminded me..."

"Of my mother?"

Her father looked at her. His eyes were haunted. "Yes." Again, as she had a thousand times, she ached for him and the horror he must have known all those years ago, when her mother was kidnapped.

Olivia felt the sting of guilt. "I'm so sorry that I ran off like that, Dad. I can understand what you must have felt. If I had it to do again, I'd do it differently."

He forced a smile. "But if you'd done it differently, would you have ended up here, in this town you say is just the place for you?"

She leaned her head on her hand and felt a musing smile lifting the corners of her mouth. "You know, I believe that I would have. I believe that somehow I would have found my way here. I believe that some things are meant to be."

Her father looked at her and shook his head. "You always were a fanciful girl."

"Hmm. Still fanciful, maybe. But not a girl anymore."

Quietly he said, "Your Jack Roper bears a striking resemblance to most of the members of the Jones family."

She took in a breath and let it out. "You've noticed."

"Has *he* noticed?"

"Not that he's admitted to me."

"Oh, Livvy. I hope you know what you're doing with
a man like that."

She reached across and patted his hand. "Dad, it's my
life, remember? I get to create my own successes. And
make my mistakes for myself."

"I know. I keep telling myself that."

"And I appreciate that you're finally letting me work
things out for myself."

"If you need anything, or even if you just want to talk,
you know I'm here."

"I know, Dad. And thank you." She watched fondly
as he unwrapped the mint he was still holding in his hand.

Lawrence and Mindy left at three Monday afternoon
for the forty-five-minute drive to Marysville where
Lawrence's plane waited. Olivia hugged them both in
turn and then stood on the porch out of the drizzly rain,
waving as they drove away.

Her small house seemed very empty after they'd gone.
She sat close to the fire and tried to read for a while.

Then she thought of calling Eden, who spent more
time at home now that she was so close to her delivery
day. Or maybe she could visit Amy or Regina. They'd
each be glad to see her. Even Delilah would probably be
home from school by now.

But in the end she did what she knew she probably
shouldn't do. She put all the cat supplies from the back
porch into two plastic bags, grabbed an umbrella and
headed for Swan's Motel.

Unfortunately the drizzle had turned to a downpour.
And a wind had come up, so the umbrella didn't do much

good. By the time she reached Jack's room, she was as drenched as she'd been the night he'd followed her from Las Vegas and picked her up on that lonely, twisting mountain road.

Since it wasn't serving any purpose, anyway, she collapsed the umbrella and then, bravely, she used the handle to knock on the door.

Jack answered within seconds. Her heart did that silly flip-flop it always performed when she saw him. He was wearing jeans and a blue chambray shirt. His feet were bare and the shirt was unbuttoned. He looked so good, he broke her heart. Behind him she could hear the drone of a TV.

She didn't miss the quick flash of gladness that lit his face nor the way he turned the gladness into a scowl.

"What the hell are you doing here?"

She held up the plastic bags and tried to display a degree of savoir faire, even though her eye makeup was probably running down her cheeks and she knew her hair was plastered to her head. "I brought the cat supplies."

He reached out and dragged her into the room, then shut the door. She was aware of a lot of plaid and pine— pine-paneled walls, a pine dresser, table, chairs and nightstand. From the unmade plaid-covered bed, Buzz granted her a sleepy cross-eyed glance.

Jack strode to the television, which was suspended from the ceiling in the corner by the door to the bathroom. He switched it off. The rain outside was suddenly a low, steady roar.

He turned and confronted her, planting a fist on his hip in a blatant display of male displeasure. "You're soaking wet."

"Very observant," she muttered, and took the few steps to the table, where she set down the bags and the dripping umbrella. She began to peel off her soaked outerwear.

"Don't take those off."

"Why not?"

"You're not staying."

She shrugged and took them off, anyway, pulling a chair over by the ancient-looking wall heater and hanging the wet things there in hopes that, by the time she left, they would be at least somewhat drier. That done, she marched right past him to the bathroom, where she grabbed a towel off the rack and dried her hair a little.

He stood in the doorway, watching her, a muscle in his jaw working furiously. She pretended to be utterly unconcerned, though her heart was racing and her skin felt prickly and warm.

She saw in the bathroom mirror that her eye makeup *was* a mess. She bore a faint resemblance to a waterlogged raccoon. Since there were no tissues that she could see near the cracked sink, she rolled off a few sheets of toilet paper and blotted up the mess around her eyes as best she could.

"Don't ever do this again," he warned, leaning in the doorway and crossing his arms over his beautiful scarred chest.

She locked glances with him in the streaked mirror above the sink. "Do what?"

"Don't come here."

"Why not?"

Suddenly he seemed unable to remain still. He left the doorway, turning for the main room. "Just don't." He muttered the words over his shoulder.

Olivia tossed her smudged makeshift tissues into the open commode and threw the towel she'd used across the sink. She went to the doorway herself and leaned in it.

"I asked you why not?" Her tone was blatantly hostile. He shot her a sharp glance, probably wondering why she was suddenly showing antagonism. She hadn't uttered an angry word around him in two weeks. Since the day he'd found her here in North Magdalene, she'd been all sweetness and light.

But something inside her had cracked. She had come here only to make another gentle, good-natured attempt to get closer to him.

But it just wasn't working. She was tired of answering his surly looks and muttered commands with sweet smiles.

It had finally happened. She was fed up with him. Jack dropped to the end of the bed.

Buzz, jostled, let out a meow of complaint and then yawned hugely, exhibiting a multitude of sharp yellow teeth.

Jack rested his elbows on his knees and looked her up and down. "You didn't get that wet running from your new car to the door of this room. You *walked* over here." It was an accusation.

She refused to be intimidated. "I'll ask you again. Why don't you want me to come here?"

Again, he didn't answer, only fired more questions at her. "What are you doing walking over here in a downpour like this? Where's that new car of yours?"

She bit her tongue and looked away.

"Answer me. Where is it?"

She made herself look back at him, square in the eye. "There is no new car. I didn't buy one."

"You said—"

"I lied."

That gave him pause. He eyed her sideways. "What do you mean, you lied?"

"I mean, I never intended to buy a vehicle this weekend. I never intended to buy a vehicle at all. Not for a while, anyway."

"Why not?"

She let out a little puff of air. "Think about it."

He raked his hair back with a hand. "I don't know what you're talking about."

"Oh, yes you do. You know. We both know. But we're supposed to pretend we *don't* know."

"You're making no sense."

"You say that. But you know it's not true. I'm making perfect sense." She kicked away from the doorway and marched over to him.

Hands on her hips, she glared at him. Then, with a low groan of frustration, she turned away. She went to the window that faced the landing. Lifting the plaid curtain, she looked out through the gray mist and driving rain at the box-shaped building across the way.

She heard him rise, though he made no sound. She felt his approach and the warmth of him so near behind her.

She didn't turn, only continued to look out at the rain. Neither spoke for a time, then she told him, "I can't take much more of this, Jack. It hurts too much. You're going to have to decide whether to stay or to go."

"I have decided." His voice was rough and low. "I'll be going. As soon as I'm sure . . ."

She dropped the curtain and whirled on him. "Sure of what?"

"That you'll be all right."

"You're telling me that you're still here because you feel responsible for me?"

"Yes."

"Liar."

He flinched, but recovered. One side of his mouth lifted in a threatening sneer. "Watch yourself."

"Liar."

"Don't—"

"Liar."

The third time was the charm. He took her by the arms and hauled her tight against his chest. He looked into her upturned face. "Stop this. Stop it now."

"No."

"Why are you doing this?"

"I love you, Jack."

"Shut up."

"Kiss me." Brazen, shameless as she'd always been with him, she stood on tiptoe, so her mouth was only inches from his. "Kiss me," she whispered, feeling his breath caress her lips. "It's what you want to do. What you always want to do."

"No."

"Liar."

"Shut up."

"Kiss me."

"I ought to . . ."

"Yes. Yes. Do it. Kiss me now."

Within the sound of the pounding rain and the angry wind, there was a silence, a moment of absolute stillness. Olivia looked into Jack's eyes. She saw the heat there. She felt his heart pounding in time with hers.

His mouth descended those final crucial millimeters. She sighed, a sigh of longing and hope.

But the kiss never happened. Instead he straightened his arms and very gently pushed her away from him. He dropped his arms.

They looked at each other. Outside the rain droned on.

He said, "I'm no good for you. We both know it."

She bit her lip and shook her head.

"I'm a guy who makes his living by keeping on the move. I'm not the right man for you. I'm . . . I'm useless to you as a partner in life."

"You are so wrong."

"You say that now."

"I'll say it forever if you give me a chance."

"Olivia . . ."

"I'm tired of playing games with you, Jack. Of going along with you so you won't decide there's nothing more to keep you here. If you're leaving, you're leaving. We can at least have honesty between us when you go.''

"What do you mean?" His eyes were wary.

"I mean there was no cougar."

He blinked. "No cougar?"

"Right. No cougar. No scary animal in the woods at all. Oggie and I cooked that up to get you to come to my rescue, since you were avoiding me completely at the time.'' She sucked in a breath and told the rest. "And I never planned to get a car until things were worked out between you and me. If I bought a car, then how would I talk you into driving me to Grass Valley to buy groceries?'' Raising her chin, she looked at him as proudly as she could. "So now you know how I've lied to you just for the chance to be near you."

"Olivia—"

"I'm not through. I said I lied. And I did. But at least I knew exactly what I was doing. But you're telling the worst kind of lies, Jack. You're lying to yourself. You're here for more reasons than because you feel responsible for me. I know it. Oggie knows it. Everyone in town knows it. Except you, apparently." Swiftly she strode to the chair and grabbed her wet things. Then she snatched up the umbrella. "And I just hope you get honest with yourself before it's too late."

With that she turned for the door, flung it wide and walked out into the storm.

She didn't get far. Jack caught up with her in his car just as she reached the turn from Pine Street to Rambling Lane. He rolled up beside her, leaned across to the passenger door and pushed it open.

She stopped, turned and looked at him as the rain poured down on her and the wind whipped at her clothing. Here she was, all over again, being rescued from a rainstorm by Jack.

"Get in."

She slid into the seat and pulled the door closed. He turned from the curb and drove straight to her house. As soon as the car stopped, she leaned on her door. But he reached across and held her there.

She looked straight ahead. "What is it, Jack?"

He said nothing.

She faced him. "You don't know what to say, do you? Because there's nothing to say. Until you make up your mind."

"I have made up my mind."

This was the same impasse they'd reached in his room. She'd had enough of it. "Let me go, Jack."

He released her. She slid from the car, ran up the steps and into the house.

Chapter Fifteen

Jack drove back to his room knowing the time had come to leave. As Olivia had so forthrightly confessed, there was no cougar and she could buy a vehicle anytime she wanted one.

And there was more. He'd seen it in the proud, high set to her shoulders, in the uncompromising glint in her eye. Somehow, during the brief time she had been in this small mountain town, Olivia had come into her own as a grown woman at last.

"R-rrreow?" Buzz was waiting by the door when Jack let himself into the room.

Jack shrugged out of his jacket. Then he bent and picked up the cat. As he idly rubbed Buzz's stubby head, he noticed that the message light on the phone was blinking.

The call was from a lawyer friend, Del Goldwaite.

"He wants you to call him back as soon as you can," Chuck said when Jack checked for the message. "He'll be at his office if it's before six. After that you should call him at his house."

It was quarter of six, so Jack tried the law firm where Del was a partner. The receptionist put him on hold and then came back to say Del was on another line and would call him back in five minutes.

Jack waited ten minutes and then the phone rang.

"Roper here."

"Jack, old buddy."

"Del. What's the deal?"

"It's like this. A client of mine called me. His wife's run off, cleaned out their joint bank accounts and disappeared with her hairdresser—or so the client thinks, anyway. The man is out of his mind. He has reason to believe the woman's in Mexico, and he wants to hire a man to go down there and find her. He wants the best. I said I'd do what I could and I thought of you."

"Okay."

"But there's a glitch."

"Yeah?"

"Since I couldn't reach you right away, the man's found someone else. I just got off the phone with him. I was pitching you like crazy. So now he says he'd like to talk to you before making a final decision. How soon can you get here?"

Jack considered. The job itself didn't thrill him, doing the footwork for a jilted husband who probably had revenge on his mind.

"Jack? You with me there?"

"What kind of money are we talking about, Del?"

Del told him.

Jack whistled under his breath and then did some fast calculating. Money like that could put him back in the black. He had to get real here. He'd just given himself what amounted to an extended vacation, looking out for a woman who didn't need looking out for anymore—if

she ever really had. It was past time to get back to the real
world.

"Jack? How long until you can get here?" Del was
starting to sound impatient.

"Assuming I can get a flight right away, maybe three
or four hours."

"Where are you, Jack?"

"Northern California. About eighty miles northeast of
Sacramento."

"No." Jack knew his friend was shaking his head. "It
won't work. I was thinking an hour, two, max. The man
is angry. He wants action now. He won't wait, even for
the best."

"But Del—"

"Look. Sorry. It's a no-go. But maybe in a few days,
if the competition doesn't deliver. In the meantime, get
back here to the city, so I can pull you out of a hat at the
crucial moment. Understand?"

Jack understood. "Yeah. I'll be back in town by tomorrow."

"That should do it. Don't let any moss grow on it."

"I hear you. See you then." Jack hung up.

"R-r-reow?" Buzz, who'd made himself comfortable
in an easy chair, paused in the bath he was giving himself to look up at Jack with cross-eyed curiosity.

Jack made his decision. Whatever had kept him hanging on here wasn't going to keep him any longer. If he
didn't get back soon, he'd have no business left when he
returned.

"The time has come, Buzz, my man. We're heading
out."

Buzz appeared unconcerned by the news.

Jack suddenly felt charged with nervous energy. He
began pacing up and down on the strip of carpet at the
foot of the bed. He rubbed the back of his neck.

He had to talk to Olivia, to say goodbye. And then that was it. He was out of here.

"You're leaving," she said softly, when she opened her door and looked in his eyes.

He nodded, tipping his collar up. It was growing colder now that night was approaching. The rain had eased off. It was a steady drizzle again. It dripped from the eaves of the porch all around him.

She stepped back a little. He could feel the warm air from the fire behind her. It looked cozy in there. "Will you come in?"

"No." He held out his hand. "Here."

She took what he offered, a fifty-dollar bill.

"I didn't forget," he said, shoving his hands back into his pockets for warmth.

She set the bill on the little table by the door, then came outside, pulling the door shut behind her. She wrapped her arms around herself to keep warmer and huddled with her back against the door. "I didn't care about the bet." She looked away, as if collecting herself, and then she faced him again. "The money never mattered, Jack."

"It isn't the money."

He watched her eyes fill. They glittered like sapphires in the fading light of day. "I guess I know that." She bit the inside of her lip. He could see she was willing the tears back.

"Olivia, I..." He didn't quite know how to continue.

"What? Say it. What?"

He took in a breath, which came out as mist when he spoke. "I know this is for the best."

She looked down at her shoes. "Oh, great. That's great to hear. I'll get a lot of comfort from that—and so will you."

He ached for her, so much that he forgot himself for a moment. He pulled his hand from his pocket and reached out. "Olivia—"

She batted his hand away. "No."

He stepped back, shoved his hands in his pockets again, looked down at the porch boards, over at the rain dripping from the eaves. Anywhere. Anywhere at all but at her stricken face.

He tried to think of the right thing to say. But all that came out was, "In a few months, you'll forget all about me."

She let out a tight little sound. He made himself look at her. Her eyes were still glittering, but with anger now, not tears.

"You're a fool, Jack Roper. A cross-eyed tomcat has more sense than you. A scrawny old alley cat knows enough to take his chance when it comes to him."

"I'm not Buzz, Olivia." He spoke quietly, feeling proud of how reasonable he sounded. "Buzz is a cat."

"Right." She looked away again. "Right. Sure." And then her eyes were pinning him. "You're not a cat. You're a man. And that gives you an excuse to let what happened to you when you were just a boy ruin your chances of ever finding love."

He felt his whole body stiffen, as something like panic stabbed through his outer calm. "I don't know what you're talking about."

"Oh, yes you do." She glared at him. She was shivering from the cold. "You know. You know very well."

"Look—"

"No, *you* look. I love you. With all my heart. And I honestly believe that you love me. But I've done all I can to get you to see what we could have together. There's nothing more I can do without your meeting me halfway. I only hope you wise up and change your mind about this before I get tired of waiting for you."

"Olivia—"

"Goodbye, Jack."

She turned, pushed open the door and went back inside, closing it firmly in his face.

There was nothing more to do. Jack knew it. He returned to his room to gather up his few belongings.

The phone rang just as he finished packing.

Olivia, he thought, despising himself for the way his heart was suddenly racing and his chest felt tight.

He reached over and picked up the receiver on the second ring. "Roper here."

"So, you're leavin' town, eh?"

Jack knew the voice. Oggie Jones. Dread curled like a small, cold snake in his stomach, though why that should be, Jack swore he didn't know.

"Hey. You there?"

Jack made himself speak. "I'm here. And yeah, I'm leaving town."

"Then listen. The Hole in the Wall's closed today. But Eden's got the boys running in and out all the time, polishing bottles and checking stock. By midnight, though, the place'll be completely deserted. Meet me there then. Go in the back way. I'll leave it open for you."

"Look, there's no reason for—"

The old man grunted. "You're outta time, boy. You put me off until the end. And this is it. You ain't gettin' away from me without hearin' the things I intend to say. Midnight. Be there."

"Listen, old man—"

But Oggie had already hung up.

Jack hung up his end, swearing to himself that he wasn't putting off leaving, not for anybody, and especially not for some crazy old coot like Oggie Jones.

"Damned old fool," he muttered to himself.

Buzz, from a nest of covers he'd made on one side of the bed, lifted his head and blinked at Jack.

Jack saw the cat staring at him.

"We're leaving. Now," he said.

Buzz yawned. The animal looked way too knowing for a cat whose eyes didn't even focus right.

"I'm not meeting that crazy old man. That's all there is to it."

Buzz said nothing, only continued to regard his master with that irritating cockeyed stare.

Chapter Sixteen

By midnight the rain had stopped.

The back door to the Hole in the Wall was unlatched, just as the old man had promised.

Jack went in and tugged the door shut behind him. He found himself in a dim hallway, which was lit with one meager fixture halfway down toward the main part of the tavern. Jack started walking.

When the hall opened up into the main room and he was a few feet from the bar, he could see the light coming through the curtains to the back room. He went through the curtains and there was Oggie, in the same chair he'd been sitting in that first day, when Jack came looking for Brendan Jones. The old man was reading the local newspaper. The smoke from his cigar curled up toward the hooded fixture over his head.

Oggie looked over the top of the paper. Jack met his eyes.

Slowly Oggie folded the paper and dropped it beside his chair. Then, his cigar in the corner of his mouth, he put his hands over his belly and stared at Jack long and hard. Jack stared back, thinking that the old rogue looked a thousand years old, his eyes red and watery, smoke swirling around him, the light from above casting every wrinkle on his face into road map relief.

Jack waited what seemed like forever for Oggie Jones to speak. When Oggie remained silent, Jack prompted coldly, "Okay, I'm here. Whatever it is, say it now."

Oggie coughed, then puffed on his cigar some more. At last he suggested, "Have a seat."

"I'll stand. Talk."

Oggie fiddled with his suspenders. He studied the glass ashtray on the green felt cloth that covered the table. Finally he said, "I got a story to tell you."

"A story about what?"

"About a cardsharp named Oggie Jones." Oggie reached out and idly spun the ashtray. "And about the cardsharp's lady, Alana Dukes."

The sound of his mother's maiden name on the old man's lips hit Jack like a freezing wind. He wanted to turn and run back out the way he had come.

But he didn't. What point was there in that now? He'd heard just enough that he wasn't going to be able to hide from the truth anymore. He might as well hear the rest.

"You sure you won't sit down?" The rough voice actually held a note of concern.

Jack decided maybe the suggestion was a good one, after all. He yanked out a seat and dropped into it. "All right. I'm listening."

Oggie moved in his chair, settling in, getting as comfortable as his old bones would allow him to be. He crossed his legs, then uncrossed them, grimacing a little with the effort.

Jack waited, uncomplaining. He was feeling a little numb, suddenly. A little sick. And whether the old man told the story fast or slow didn't matter much, anyway.

Oggie sat back with a long exhalation of breath. "I met Alana in Saint Louis at a little place called the Red Garter. It was after the second great war. The country was prospering."

The old man scratched the side of his face, his black eyes narrowing. "It wasn't love. Back then, I didn't believe there was such a thing as love. But it was close to love. As close as a drifter like me had ever come to it, anyway. We respected each other, Alana and me. And we suited each other, too."

The old man tipped his head and stared at the ceiling, pensively rubbing his chin, as if he saw the face of Alana Dukes up there in the shadows and smoke. "Ah, she was a beauty, white-blond hair and big green eyes. Kept the suckers goin', she did, smilin' and flirtin', while I raked in the winnings. We were a hell of a team." Oggie shook his head, bent forward with a grunt and stubbed out his cigar in the ashtray. Then he was looking straight ahead again, though his eyes were still decades away.

"We lasted five years together, Alana and me. We prospered like this great land. A pair of entrepreneurs, that's how we thought of ourselves, doin' well off the extra cash in other people's pockets. Movin' West, we were. Carryin' our nest egg in one of Alana's nylon stockings.

"But then we hit Bakersfield." The old man took a minute for the ritual of lighting a fresh cigar, spitting the end on the floor and putting the match to it, puffing until it glowed red.

"And?" It was Jack's voice, though it sounded so ragged he hardly recognized it as his own.

Oggie examined the red coal at the end of his new cigar. "And Alana fell in love with another man. It happened overnight. One night she was sleepin' with me, like always. And the next night she was gone. She'd met him because she loved apricots, she told me. She'd stopped at this little roadside stand—*his* roadside stand, it turned out, to buy some apricots. And there he was. A farmer. John Roper. A real upstandin' guy, John Roper was. He claimed he was willin' to forgive Alana's checkered past as long as she married him and put her wild life behind her for good." Oggie cleared his throat. "She came to me and told me she was leavin'."

"What did you do?"

"What the hell could I do? It was her life. I wished her well. We split the nest egg. Then I went out and got good and drunk and gambled my half of our savings away in one night." The gnarled hand tapped the cigar on the edge of the ashtray. Jack watched the cinders drop. "I was sulkin', see? But hell. I could see she'd found her man. I'd thought we had it good together, but after seeing the look in her eyes when she talked about Roper, I realized I didn't have a clue what *good* was. And eventually I had to admit to myself that things had been fadin' between the two of us for a while anyway."

"And then?"

Oggie's shrug said it all.

"You left."

"You bet. I went on my way, with nothin' in my pockets and no prospects to speak of. I came here, to North Magdalene. And I met Bathsheba." At the mention of the strange, biblical name, the old man's face changed. It seemed to glow from within. "We married within a month of our meeting, and had a son within the year."

"Jared."

"Yeah." The old man's eyes were on Jack. They burned right through him. "I thought," Oggie said quietly, "that Jared was my firstborn. But now—"

It was enough. Jack's chest felt so tight he could hardly draw breath. "Look. I get the point."

"Do you?"

"Yeah."

Gently Oggie said, "I didn't know you existed, son."

Jack looked away, then made himself look into those wise eyes once more. "I understand. And it doesn't matter."

"That ain't true."

"Yes, it is. You didn't know about me. It wasn't your fault. It just happened."

"Naw, it didn't. Didn't your mother ever—"

Jack cut him off. "Look. It was like you said. She loved John Roper. She wanted to believe I was his. She swore I was his."

"But you weren't. And John Roper knew it, too, didn't he?"

"I think so. I don't know. And what's the point in speculating? I'm a grown man now. This is ancient history."

"No, son. You live it now. You live it every day of your life."

"No."

"Yes." Oggie waved a hand. His eyes were like broken shards of black glass. He went on, his sandpaper voice growing urgent. "It *is* important. It's made you what you are today. When John Roper realized you weren't his blood son, he turned away from you. He was your dad, and he turned away. That's what happened, ain't it? He turned away from you *and* your mama. And your mama blamed you, didn't she? Your mama never loved you right, either, because she couldn't forgive you for being born and losing her the man she loved. You grew up belonging nowhere, claimed by no one."

"Stop." Jack squeezed the word out past the knot in his throat. He sucked in air. "I already said it doesn't matter."

The old man was relentless. "Yeah, it does. A man needs to know his people—and his place. Or else he wanders. He lives outside the circle of life. He can't give himself to anything. A place. A woman. The raising of a child."

"No."

Oggie went on as if Jack hadn't spoken. "But now, I'm here to tell you I know you're mine. And I do claim you, son. Hell, I woulda claimed you way back then if I'da known."

It was too much. Jack stood, shoving his chair away so violently that it hit the curtain and fell on its side behind him. "I said stop this." He leaned across the table. "Let it be, you crazy old fool."

"No." Oggie looked up at Jack, unflinching. His rheumy gaze was so intense it raised the short hairs on the back of Jack's neck. He calmly explained, "A Jones don't never stop. And I'm a Jones. Just like you're a Jones, no matter what damn name you go by."

"*No.*"

"Yeah." Oggie pushed himself painfully to his feet, his knotted knuckles white on the green tablecloth. "You're mine." He craned toward Jack so that not more than a foot of charged air separated the two of them. "I knew you were mine the minute I set my eyes on you that day you came lookin' for that lost woman of yours. *Mine*, Jack Roper. One of my kids. As much a part of me as Jared or Patrick, Delilah or Brendan."

Jack hit the table with his fist and spoke through teeth so tightly clenched that they ached. "I don't even *know* you, old man."

"You will, if you just let yourself."

"No."

"Yes."

Jack swore, a short, dark oath. He turned. And then, kicking aside the chair that lay across his path, he shoved through the curtain and got the hell out of there.

"Run if you want!" The old man called after him. "But you'll never get away. A man is what he is, and he never finds peace until he looks in the mirror and understands what he sees. Son! Son, you listen to me!"

Once he reached the back parking lot, Jack leaned against the old Cadillac that belonged to Oggie and gulped in air like a man just saved from drowning. When at last he began to believe that maybe his rubbery legs would hold him upright, he straightened. Then he headed for Swan's Motel.

But his feet didn't take him there. Instead they turned on Pine Street and then again on Rambling Lane. He broke into a run. He pounded up the long, twisting street toward the little white house with the green trim. He was breathing hard when he mounted the porch.

The light was off. The house was dark. He imagined she was sleeping. He had no right to hope she would welcome him. But right then his need was so great that he knocked anyway.

The porch light came on, blinding him in a cold spill of brightness. He felt naked. And then she peeked through the curtain of the window beside the door.

Her sweet face was pale, scrubbed clean of makeup. They stared at each other. He knew he should turn and leave. He prayed she'd let him in.

She dropped the curtain. Then he heard the lock being turned. She pulled the door open and stepped back.

He went in.

She closed the door behind him and turned to face him, clutching her robe at the neck. "You talked to Oggie."

He stared at her, then accused, "You know."

She nodded. "Oggie made me promise not to tell you. He said you didn't want to know."

Jack heard a laugh. It came from his own mouth. It sounded a lot like a groan. "He was right. But deep down, I *did* know. I think I knew the minute I saw him, that first day I came looking for you. But I could pretend I didn't know. As long as no one told it straight-out to my face. As long as no one mentioned names. Places. Details. But that old bastard just couldn't let it be."

"Oh, Jack." Her eyes were full of love. Of understanding. He hated her right then, almost as much as he yearned for her. "He wants another chance," she said. "He wants to be your father."

"Damn it, Olivia. I'm forty-one years old. I am what I am. It's a little late now."

"No, Jack. It's not. It's never too late."

"Yeah, it is. Knowing the truth doesn't change who I am. It just makes it all... sadder, more pathetic, somehow."

"Only because you let it be that way."

"You're a damn dreamer. You always did live in a fantasy world."

"No, Jack. I don't live in a fantasy world. Not anymore. I live in the real world, a world I'm creating. Day by day."

Her pretty chin was held high, her blue eyes shone. He wanted to grab her and shake her until she admitted he was right, that her head was full of pointless fantasies, which she insisted on calling dreams.

He also wanted her to reach out her hand and pull him out of the darkness in which he suffered and into the light that seemed to glow all around her.

He knew that neither of those two things would happen. He knew that there was a hard shell around his heart. Olivia was the only one who'd seen through the shell, down into the depths of him. But she couldn't break the shell. Nothing could do that. It was too much a part of him.

She asked the question. "Why are you here, Jack?"

He gave her the brutal truth. "Because I want you. I'll always want you. And I couldn't stay away. Not tonight, not after listening to all those things I never wanted to hear. But I'm leaving at daylight, just as I planned." He looked at her, at all of her, from the tangle of sleep-mussed gold curls to the bare pink toes that peeked out beneath her robe. He said roughly, "I want to be inside you. One more time."

Three steps separated them. She bridged them without seeming to move.

"All right." Her little chin was still high. But her tender mouth quivered. Two bright spots of color stained her cheeks.

Shame flooded through him, tempering his anger, his pain...and his desire. He hung his head. "Get smart. Don't let me use you. Send me away."

"Shh. I love you."

The words pierced him. He hadn't known how he had wanted to hear them until she had uttered them.

"Say it again." His voice was like the sound of something tearing.

"I love you."

"Again."

"I love you, love you, love you..."

Her soft hand framed the side of his face. She came up on tiptoe and pressed her lips to his. His mouth burned at the contact. His body was on fire with need of her. Yet he forced his hands to stay at his sides. He let her do the kissing.

She did a damn fine job of it, too. She nibbled and tasted, licked and caressed. Her scent, that scent of flowers and freshness, swam all around him. He was hard, achingly hard. He could feel his manhood, pushing at the placket of his jeans, wanting to be out and inside of her, where it was safe and warm, where heaven was.

With a groan, though he kept his hands to himself, he pressed his hips against her. She sighed and pressed back. He thought he would die—and be happy to go.

Still kissing him, cradling his face in her tender hands, she lifted her hips and rubbed boldly against the ridge of him. He groaned again.

She stepped back then.

Stunned, starved for her, he opened his eyes. If she refused him now—

But she wasn't refusing him. "Take off your jacket."

He did as she asked, tossing it across a chair.

She was holding out her hand. "Come on. Let's go to bed." When they reached the bedroom, Olivia let go of Jack's hand. Then she crossed the room and turned on the little lamp on the nightstand.

She was very frightened. But absolutely sure that she was doing the right thing. She loved this man. And if tonight was the last one they'd have together, it was better than no last night at all.

She had condoms, which she removed from the drawer in the stand and set beside the lamp. A wave a sadness washed over her, as she thought of how she had bought them two weeks ago, so certain that she and Jack would work out their problems soon, wanting to be prepared when their moment of tender reunion came.

Well, she was prepared, all right. But the reunion, it seemed, would never be. This was more in the nature of an intimate farewell.

She knew he was looking at the condoms, and she gave a little shrug. "Okay, I admit it. I want you, too." She forced a smile. "I always will. And this is a better way to end it than me calling you a fool and closing the door in your face, don't you think?''

From the shadows she could feel his eyes caressing her with heat and hunger. "Yeah. Take off the robe."

Her body responded instantly to his command. She felt her nipples grow to hard little nubs. Down there, the luxurious heaviness, the warmth and the wetness had begun.

"Take it off."

She bit her lip. The robe was of thick, pink chenille, hardly the type of thing one wore when one planned a seduction. Regina had given it to her. And Jack wanted her to take it off.

She did, not daring to look at him across the room. She paid great attention to her task as she untied the belt and dropped it to the ground. Then, one shoulder at a time, she shrugged out of the sleeves. It dropped in a pink pile at her feet. She looked down at it, as if wondering how it got there.

Now she wore only a pink flannel nightgown, which was also a hand-me-down from Regina.

"Come here." Jack's voice was gruff.

She looked up then, into his eyes. And she was captured. She couldn't look away. Slowly, like a sleep-walker, she approached him. And when she stood right before him, he reached out, cupped her face and brought her mouth to his.

The kiss was hot and consuming, as purely carnal a caress as she had ever known. His tongue swept her mouth, claiming it, leaving no room for anything there but the taste, the feel, the reality of him.

His hands slid down her neck, out over her shoulders, rubbing, pressing. And then, swift and knowing, they were at her hips, bunching her modest nightgown, sliding it up her legs and holding it at her waist.

She wore no panties. From the waist down, she was bare. He touched her, touched the womanly heart of her, as he went on kissing her in that total, consuming way. He felt her wetness, her readiness, and he groaned into her mouth.

She might have been embarrassed. But there was no space, no time, for such a trifling emotion. His need was on him, and she was ready for him.

His mouth still locked with hers, he took her shoulders and slowly, inexorably, pushed her back, toward the bed and the nightstand and the pool of light the lamp made in the night-dark room. When they reached the bed, his hands left her, though his mouth went on tormenting hers. He fumbled with his jeans, ripping them open, shoving them out of the way, surging against her, so she felt his hardness touch her belly through the fleecy fabric of her gown.

He fumbled on the table, still kissing her, seeming to drink her very being from her mouth. He found one of the condoms and tore it open, tossing the little foil package away. He slid the condom in place.

"Now," he said into her mouth. "Inside you. Now."

He took the gown and gathered it up, out of his way. Then he pushed her down, back across the bed, mouth still locked with hers. He nudged her legs apart and positioned himself between them.

And then, in one long, deep stroke, he was inside.

Her body opened to him easily. It was so good to feel herself expanding to take him, to have him inside, to hold him there, for as long as he would stay.

Until daylight.

Not long enough. But better than not at all.

He sighed, a sigh of relief that seemed to border on pain. The sigh trailed across her cheek as he released her mouth and buried his head in the curve of her shoulder.

"No one like you. Ever."

She whispered, "Please . . ."

He vowed, "Soon. Soon."

And yet he didn't move.

And suddenly it didn't matter. Because her completion happened, anyway, so suddenly it was as if it spun into being out of nothingness. Olivia cried aloud, pressing herself up, feeling the sparks inside, like stars bursting, sending light flooding out to every limb. He stiffened, pressing into her so hard and deep. She knew he'd reached his release as well. Their bodies moved apart, limp. They both were breathing hard.

But then, all at once, he was kissing her again in the soft hollow of her throat. And down over her breasts, her belly. Into the bronze nest of curls. He parted her and tasted her.

She moaned. She clutched his head. He looked up, his face cruel, ruthless with desire.

"I must remember."

"Never forget."

Until daylight.

She encircled him with her hand. He threw his head back, sent a feral cry to heaven. She stroked, faster and faster. He spilled, hot and quick, across her hand.

They rested.

And it started again.

She dared to recall her vain hope from their night in Las Vegas. Maybe she would win out over time at last. Maybe daylight would never come. Maybe they could go on forever, in the velvet heart of midnight. Rising and falling. Resting. Then reaching out once again.

He filled her, a long, gentle slide inside. He moved slowly within her. She thought of the movements of the sea, far from shore, an extended, heaving rise and fall. When fulfillment came it was like an expansion, like something that grew and increased until she could no longer contain it. It overflowed the frail vessel of her body and set the night afire in a river of flame.

Later she lay tucked against him. His leg between hers, his arms tight around her. He reached down and found the covers, pulled them up.

"Jack?"

"Shh. Rest now."

"One thing."

"Shh."

"Don't leave me when I'm asleep. Promise."

"I promise."

"You'll wake me?"

"I will." He tucked the covers around them.

"It's late," she said.

He gave her the answer. "So late, it's practically early."

They both closed their eyes. Sleep embraced them as one.

They were together.

Until dawn.

But in the back room of the Hole in the Wall, Oggie sat alone. He knew he should go home to his warm bed at his daughter's house. But he hadn't the energy.

He was tired. The plans and schemes that usually filled his mind were gone. For the first time, besides being old, he felt old.

His eyes drifted closed.

A sad dream engulfed him. Slowly one lone tear slid over the wrinkles on his cheek and plopped onto his gnarled hands.

His dream turned cruel. He shuddered, and his lighted cigar dropped from his lips onto the folded newspaper that lay on the old plank floor.

For a while the coal at the end of the cigar only smoldered, slowly scorching a black hole in the center of the front page. But then a tiny tongue of fire rose up. It flickered, died, then rose again.

Soon enough it danced up strong and then forked out, to claim the shadows and snake in blazing ribbons along the tinder-dry floor. By the time the old man coughed and looked up, the curtain to the main room was a wall of flame.

Chapter Seventeen

Olivia heard the church bell clanging madly. The long wail of a siren joined in.

"What?" She woke fully. Jack was already rolling from the bed. "What is it?"

He shoved his feet into his jeans, pulled them up, buttoned them. "I don't know. A fire, maybe. Or an accident." He sat down and yanked on his socks and boots.

Olivia threw back the covers.

"Stay here. I'll see what it is," Jack urged.

"No way." She grabbed for a pair of jeans of her own, as well as a sweater, shimmying into them swiftly, then reaching for a pair of socks.

He was already dressed, anxious to be gone.

"Just a minute more," she told him as she found her socks and shoes. She jerked them on, fast as she could, then stood. "Okay. Let's go."

She grabbed a heavy cardigan off the coatrack in the hall. Jack took his jacket from the chair in the front room. They ran out into the night, where the church bell clanged louder and another siren had joined the first one.

Jack pointed. "Look. See the smoke. It looks like a fire. Probably on Main Street."

She glanced around for his car.

He seemed to know her thoughts. "I didn't bring it. Come on. If you're coming, let's run for it."

He held out his hand. She put hers inside it. They ran, the night air cold in their lungs, their breath emerging as fog into the darkness.

Each house they passed had a light on inside. People stood on their porches. And some ran, with them, toward Main Street. They turned onto Pine, Jack ahead, towing Olivia along. She had a stitch in her side and nursed it. But she did her best to keep up. She wanted to see what had happened, to help if she could.

They reached Main Street.

They saw the source of all the furor at the same time.

"My God! The Hole in the Wall."

There were fire trucks, with the big canvas hoses already unrolled. There were four-by-fours with racks of red-and-blue lights on top. And there were people everywhere.

Olivia forgot the stitch in her side. She ran with Jack to the section of street right in front of the bar.

There, the night was bright as day. The heat from the flames pushed back the autumn coolness. The faces all around were lit with eerie reflected light, the expressions stunned and awed. Above, a forest service helicopter circled, blades beating.

"I'll see if I can help." Jack left her, making his way over to where the volunteer fire crew, which included the Jones men, held the hoses and aimed them through the broken windows. The hoses spewed fat shafts of water. The water sizzled as it hit the flames. But the fire was well along, and the Hole in the Wall was aged, dry wood.

They were trying for containment. Even Olivia could see that.

"It's spread to the Mercantile, look there," someone said.

Olivia looked and saw the garish light inside the brick building that meant there were flames inside of it, too.

"Must have gone through that center hall," someone else said.

"Please. Keep back." It was Eden's voice. Olivia looked and saw her, her bathrobe barely meeting around her huge stomach. "Keep back. Don't worry. It's only a building. We have insurance, after all."

"There's no one inside, then?" Nellie Anderson, who practically ran the community church, wanted to know.

"No one. They all went home hours ago," Eden soothed.

"Thank the Lord." Linda Lou Beardsly, Nellie's friend, clasped her hands together and tipped her head toward the sky.

But then Delilah ran up, her black hair loose and flying. "Have you seen my father? Has anyone seen my father? He's not in his bed. I can't find my—"

Olivia knew, with a sudden sick lurch in the pit of her stomach, where the old man must be. After all, he and Jack had met only hours before. The Hole in the Wall would have been the perfect place that time of night for a man to tell the hardest truths to his son. Quiet. Deserted. A place where no one else would hear the things they said.

"Oh, no..." The words escaped her lips as she turned to look for Jack. He stood by the other men. And he had heard Delilah's cries.

Jack saw Olivia. Their eyes locked. And she knew what he was going to do.

He spoke to Jared. Jared shook his head. But Jack grabbed the other man and muttered something low and intense, as he pointed toward the place where Eden stood. Olivia knew the gist of what Jack was saying.

You've got a wife and baby. You can't risk it. But I've got nobody. I'm going in....

Right then, Delilah grabbed Olivia's arm. "Olivia. Have you seen him? My father, do you know where he is?"

But Olivia didn't answer. She was watching Jack and Jared. She saw Jared nod. Jared picked up a bucket that stood near his feet and doused Jack with its contents. Then he shrugged out of his heavy fire-resistant jacket and handed it over. Jack slipped it on. Jared set his hard hat on Jack's head.

"No! Jack, no!" Olivia yanked her arm from Delilah's grasp and shoved her way through the crowd.

But she wasn't fast enough. Jack was already disappearing into the roiling smoke beyond the double doors, as Jared shouted orders to the other men. "Keep the hoses going in the windows, wet it down!"

"Jack! No! Don't do it!" Olivia ran for the doors, thinking wildly that if he was going into that inferno, he was going to have to drag her right along with him.

But then, in midflight, she felt a hand close over her arm. She was yanked backward. Another hand grabbed her other arm.

She kicked, she screamed. "Let me go! Don't you see? He'll die in there, don't you see?"

But the strong hands held her fast. "Easy, Olivia, settle down." Jared spoke gently. But his grip was firm. She knew he wasn't going to let her go.

Jared shouted more orders. "Patrick, go around back. See if any of the guys back there have seen a sign of Dad."

Patrick shot around the back of the building.

Olivia forced herself to speak reasonably. "Jared, please. I'm all right. You can let me go now."

Jared only shook his head and held on.

* * *

Jack could hardly see. The smoke was too thick. All around him was the hissing of water hitting fire, the roar of hungry, undoused flames, the crackling of boiling pitch and the creaking of burned beams about to give.

Smoke clogged his lungs, stinging. It burned to draw breath. He yanked his shirt over his mouth. The shirt was wet, thanks to Jared. It helped a little to screen out the acrid smoke. But not much.

To his left there was the sound of bottles exploding behind the bar. Then a long, whiplike *snap*—the big mirror cracking from the heat. Next, a tinkling like a thousand tiny bells as the mirror disintegrated and collapsed onto the floor.

Jack peered through slitted eyes, trying to get his bearings, to see his way to the back room. He looked from side to side. Jets of water from the hoses shot by through the windows behind him. He had to be careful not to stumble into them. Their pressure was great enough to knock him off his feet and push him into the blaze that raged all around.

He coughed, swiped at his burning eyes, then peered toward where he thought the back room should be. He saw a hole there, where the curtain had hung. And beyond it, a fire storm. It looked like the whole back room was alive with flame.

He heard an ominous crack, like a gunshot in the roar and whisper of the fire. And he watched, stunned and sickened, as the ceiling in the back room crashed down to meet the floor.

If Oggie was still in there, he'd been burned alive. And now the charred old bones were crushed as well.

Jack tried to see if there might be a way through the fire, out the back hall through which he'd entered earlier that night. But the back hall looked like a tunnel of flame.

Jack dropped to the floor, starving for air. He sucked it in, smoky, but at least breathable this low down. Over behind the bar more bottles exploded, more glass rained down.

He looked around again and saw that the support beams in the middle of the floor were afire. The flames licked and ate at them.

Overhead the ceiling seemed to be moaning.

Jack knew there was no time. He knew that if the old man wasn't outside somewhere right now, he was dead. If Jack wanted to save himself, it was time to get out.

And yet he didn't move.

He thought of the people he had saved in his life.

He'd dragged a buddy, half-dead, through a jungle on the other side of the world. The buddy had lived.

He'd pulled a baby from a burning hut. The baby had lain so still, he'd thought life had left it. But when he put his mouth on the tiny blue lips and gave the gift of breath, the baby coughed and puckered up its little face and let out an angry cry.

He'd tracked a little girl to a mine shaft where her kidnappers had left her to die. She was so weak she couldn't hold on to him. She lay limp, her head lolling, as Jack carried her out. After a few days in the hospital she'd been fine.

But Oggie Jones was not going to be fine. Jack's own father, and he'd come too late to save him.

Jack's eyes were full, burning, wet. And it wasn't just the smoke. Something was breaking inside of him, like a wall going, a shell cracking.

"Oggie! Damn you, Oggie, are you here?" he shouted, knowing it was useless, knowing the old man was dead.

But what had it been for, all those people he had saved, all the women and the children, the buddies and the babies? He knew what for. To give them a chance to return to what Jack had never known: a home and a family. A place that mattered and people who cared.

And this time? This time was different. He didn't want to admit it. He fought admitting it. But this was for *him*. He'd been a fool to turn away from the old man. He could see that clearly, now that it was too late.

He wanted the old man alive. He wanted a chance with him. He *wanted* the family he had never known. . . .

Overhead the ceiling gave an ominous, extended moan. Not more than a minute—two, at the most—and it would come crashing down.

"Oggie!" Jack shouted one more time. And then, after a short fit of coughing, he screamed, "Father! Father, where the hell are you?"

More bottles exploded. The water from the hoses hissed and popped in a futile effort to douse the conflagration.

Jack's body, which had learned the habit of survival in a thousand different trials, pushed to go on living. He began to crawl backward.

He was almost to the door when he heard the groan.

It sounded human.

He froze, peering to his right, where he thought he'd heard the sound. Smoke eddied and swirled. Then he saw it. Sticking out from the overturned table not five feet away. An arm and a gnarled, aged, human hand.

With a cry like an animal in pain, Jack slithered closer. The arm disappeared beneath the overturned table. Somehow Oggie had made it this far.

Jack shoved the table up and over. It fell into the nearby flames with a muffled crash. The old man rolled his head and groaned once more, unconscious, but definitely alive.

Jack lifted himself to a crouch, pulled the limp body up by an arm and positioned himself.

In the middle of the room, one of the support beams collapsed. It broke in the middle and gave. Sparks showered. The ceiling cracked and groaned. Jack could hear it beginning to go.

With a yank that made the unconscious man moan, Jack pulled his father onto his back. Then he rolled to his feet, still crouching beneath his load, and aimed himself at the door.

"Everybody back!" Jared shouted, taking his own advice and pulling Olivia along with him. "The roof's going!"

Olivia, numb by then, staggered back because she was pulled that way. She stared, awestruck, broken inside, as the Hole in the Wall saloon caved in upon itself. She heard the groaning, the cracking, and then the center gave, pulling the rest in with it.

Sparks shot up to heaven. The red glow inside peeled open to expose itself to the night. It was savagely beautiful.

And it meant Jack was dead.

And just as she allowed her mind to frame her loss, it happened.

A bent, distorted figure burst through the double doors.

Chapter Eighteen

"Look!" someone shouted.

"Woo-ee, lookee there!"

"Do you believe it?"

"It's Roper."

"He's got Oggie."

"He's saved the old man!"

Olivia blinked. And joy shot through her, sharp as a lance, painfully sweet. "Jack!" She yanked against Jared's restraining hands. This time he released her.

Olivia ran. It wasn't far.

But she wasn't quite fast enough. There were others ahead of her. They'd already formed a circle around Jack and his burden. So she stood on tiptoe behind Rocky Collins, peering over his shoulder, trying to see what was happening in the center of the circle where Jack was.

Olivia glanced from face to face. Brendan was there. And Amy. Delilah. Patrick. Regina. Eden. All of them. All the Joneses. Even Jared managed to slip past the outside of the circle to get to his father's side. Except for the men who had to stay with the fire, everyone crowded around Oggie Jones.

Carefully Jack knelt and laid the old man on the ground.

Delilah knelt beside Jack. "My sweet Lord." Delilah looked at Jack. There were tears in her dark eyes and a warm, exultant gratitude. "You did it. You brought him out."

"Come on now, folks, let us through. Let us see to this." It was the calm voice of Will Bacon, the practical nurse who ran the local medical clinic. People moved aside for Will, who was followed by Bertha Potts. Bertha drove the ambulance and assisted Will at the clinic.

Will crouched beside Oggie, who was coughing and coming around.

"Just take it easy, Oggie," Will said. "Looks like you're going to be all right."

Oggie coughed some more and tried to speak, but another bout of coughing racked him.

"You just lie down. Bertha, a pillow, please. And bring the oxygen tank."

But Oggie shoved the pillow away and sat up. "Let a man get his breath, will you, Will Bacon?"

"All right, all right."

"What happened, Oggie?" someone asked.

Bertha tersely instructed, "Don't bother him with questions now. Can't you see the man can hardly breathe?"

Oggie coughed some more. But all eyes were on him. He wasn't passing up an opportunity like that. He shoved away the oxygen mask that Bertha was trying to put over his mouth. "I woke up from a little nap. The damn place was alive with flames. I couldn't find my cane. I staggered out through the burnin' curtain, into the main room. I made it almost to the door. And then I tripped.

Grabbed on to a table, and it came down over me. It's the last thing I remember—until I heard someone calling me." Oggie hacked and spat.

"It was that cigar of yours, wasn't it, Father?" Delilah's tears had already passed. Now she was looking more herself.

Oggie grumbled and hacked some more. "Don't get on me, Delilah, damn it. Can't you see I almost died?"

"But if I've told you once, I've told you a hundred times—"

"Shh, sweetheart," Sam Fletcher said gently, behind his wife.

Delilah looked up at him. "But Sam—"

Sam shook his head. Delilah said no more.

And now Oggie was looking at Jack's soot-smeared face. "It was you, wasn't it? You were callin' me." Oggie grabbed Jack's hand. "You pulled me out, didn't you, son?"

Jack nodded.

"You called me *Father....*"

Jack nodded again.

Will Bacon shook his head. "Can you folks go into all this later and let me and Bertha do our job? Oggie, you've got one heck of a goose egg here. And you've got several burns that need attention."

"Well, I told you, I fell down and hit my head. And I was just pulled from a burnin' buildin'. It makes sense I got burned. But right now I'm tryin' to talk to my son here. This is important. This is priority number one, you hear what I'm tellin' you, Will?"

"Take it easy. Bertha, let's get him into the ambulance."

"What the hell's the matter with you, Will?" Oggie demanded to know. "Can't you see what's happenin' here?"

"Settle down," Jack soothed. "Settle down. Will's right. You need care. And we can talk about this later." Jack smiled.

"You hear that?" Oggie gave in to another coughing fit. But as soon as it passed, he went on, "You all hear that? He's gonna talk to me. We got a lot to say to each other. 'Cause, you see, I'm his dad."

Delilah grunted. "Oh, well. What a surprise," she muttered, not sounding surprised at all.

Jack blinked and stared at his half sister, while those nearby in the crowd whispered knowingly among themselves.

Delilah rolled her eyes. "Oh, please. It was so obvious, right from the first. I grew up with three other brothers just like you, after all." She put her hand on Jack's shoulder and stared into his eyes. Suddenly she was looking emotional again. "And I'm glad we've found you...." She sniffed a little. "Though I admit, I'd like to hear you tell me that my father never cheated on my mother. That's the one thing I've always respected about my brothers and my father. They drive the rest of us crazy, but they never cheat."

"He didn't," Jack said gruffly.

"Damn straight I didn't," Oggie groused. And then he yelled at Bertha. "Hey, easy there. Can't you see I'm old?"

"Quit your bellyaching," Bertha advised. By then Oggie was on the gurney.

"Everyone, clear the way."

The crowd cleared a path as they wheeled the old man toward the ambulance.

Jack watched them take his father away. And then he handed Jared back his hard hat and jacket and turned to scan the crowd.

Olivia waved. He saw her. She smiled at him. He pushed through the crowd until he reached her side. He held out his hand.

She took it.

Right then, in the circle where Oggie had been, Eden groaned and clutched her huge stomach.

"Eden, honey?" Jared's usually stern face was a portrait of stark fear. "Is it—?"

"Yes." Eden's contorted expression slowly relaxed. "There. Got through that one."

"Oh, my God."

"Jared, it's okay."

But Jared was already shouting. "Hey, I need help! Bertha, Will, get the hell over here. Eden's having the baby now!"

"Jared. Jared, settle down." Eden reached for her husband's hand and brought it to her lips. "I'm fine. And anyway, first babies take a while." She glanced at the Mercantile Grill, which was still ablaze inside. She sighed. "Well, it could be worse. The Mercantile building is brick. They'll be able to save the structure at least."

Right then the front wall of the bar gave way. It collapsed inward like a toy stepped on by a thoughtless child.

Rocky Collins, who practically lived at the Hole in the Wall, stared at the disintegrating building as if he were losing his best friend.

Tim Brown, another Hole in the Wall regular, patted Rocky on the back. "Don't worry, Rock. You know Eden. She'll have them rebuilding in no time flat."

"Yeah. Sure. You're right, Tim." Rocky tried to keep his chin up. "Somehow, I'll get by till the Hole in the Wall's standin' again."

By that time Will Bacon was at Eden's side. "I think you'd better ride along with us to the hospital, don't you?"

Eden cried out as another contraction gripped her. When it eased, she agreed. "Yes, I think you're right."

Jared helped his wife into the ambulance, where Oggie was already waiting. "I'll follow in the truck," he told Will Bacon. Patrick and Brendan promised they'd watch over things until the fire had burned down to nothing and everyone went home. The ambulance pulled away. As soon as it disappeared around a bend, everyone turned back to watch the burning buildings and the relentless efforts of the volunteer firemen.

At last, as the sky to the east began to turn pale, the fire was declared contained. A few random threads of smoke still spiraled up from the ruins, but nothing was left burning. The Mercantile stood gutted, a black shell. The Hole in the Wall was no more.

Slowly, in groups of twos and threes, the townspeople left the scene and trudged back to their beds.

Except for Olivia and Jack.

They stood side by side, holding hands, until the last fire fighter had gone home. Then, together, they turned to face the eastern mountains where a new day was being born.

Olivia watched the thread of gold that was the sun as it strove to breach the crest of the highest hill. She was thinking that only a few hours before, she'd wanted to hold back the dawn.

Now she smiled in welcome, as morning claimed the world. "You understand now. Don't you, Jack?" she asked him quietly.

He nodded. Then he lifted her hand and pressed it to his lips.

She looked at him, into those beautiful obsidian eyes. "And we're staying here, we're living here."

"All right." They were only two little words. But they meant everything to her.

But Jack was still a realist. He tipped his head toward the burned-out Mercantile. "I want to point out, however, that we're both unemployed, as of now."

"We'll find something. The family will help. And I'm rich, after all."

She didn't say which family. He knew. The Joneses. The family that had taken her in and helped her to find the incredible woman inside herself. The family that seemed to have been his all along.

"I won't live off your money."

"Of course you won't. But this is our place, Jack." Her face glowed in the new light of day. "The place we really found each other. The place we're meant to be, where our children will grow up. It's going to be a great life we'll have, Jack. I know it. I feel it in my bones."

The sun broke above the mountains. Jack Roper reached for the woman he loved. They kissed, there in the middle of Main Street, with the dawn on one side and the burned-out buildings on the other. Then, hand in hand, they turned for the little house on Rambling Lane.

They made only one stop on the way, at Swan's Motel, where they let Buzz out of Jack's room. The cat followed behind them, loyal as a dog, all the way to the white house with green trim.

Inside they undressed and showered quickly, together. Then they climbed wearily into bed.

He gathered her into his arms. "I love you."

"I know. And I'm so glad you're willing to say it at last."

"We're getting married. As soon as we can get a license. Today. Tomorrow, at the latest."

"Can we get some sleep first?"

"All right. But as soon as we wake up, we're looking for the nearest justice of the peace."

"Absolutely." She yawned and snuggled up close.

Jack nuzzled her damp hair. She smelled, as always, of soap and of sweetness.

Her breath was even, her body limp. She was already asleep.

Jack lay holding her, thinking about the shell, vanished now, that had for so long encased his heart. Olivia had seen beyond it. She'd led him to this town where his family waited.

And then she and the town and a crazy old man had set to work on him, to crack open the shell.

Jack Roper was a realist. He didn't believe in fate. Yet, somehow, while hunting down a poor little rich girl, he had found everything that had been missing in his life: a family, a life's mate and a true home at last.

In his arms Olivia stirred. "Jack?"

"Umm?"

"Stop thinking, Jack. Get some rest."

"I think we should be married in Vegas."

"Great idea." She yawned. "Now please. Rest."

He kissed the crown of her head. "Shh. All right."

At the foot of the bed, Buzz lay purring. Jack Roper, home at last, closed his eyes and went to sleep.

Epilogue

Jack and Olivia were married in Las Vegas the next day. When they called to tell the family about it, they learned that Eden Jones had delivered a baby girl, Sally Louise.

In the following spring Regina Jones had a daughter. They named her Anthea Jane.

Also in the spring, the calico cat that Olivia had befriended produced four kittens. Two of them bore a startling resemblance to Buzz.

The Hole in the Wall and the Mercantile Grill reopened eighteen months after the fire. Six months after that, Olivia became head chef there.

Jack found a job at the local sheriff's station as a deputy. When the county sheriff retired, Jack ran for his job and won.

At one hundred and three years old Oggie Jones was interviewed by a reporter from the *Sacramento Bee*.

"To what do you attribute your long life, Mr. Jones?" the reporter inquired at the end of the interview.

"Fortitude, orneriness and having known the love of a good woman—not necessarily in that order. Anythin' else you want to know?"

"No, Mr. Jones," the reporter replied. "I think that just about says it all."

* * * * *

Montana Mavericks

Stories that capture living and loving beneath the Big Sky, where legends live on...and the mystery is just beginning.

This October, discover more MONTANA MAVERICKS with

SLEEPING WITH THE ENEMY
by Myrna Temte

Seduced by his kiss, she almost forgot he was her enemy. *Almost.*

And don't miss a minute of the loving as the mystery continues with:

THE ONCE AND FUTURE WIFE
by Laurie Paige (November)
THE RANCHER TAKES A WIFE
by Jackie Merritt (December)
OUTLAW LOVERS
by Pat Warren (January)
and many more!

Wait, there's more! Win a trip to a Montana mountain resort. For details, look for this month's MONTANA MAVERICKS title at your favorite retail outlet.

Only from **Silhouette®** where passion lives.

MILLION DOLLAR SWEEPSTAKES (III)

SWP-S994

The Loop™

Is the future what it's cracked up to be?

This September, tune in to see why Jessica's partying days are over in

GETTING IT RIGHT: JESSICA
by Carla Cassidy

She had flunked out of college and nearly out of life. Her father expected her to come crawling home, and her friends expected her to fall off the wagon…but Jessica decided she'd rather sell her soul before she screwed up again. So she squeezed into an apartment with some girls she barely knew, got a job that barely paid the bills and decided that things were looking up. Trouble was, no one knew better than her that *looks* could be deceiving.

The ups and downs of modern life continue with

GETTING REAL: CHRISTOPHER
by Kathryn Jensen in October

GETTING PERSONAL: BECKY
by Janet Quin Harkin in November

Get smart. Get into "The Loop!"

Only from

Silhouette®

where passion lives.

LOOP2

WILD RIVER

Maddening men...winsome women...and the untamed land
they live in—all add up to love!

A RIVER TO CROSS (SE #910)
Laurie Paige

Sheriff Shane Macklin knew there was more to "town outsider"
Tina Henderson than met the eye. What he saw was a generous
and selfless woman whose true colors held the promise of love....

Don't miss the latest Rogue River tale, A RIVER TO CROSS, available
in September from Silhouette Special Edition!

SEWR-5

BABY'S CHOICE

Join Marie Ferrarella—and not one, but two, beautiful babies—as her "Baby's Choice" series concludes in October with *BABY TIMES TWO* (SR #1037)

She hadn't thought about Chase Randolph in ages, yet now Gina Delmonico couldn't get her ex-husband out of her mind. Then fate intervened, forcing them together again. Chase, too, seemed to remember their all-too-brief marriage—especially the honeymoon. And before long, these predestined parents discovered the happiness—and the family—that had always been meant to be.

It's "Baby's Choice" when angelic babies-in-waiting select their own delivery dates, only in

V*Silhouette* ROMANCE™

Premiere

The stars are out in October at Silhouette! Read
captivating love stories by talented *new* authors—
in their very first Silhouette appearance.

Sizzle with Susan Crosby's
THE MATING GAME—Desire #888
...when Iain Mackenzie and Kani Warner are forced
to spend their days—and *nights*—together in *very* close
tropical quarters!

Explore the passion in Sandra Moore's
HIGH COUNTRY COWBOY—Special Edition #918
...where Jake Valiteros tries to control the demons that
haunt him—along with a stubborn woman as wild as the
Wyoming wind.

Cherish the emotion in Kia Cochrane's
MARRIED BY A THREAD—Intimate Moments #600
...as Dusty McKay tries to recapture the love he once
shared with his wife, Tori.

Exhilarate in the power of Christie Clark's
TWO HEARTS TOO LATE—Romance #1041
...as Kirby Anne Gordon and Carl Tannon fight for custody
of a small child...and battle their growing attraction!

Shiver with Val Daniels'
BETWEEN DUSK AND DAWN—Shadows #42
...when a mysterious stranger claims to want to save
Jonna Sanders from a serial killer.

Catch the classics of tomorrow—*premiering* today—
Only from

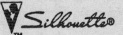

Silhouette®

PREM94

SILHOUETTE... Where Passion Lives

Don't miss these Silhouette favorites by some of our most
distinguished authors! And now you can receive a discount by
ordering two or more titles!

SD#05750	BLUE SKY GUY by Carole Buck	$2.89 ☐
SD#05820	KEEGAN'S HUNT by Dixie Browning	$2.99 ☐
SD#05833	PRIVATE REASONS by Justine Davis	$2.99 ☐
IM#07536	BEYOND ALL REASON by Judith Duncan	$3.50 ☐
IM#07544	MIDNIGHT MAN by Barbara Faith	$3.50 ☐
IM#07547	A WANTED MAN by Kathleen Creighton	$3.50 ☐
SSE#09761	THE OLDER MAN by Laurey Bright	$3.39 ☐
SSE#09809	MAN OF THE FAMILY by Andrea Edwards	$3.39 ☐
SSE#09867	WHEN STARS COLLIDE by Patricia Coughlin	$3.50 ☐
SR#08849	EVERY NIGHT AT EIGHT by Marion Smith Collins	$2.59 ☐
SR#08897	WAKE UP LITTLE SUSIE by Pepper Adams	$2.69 ☐
SR#08941	SOMETHING OLD by Toni Collins	$2.75 ☐
	(limited quantities available on certain titles)	

TOTAL AMOUNT	$_____
DEDUCT: 10% DISCOUNT FOR 2+ BOOKS	$_____
POSTAGE & HANDLING ($1.00 for one book, 50¢ for each additional)	$_____
APPLICABLE TAXES*	$_____
TOTAL PAYABLE (check or money order—please do not send cash)	$_____

To order, complete this form and send it, along with a check or money order
for the total above, payable to Silhouette Books, to: **In the U.S.:** 3010 Walden
Avenue, P.O. Box 9077, Buffalo, NY 14269-9077; **In Canada:** P.O. Box 636,
Fort Erie, Ontario, L2A 5X3.

Name:_____

Address:_____ City:_____

State/Prov.:_____ Zip/Postal Code:_____

*New York residents remit applicable sales taxes.
Canadian residents remit applicable GST and provincial taxes.

SBACK-SN

Silhouette®
™